HARD TARGET

J. B. TURNER

HARD TARGET

THOMAS & MERCER

Text copyright © 2020 by J. B. Turner
All rights reserved.

Published by Thomas & Mercer, Seattle

www.apub.com

Amazon, the Amazon logo, and Thomas & Mercer are trademarks of Amazon.com, Inc., or its affiliates.

ISBN-13: 9781542014434
ISBN-10: 1542014433

Cover design by Dominic Forbes

Printed in the United States of America

To my mother

When the men arrived at his home to kill him, Trevelle Williams was five miles away at an all-night diner in South Beach, eating scrambled eggs and toast and listening to the waitress bitch about tips. Her name tag said Mariana. Sitting in his usual corner booth, he smiled politely and checked his watch, hoping that Mariana would take the hint. But she was oblivious to his craving for peace and quiet. It was 4:32 a.m.

He swallowed the last bite of toast, gulped hot black coffee, then took out his MacBook and waited for it to connect to the internet. A virtual private network server in Iceland allowed him to send and receive messages anonymously, surf the net confidentially.

His gaze wandered around the old Pullman car diner. Two clubbers still high, sitting at the counter, sipping beers, and eating pecan pie with cream. A shifty-eyed white kid nursing an espresso. And two middle-aged guys deep in conversation about a girl they had both met at the Clevelander.

"The tourists are the worst. Especially from Europe. Ugh," the waitress said.

Trevelle nodded and checked his watch again. She'd been talking nonstop for seven minutes.

She had her hands on her hips and was shaking her head. "One time, a big group of guys from Holland ordered about two hundred dollars' worth of food and beer and stuff. You know how much they left me?"

Trevelle shrugged.

"Two fucking dollars! I thought, what? Are you guys for real?"

"That's not right."

"Damn straight it's not right. I sure as hell won't be serving them if they come in again."

"I don't blame you."

"Anyway, enough about me. How's my favorite insomniac?"

Trevelle shifted in his seat, uncomfortable with any attention directed at his personal life. "I'm fine, thank you. And I'm not an insomniac. I just keep irregular hours."

The waitress refilled his coffee and picked up his empty plate. "We've got a big menu. Lot of great food. You ever thought of trying something else?"

"Not really."

"Get out of your comfort zone, so to speak."

"I'm happy in my comfort zone."

She gave a rueful smile. "You never change. Change is good."

"I like what I like, what can I say?"

"My kind of guy." The waitress winked at him, then walked away and picked up some dirty plates from an adjacent table.

Trevelle took a deep breath and looked at his computer. He'd logged on to a high-level cybersecurity chat room he occasionally contributed to, where the discussions ranged from network protection and security to software, programming, and state surveillance.

An encrypted private message popped up under the screen name CrackerHack.

It was the online handle of his friend David, who lived a hermit-like existence in New York. The guy was even more hardcore than he was.

The message said: Wondering if you've had any luck analyzing that file I sent you last week—the one from my hacktivist friend in Germany. Dude said the American company they lifted it from has ties to the Pentagon and the CIA. Told him I'd get back to him if it contained anything juicy.

Trevelle thought the message was strange. He hadn't received any file. He quickly messaged back, saying to send it again but this time to his new email hosted in Switzerland.

When you did the sort of work he did, you couldn't be too careful.

He finished his second coffee of the day.

The waitress was instantly tableside, refilling his mug. "Anything else, just holler."

Trevelle looked up and smiled. "Appreciate that." *He watched her head to the other side of the diner to take another order.*

He glanced out the window to where the edges of the sky were just beginning to lighten. He liked to spend a few hours down on the beach at the start of each day. Backpack on, laptop and cables and cell phone inside, walking on Ocean Drive, past the neon-lit signs on the art deco bars and hotels and apartments. He sometimes spent an hour or two at the News Cafe, watching the sunrise. The vibes were nice, mostly.

It made a sharp contrast to where he lived and worked.

Trevelle's operation was based in an abandoned warehouse he had bought and converted into a high-tech fortress in the Overtown area of Miami. Low rent, high crime. He had views of a run-down liquor store, a crack house, and I-95. The rumble of freeway traffic a constant companion despite the thick walls and bulletproof, triple-glazed windows. But no one bothered him there. That was the main attraction. Still, South Beach was where he felt truly at home.

The vibes were chill, if you knew where to look. European house music pulsating into the night air. He usually popped into the Deuce when it opened at eight. Maybe a Heineken with a passing barfly from out of town. A game of pool with whoever was in at that ungodly hour.

3

The ping from his MacBook indicated he had a message. Trevelle assumed it was the file his hacker friend had resent. And it was. But before he could open it, a second notification pinged. This one contained a video automatically generated by his home surveillance system.

The thermal sensor detectors had been activated.

He clicked to open the file, slipping on his wireless headphones. Real-time, high-definition footage began to roll.

Trevelle felt sick. Three men in ski masks and surgical gloves, carrying flashlights, were inside his home. Their voices were low, speaking in a language he didn't understand. They fanned out, packing up all his laptops and devices, photographing the inside of the huge warehouse he called home. How the hell had they even gotten in? He had designed the warehouse to be impregnable. Perimeter intruder detection, CCTV, security lighting, and thermal sensors both inside and outside.

He stared, transfixed, as one of the men disappeared. He returned a few moments later with a guy in a Tom Petty T-shirt and boxer shorts, who was adjusting his glasses and squinting against the light.

Trevelle had been so caught off guard by the breach that he'd forgotten that Fernandez, a genius hacker and one of his closest friends since MIT, was spending the night. Fernandez was in town to meet some financial guys who he hoped would fund his technology start-up in one of the poorest areas of Miami. Was it possible the intruders were there for him?

Through the headphones, Trevelle heard Fernandez sobbing.

The masked man pressed a gun to Fernandez's head. Then he blew his brains out. Despite the silencer visible on the end of the gun, Trevelle was certain he heard the sound echoing off the stone walls of the warehouse and that it would haunt him forever.

One

It was early in the evening, and Jon Reznick was shooting pool at a dive bar in Rockland, Maine. The woman across the table from him wore a tight-fitting Ramones T-shirt and was chewing gum. Reznick had been close to Gemma Frazier's brother, Mikey, back in their school days. And he'd always had a soft spot for Mikey's slightly wayward younger sister.

Gemma lined up a shot but missed the eight ball in a corner pocket. "Shoot!"

"Bad luck."

"Tell me about it," she said, leaning on her pool cue. "It's the story of my life."

Reznick gulped the rest of his draft beer and shook his head, smarter than to wade into those waters.

Gemma flicked some hair out of her eyes and smiled. "Well, Mikey told me that you disappeared off the face of the planet after high school and were overseas for a while. Says you still won't talk about it. Says you're a goddamn fucking enigma wrapped up in a mystery or something."

"I have no clue what you just said."

Gemma burst out laughing. "Seems a shame we didn't run into each other sooner. Though"—she gestured around at the bar—"I wouldn't have expected to see you back at the Myrtle anyway."

It was Reznick's turn to smile. He checked his watch. "I really gotta go."

She pouted. "Already? But we haven't finished our game." With a wink, she added, "And I'm winning."

"I'd better quit while you're ahead, then. Got to get up early tomorrow. Stuff to do."

"Like what?"

His cell phone rang.

Reznick pulled his phone out of his pocket, expecting it to be Lauren. His daughter was at Bennington College in Vermont, and they usually spoke once a week. But instead of Lauren's cell number on the caller ID, a number he didn't recognize flashed on the screen. He looked up at Gemma. "I need to take this."

"You want another beer?"

"Put it on my tab."

"That I can do." Gemma headed to the bar to order the drinks.

Reznick walked to a quieter corner to take the call.

The voice on the line was a whisper. "Hey, man, are you there? Reznick?"

"Who's this?"

"Your IT pal in Miami."

Reznick recognized the voice of the high-level hacker he sometimes did business with. The kid kept a low profile—not surprisingly—but Reznick had found out that his name was Trevelle Williams and that he was a former National Security Agency cybersecurity expert. The kid had helped Reznick out of numerous tight spots and investigations that Reznick had worked on for the FBI, but it was extremely unusual for Trevelle to call him out of the blue. That wasn't the only reason he sensed something was wrong—there was a tightness in the guy's voice. "You sound kinda strange. You OK?"

"I've got a situation," Trevelle whispered. "I need your help."

"A situation? What kind of situation?"

"Long story . . . Bottom line? I'm in trouble."

Reznick looked across at Gemma, who was chewing gum and drinking beer from the bottle as she talked to the bartender. "You in Miami?"

"Not anymore. I'm headed to New York. Can you meet me there?"

Reznick heard other voices in the background. "Where are you calling from? I hear other people."

"I'm on a Greyhound bus."

He pictured the kid slumped in a seat, hand concealing his mouth as he whispered into the phone. "You left Miami on a Greyhound?"

"I believe people are trying to kill me."

"Tell me what happened."

Trevelle took a deep breath. "They've already killed one person. A friend of mine. I don't want to talk about it over the phone. Will you meet me? I don't know anyone else in a position to help me with something like this. Only you."

Trevelle was a good guy. Supersmart. Whatever had unnerved him and made him think his life was in danger had to be bad. "OK, let's try and figure this out. Do you know why these people want to kill you? Do you know who they are?"

"I have a . . . I received a file." His voice, already a whisper, dropped further. "It was passed to me. I think it has something to do with that."

"What does the file contain?"

"I just opened the file a couple hours ago, but it was originally sent to me a week ago. It has national security implications."

"I understand."

"Look, man, I'm not going to sugarcoat it. Will you help me?"

Reznick was conflicted. He had decided to take a few months off—no shadowy ops, no FBI crises. But he couldn't ignore a call for help from a guy who had gone above and beyond for him in the past. "Where in New York are you going to be?"

"I can't say exactly. Just head to Manhattan. I'll know when you're there. I'll contact you again."

Two

Early the following afternoon, Reznick's flight touched down at JFK. He slung his backpack over his shoulder and headed out of the terminal. He preferred to travel light. Then he waited in line to catch a cab into the city.

The Manhattan skyline came into view through the taxi's windows. New residential towers sprang up each time he visited. A vista forever changed since 9/11. Thinking about it always left him empty. His young wife, Elisabeth, had died in the Twin Towers. That day had not only changed America and destroyed thousands of lives but also set the country on course for war. A dirty war that was still playing out in Afghanistan. The memories of Iraq were seared in his brain. As a young Delta Force operator, he had seen firsthand the destruction, the blood, the dead, and the dying. It never seemed to end. And for what?

His cell phone rang, snapping him out of his dark thoughts.

"You're here." Trevelle sounded relieved.

Reznick looked out the window, bemused. "How do you know I'm in town? My phone is secure."

"Not as secure as you think. It's three years out of date."

"It is?"

"Standard-issue FBI encryption. I pioneered it eight years ago and sold them the patent."

Reznick glanced at his phone, then returned it to his ear, displeased. "So this phone is vulnerable?"

Trevelle laughed, seemingly back in his comfort zone. "You have no idea. I've got some great encryption software for my high-end clients. You want me to download the software to your cell phone?"

"And it works?"

"Trust me. This version is being used by the Israelis. Shin Bet has issued this to most of their senior people."

"Fine, send it over."

"Good stuff. I'm loading the software onto your cell . . . now."

Reznick heard a ping from his phone. "That's it?"

"That's it."

The cab driver glanced in his mirror.

Reznick stared at the man, who looked away. "When did you get into town?"

"Early this morning."

"Where are you?"

"I'm on the west side. West Thirty-Fourth between Eleventh and Twelfth. Northern entrance to the High Line. You know it?"

"I know it. Where will you be exactly?"

"Not far. I'll find you."

"Gimme ten minutes."

A silence stretched between them.

"You still there, son?"

"Mr. R., I just wanted to say thanks."

"What for?"

"Trying to help. Believing me. Trusting me."

"See you soon, kid."

Reznick asked to be dropped off three blocks away from his destination, trying to minimize the risk of being tailed. He walked into the Javits Center and headed across the lobby. Then he strode out of an exit directly opposite the High Line entrance.

He crossed the street and passed a line of tourist buses gearing up for tours of the city.

Then he headed up the iron stairs, and he was on the High Line. He walked south along the elevated former freight rail line, now a beautiful mile-and-a-half-long walkway that led down to the edge of Greenwich Village.

He walked for fifteen minutes.

The semi-industrial landscape fringing the Hudson River soon gave way to superhigh residential towers and the Chelsea neighborhood below.

Reznick caught sight of a hunched figure in the distance. The skinny black kid was sitting on a wooden bench, headphones on, backpack at his feet, shades on. He wore a gray sweatshirt with a hood, dark jeans, and black sneakers and exuded a cool anonymity. Reznick figured the kid was in his late twenties, early thirties max. He walked toward him and sat down.

Trevelle took off his headphones. "Appreciate you coming, man."

"You sounded more than a little shaken up on the phone."

"You could say that."

Reznick turned and looked at Trevelle, who was peering over his sunglasses. His bleary eyes reflected lack of sleep, and they darted from one side to the other, as if he expected someone to walk up and attack him at any moment.

How likely that was, was something Reznick needed to determine. He let his gaze wander farther down the High Line. Tourists taking selfies, skyscrapers all around. It all seemed innocuous. "OK, we are where we are."

Trevelle looked around, then raised the wrist wearing his watch. "Wearable prototype jammer. Can't be too careful, but we should be able to talk securely here."

Reznick stared at the watch. "And that blocks all signals?"

"It's been activated and we're safe. For now."

Reznick waited until a couple ambled past before he spoke. "So what's this all about? I mean really about. Someone has sure put the fear of God into you."

Trevelle bent forward and picked up the backpack at his feet. He unzipped it, reached in, and pulled out a MacBook Air. He flipped open the lid, logged on, and maneuvered the laptop so Reznick could see it. "I need to warn you, I'm going to play a video clip. And it ain't nice."

"Hit it," Reznick said.

Trevelle pressed play and the footage began.

Reznick watched the screen. Masked men with flashlights scoured an industrial building that looked like a warehouse. "Where is this?"

"This is my workspace. My home. Same place you visited a few years back, in Overtown. I live, work, and do everything there."

"I thought it was supposed to be off the grid or something?"

"So did I. I've never had one intrusion in all these years."

Reznick stared at the screen. "So who are those guys? And how did they find you?"

Trevelle shook his head. "No idea who they are. Faces covered, very professional. How did they find me? I'm guessing they could have followed a friend of mine who was staying with me. He's the one they killed. At first, I thought maybe he was their target. He's an acknowledged leading light in signals intelligence. He might've popped up on the radar of some bad dudes. But then . . ."

Reznick watched as the men went around gathering up computers and hard drives. Though the sound was low, he could hear them speaking in a foreign language.

"Fernandez had his own gear with him. As far as I can tell, they only took my stuff." Trevelle gestured at the screen. "This is when it gets crazy."

A masked man hauled a frightened, bespectacled twentysomething into view and pointed a gun at the young man's head.

"That's Fernandez," Trevelle said, shaking his head. "Can't believe it."

Reznick stared at the screen. The masked man pulled the trigger, and Fernandez dropped like a stone, blood pooling on the concrete floor. A wave of revulsion washed over Reznick. He had done the same to high-value targets in Afghanistan and Iraq. Time after time. But to see a young kid, who'd probably done nothing wrong, neutralized like that sent an icy chill down his spine.

Trevelle closed the screen and returned the laptop to his backpack, zipping it up once more. "He was my closest friend in the world."

"How exactly did you know Fernandez?"

"We met at MIT. And we both worked at the NSA around the same time. Different facilities at Fort Meade. But we met up for coffee, and beers on the weekend. He stayed in Naples with his parents most of the time."

Reznick nodded. "Dumb fucking luck that he was staying with you."

"He's been trying to raise funding the last few weeks from some firms in Miami and Silicon Valley. He was talking about buying a cheap industrial space in Overtown and turning it into a cybersecurity hub. He had visions of employing hundreds, maybe thousands of people, as contractors for the government. He talked about hiring smart kids from the area—kids who were otherwise susceptible to gangs and drugs—and training them."

"You said at first you thought he was the target. But now you don't?"

"No, I don't. Maybe. Shit, I don't know."

Reznick squinted as the glass towers surrounding them reflected the fierce sun. "Don't beat yourself up. Whoever those guys were after, his death wasn't your fault."

Trevelle shook his head and sighed.

"You mentioned a file that was sent to you. Tell me about that."

"God, I wish I could turn the clock back. I thought I was doing a favor for a friend by agreeing to decrypt the file. A friend of mine here in New York, David. He was sent the encrypted files from a hacker friend in Germany."

"Why couldn't the friend in Germany have accessed the information?"

"I don't know. Sometimes we share these files with friends or associates, covering our tracks, that kind of thing. We have them analyzed, and then when it's agreed, they might be released to the outside world."

"You're talking WikiLeaks?"

"Precisely."

"So this friend in New York, not Fernandez, he sent you the file?"

"Yeah, he sent the file just over a week ago. He was inundated with requests to decrypt and analyze sensitive files. He was swamped. So, he sent it on to me. I never got it, which seems strange now that I think about it. So yesterday, it's before dawn, I'm sitting in an all-night diner." He looked at Reznick and shrugged. "I don't sleep too well. Anyway, this friend, David, messages me, asking if I'd looked at the file yet. I tell him to send it again. The same time it arrives, I get the alert that those guys are creeping around my place."

"Have you spoken to this friend in New York since this happened?"

Trevelle hesitated. "I was heading up here to see him in person, but I've been so freaked out, I wanted to talk to you first. I sent him a message—nothing specific, just a hey, wanted to touch base about a project, but no reply. That's not unusual, though. If he's deep into a hack, sometimes I don't hear from him for weeks, or months."

"I need to know more about the file. What kind of file is it? What does it contain?"

Trevelle leaned forward, unzipped the backpack again, and flipped open the MacBook.

Reznick watched as the kid signed in to a virtual private network, this time accessing the internet via a secure server in Germany. Two passwords were inputted as random metadata scrolled across the screen. Trevelle typed in one more password. The weird gobbledygook file dissolved, and the decrypted file appeared before Reznick's eyes. Trevelle turned the screen more toward Reznick. "Check it out."

Reznick leaned closer and read the document quickly. It was a memo. Calling for a woman's assassination.

"You familiar with this kind of thing?" Trevelle asked.

Reznick sat back on the bench. "Yeah. The memo appears to indicate that an operation has been set up, something similar to a special access program. That means the operation is considered highly classified, and information is severely restricted to a select few. Even people with top security clearances might not have access. Maybe only those in the higher echelons of the military, the chair of a congressional committee, and a few others would know. This kind of thing is black ops, sometimes. I would guess it's a government operation."

"Except it's not," Trevelle said. "It appears government from the terminology. But I know that this memo definitely did not originate from within the US government or the Pentagon."

"So who's it from?"

"This is where it gets interesting. It's from a private security company based here in New York. Geostrategy Solutions."

Reznick speed-read the document again. It gave permission for a back-channel operation conducted by an unnamed foreign intelligence service to neutralize—assassinate—an American woman.

Geostrategy Solutions. Reznick doubted they'd instigated this on their own. He wondered if the assassination was a government operation that had been subcontracted to a private security firm. Compartmentalized assassination. Need to know. It gave the government plausible deniability. "It's interesting. But how do we know this is authentic and not some elaborate hoax?"

Trevelle waited until a group of excited school kids passed by with their frazzled teachers before he picked up the conversation. "The guy who sent this to me and the guys who sent it to him don't play pranks. They're serious dudes out to expose government corruption. Besides, all the metadata points to it being legit."

"So this is for real. The woman referred to in this document . . . Do we know who Rosalind Dyer is?"

Trevelle logged out of the VPN and reaccessed the internet using a server in Switzerland.

"Why use a server in Europe?" Reznick asked.

"They're way more into privacy. And we can cover our tracks."

"Figures."

Trevelle typed in the name Rosalind Dyer, and the screen showed a picture of an attractive fortysomething woman. "Here she is. This is who they want to kill."

Reznick studied the picture. The woman looked well dressed. But not flashy. "Who is she? What does she do?"

Trevelle took off his sunglasses and lowered his voice. "This is where it gets interesting. She lives in DC. And she works for the government."

"What part of government?"

"She's a special agent. An investigator."

Reznick's brows rose. "FBI?"

Trevelle shook his head. "Defense Criminal Investigative Service. DCIS. The investigative arm of the Department of Defense Office of Inspector General."

Reznick frowned at the picture. "Never heard of them."

"They ensure American tax dollars are being spent correctly. Think defense contracts."

Reznick pondered that. "Billions of dollars at stake."

"She must know something," Trevelle said. "And that's why someone wants to silence her."

Reznick nodded. "Listen, son, I don't know if I'm the best person to help with this."

"Why not? I thought you'd be the perfect person."

"I think we need to turn this over to the FBI. This is what they do. They'll protect you. And they can figure out what to do about this woman and the people who want to kill her."

Trevelle turned away as if disappointed.

"What?"

"I'm not handing myself in. I'd never see daylight again."

Reznick sighed. "You're not making this easy."

"Listen, I'm not ruling out speaking to the Feds about this. At some point. But I'll need guarantees."

"I don't think they do guarantees. But I can talk to them."

"In the meantime . . . what do you think? Am I overreacting?"

Reznick gave it some thought. "The timing is odd. These guys descending on your place right when you receive the file. But if, as you say, your friend originally sent it a week earlier, that might have given them time to discover they were hacked and trace the recipients. The sort of work you do, I trust you'd know if this was coming from any of your other jobs."

"So what would you do, if going to the Feds isn't on the agenda?"

"I really think that's your best and safest option."

Trevelle shook his head. "You said you know the sort of work I do. Then you know they'd lock me up and never let me near a computer again."

"Well, then I guess you need to warn your hacker friend in New York and Special Agent Dyer. Both of their lives may be in danger."

Trevelle nodded. He shut the MacBook and placed it inside the backpack. He zipped it up and got to his feet, slinging the bag over his shoulder.

"How far away does your friend live?" Reznick asked.

"He's a fifteen-minute walk from here. He lives down in the Village."

Reznick stood up. "So what're you waiting for? Let's go talk to him."

Three

It was a short walk from the High Line to Hudson Street, lined with upscale shops and fashionable bars and restaurants in Greenwich Village.

Reznick looked around the area. "Nice place. Costs a fortune, I'll bet."

"David—that was his handle, as in David and Goliath—bought Bitcoin when it was two cents. He bought the whole townhouse and rents out the floors below him."

"Smart dude."

Trevelle stepped forward and buzzed apartment 6. He tried a few more times. No reply.

"Maybe your friend went out for coffee?" Reznick said.

Trevelle shrugged. "Doesn't sound like him."

"Why not?"

Trevelle pulled out his cell phone. "He's agoraphobic."

"So he doesn't leave his apartment? Ever?"

Trevelle shook his head. "He opens the window and sits on the balcony in the summer."

"He doesn't go out? Seriously?"

"He's a fucking hermit, what can I say? It's weird, I know. But he's a nice guy."

Reznick took a step back and stared up at the top windows. "Give the guy a call. I'm assuming he has a cell phone."

Trevelle rolled his eyes. "Man, you need to chill." He called the number and pressed his cell phone tight to his ear. A minute later, he ended the call and shrugged. "Voice mail."

Reznick wondered why the guy wasn't answering. "Buzz him again."

Trevelle held down the buzzer for a full two minutes. Still nothing. "That's pretty weird for him. He gets his groceries, coffee, water, everything delivered to his apartment. I swear, he's a bigger recluse than me. When I visited, about a year ago, he showed me his medication. Xanax and a couple of other drugs to chill him out."

"So it's unusual that he's not answering?" Reznick said.

"More than unusual. But maybe he's got his headphones on, zonked on Xanax and weed."

"Does he get his weed delivered to his apartment too?"

"Usually."

Reznick shielded his eyes from the glare of the sun as he looked up at the fire escape. "And he's on the top floor?"

Trevelle pointed to a window. "Yeah."

Reznick opened up his backpack and pulled out his flashlight which he placed carefully in his waistband next to his Beretta.

"What are you doing, man?"

Reznick stepped forward, jumped up, and pulled the iron fire escape down to street level.

"The hell are you doing, man?"

Reznick put one foot on the ancient creaking ladder. "What does it look like I'm doing?"

"You breaking into his apartment?"

Reznick shook his head as he began to climb the outside of the building. "The guy might've fallen asleep stoned, watching cartoons."

"I guess. Maybe. Listen, people will call the cops."

"Relax, it's New York. This sort of thing happens all the time." He got to the top floor and looked at Trevelle on the ground. He pointed at a window adjacent to the fire escape. "This it?"

"Got it."

Reznick peered through the dirt-encrusted window. He could just make out empty pizza boxes, cans of Red Bull, and candy wrappers strewn on the floor. He knocked hard on the window. No answer. He knocked again. "Jesus Christ, never a break." He tried to lift up the window. But it wouldn't budge.

He took a knife out of his back pocket. He tried to pry the window open, sliding the knife underneath the wooden frame. But nothing. It was stuck, as if months and years of dirt, dust, and grime had cemented it.

Trevelle shouted up, "He's very security conscious."

"Thanks for telling me now."

Reznick pulled his flashlight out of his waistband and smashed it hard into the window. The glass shattered. He reached through the broken glass shards to the window lock and slid it open. He lifted up the smashed window, careful to avoid getting cut by the jagged glass.

He climbed inside. The smell of stale weed smoke filled the dank air. Reznick looked around. Dirty coffee mugs were lying on the floor. The place was dingy and dark despite it being daytime.

He switched on the flashlight and looked around. He thought it strange that the hermit hacker wasn't around. There was no sign of any computer equipment.

Reznick headed into the hallway and combed the rest of the apartment carefully. It was a complete mess. Old computer magazines lying around, clothes strewn over chairs and the floor, grungy sneakers. He checked the bathroom. Then a small galley kitchen, with dirty dishes piled high. How could someone live like this?

Movement sounded in the apartment below. No doubt a neighbor who'd heard the breaking glass.

Reznick went back through the apartment and into the living room. He saw a closet at the far end. He opened it up and shone the flashlight inside. On closer inspection, he saw the ceiling contained an attic hatch.

Reznick reached up and pulled the dangling rope. Wooden stairs unfolded neatly into place.

Reznick climbed up the steps into the attic. He shone the flashlight around the darkened space between old oak beams. Then the light caught something moving. A pair of sneakers, swaying in midair. His stomach knotted as the light bathed the far end of the attic. Dust particles backlit from a dirty skylight in the attic roof. Flies and moths buzzing around.

And hanging by a nylon cord from a wooden beam, a twentysomething white guy, eyes wide open but seeing nothing.

Four

Max Charles was clocking his fiftieth lap on the elevated indoor running track of the prestigious New York Athletic Club during his lunch hour. At seventy-eight, he was probably the oldest member working out, but his creaking bones and knee joints didn't worry him. He ran on, endorphins kicking in. Making him feel good again.

Down below on the basketball courts, J.P. Morgan hedge fund guys were high fiving each other after their game. He noticed their relaxed demeanor, their well-bred features, and all the signs of privilege.

He slowed down and rested up.

Charles felt the sweat sticking to his shirt. He checked his heart rate on his watch. Barely raised. His decades of running, rowing, and walking had left him with more energy than men half his age.

He headed down to the boxing gym and did some serious heavy bag work. Punching, jabbing, moving.

By then he was drenched in sweat. He ended his daily early-afternoon fitness regimen the way he usually did. Twenty laps in the club's pool.

Afterward, he showered and put on his gray Savile Row suit, pale-blue shirt, navy tie, and shiny black leather shoes. He walked out of the club, said goodbye to Ramono at the door, and headed back toward his office, briefcase in hand.

Charles liked routines. He liked order. He lived an orderly existence. It was only a short five-minute walk to his office in a glass skyscraper on Lexington Avenue. He rode the elevator to his thirty-eighth-floor corner office.

Charles pressed his index finger to the digital biometric reader on the door. A metallic *click*, and he pushed open the door. It closed slowly behind him, clicking back into secure mode.

He placed his briefcase beside his desk, fixed himself a coffee from the machine as his gaze wandered around his office. The walls showed the world who he was. Black-and-white photos he'd had framed of himself as a boy in New Jersey all those years ago. He'd grown up poor. The oldest of a family of nine. And he had been working since he was a child.

How far he had come from those early years. Hauling crates of fruit from wagons, meat packing—he'd done all the dirty work. And he'd loved it. It was hard, brutal labor. But as a child, he'd been a vital moneymaker for his family. The first time he'd handed over his wages to his mother, she'd cried and hugged him tight, grateful for the money coming into the household.

Now look at him. It was scarcely credible.

Charles sipped his afternoon coffee and stared out the windows onto the bustling Midtown streets below. He'd come a long, long way. Sure, it was just across the bridge to Jersey. But to him, it felt like the end of the earth.

He let his mind drift. He always enjoyed the silence the ten or fifteen minutes after his workout. The peace. It gave him satisfaction to think of how much he had achieved. It allowed him the space for his head to clear and get focused for the rest of the afternoon.

His company, Geostrategy Solutions, was grossing five hundred million dollars a year. Hundreds of employees relied on him. Their families relied on him. He knew all about responsibility. Had since he was a boy.

Charles gazed around the rest of his office. The floor-to-ceiling bookshelf was stacked with biographies of military and intelligence figures. He had written a highly regarded book on Allen Dulles, the first civilian director of the Central Intelligence Agency. More photos of Charles pictured with Kissinger, with the late President George H. W. Bush, and his favorite, one of him and his wife with the pope, taken five years earlier at a private meeting at the Vatican. He cherished the memories.

Where had the years gone?

The reality was that a lot of his adult life had been spent abroad. Serving the United States. But since he had retired from the Agency, he was glad to be back in the city he loved. A brash, crazy city that had an irresistible energy. No wonder everyone wanted a shot at the American Dream. It was available if you worked hard enough and took chances. The immigrants were still pouring in, just like his forbearers from Ireland had all those decades earlier.

The phone on his mahogany desk rang, snapping him out of his reverie.

Charles put down his coffee and picked up, cleared his throat. "Max Charles."

"Sir, I've got an update for you."

"Is your line secure?"

"Yes, sir, of course."

"So spit it out. How was the Miami operation?"

"That's where we've got a problem. Trevelle Williams is missing."

"Who's he?"

"He's the guy Marty traced the stolen document to. He still believes it was a hacker group based in Europe who initially breached our system about a week ago. They sent the file to a guy in New York who's loosely associated with WikiLeaks. As you know, we dealt with him within a few hours of Marty discovering the breach."

Charles felt his blood pressure rise a notch. His company prided itself on state-level military encryption. A breach of any sort was unacceptable, but he'd deal with that after the leak was contained. "And why did he pass the document to this Williams guy?"

"It sounded like a fluke, like he just didn't have time to decrypt it and outsourced the work. Williams is an ex-NSA contractor gone rogue, a computer genius, apparently."

"Christ, he sounds like Snowden."

"There are similarities. He's not in Moscow, though. This guy was living in some run-down shithole Miami warehouse which no one seemed to know about for the better part of seven years. But we tracked him down."

Charles sighed. "You say in Miami. Where is he now?"

"We sent a team in awaiting his return, but there's no sign of him. Our intelligence pointed to Williams always being back at the warehouse at oh-seven-hundred hours, at the latest. But he never turned up. We had to take out a friend of his. We couldn't take any chances."

"You killed him?"

"He's dead, yes."

"Shit."

"We are working very hard to locate Williams."

"Not good enough. Where the hell is he?"

Charles's computer pinged.

"I just sent you a photo."

Charles maneuvered the mouse and clicked on the photo. A grainy color photograph of a twentysomething black guy wearing shades, a Dolphins ball cap, and a backpack. "Where was this taken?"

"North Miami Beach bus station. Oh-five-twenty-two hours, yesterday. The bus was headed to New York, but he could've gotten off anywhere. His phone and computer have dropped off the grid. So he's clearly using jamming software."

"We're running out of time. Find him. Quick."

"Understood."

"If Trevelle Williams figures out what's in that file, we are all in serious trouble. People are relying on us to deliver. They pay us handsomely to make problems disappear. To make people disappear. Am I making myself clear?"

"You still want Williams neutralized?"

"Listen, you dumb fuck. Assemble whoever is available. Find Williams. Kill him. No more distractions."

Five

Trevelle sobbed hard as he sat in the passenger seat of the rental car.

Reznick threw their backpacks into the trunk of the BMW SUV, started up the car, switched on the air-conditioning to high, and pulled away. He drove down Varick Street and headed through the nearby Holland Tunnel toward New Jersey.

"I can't believe this," Trevelle said, blinking away tears. "Two friends of mine, both dead. I'm responsible. I killed them!"

Reznick snapped, "Stop that self-pitying bullshit! You didn't kill them."

Trevelle dabbed his eyes. "My actions killed them."

"Bullshit. David sent the file to you. And Fernandez crashing at your place was bad fucking luck, that's all. Besides, wasn't it some hacker group in Europe that stole the file?"

Trevelle nodded. "Yeah."

"There you go. You and your two friends—dead friends—were drawn into this without asking for it. The group accessed highly sensitive information. And it got your friends killed. You'd be dead, too, if you'd been home."

"They didn't deserve to die."

"I didn't say they did."

"I feel like I'm in a nightmare."

"You need to wake the fuck up, man, and deal with it. Get some backbone. We need to think strategically. These guys aren't just going to drop it; they're going to keep coming after you. You think this is a fucking game. This is no game, trust me."

Trevelle closed his eyes, unable or unwilling to contemplate what was happening.

"Did you hear what I said?"

"I heard. I just wish you'd lay off me for a minute."

"We need to get a grip on this situation."

"They were both good guys."

"Good guys get killed all the time." Reznick sighed. "It's life. It sucks. Look, I'm sorry, I shouldn't have been so hard on you. It's tough, I know, losing a friend."

"Correction, two friends. One murder and one apparent suicide."

"For what it's worth, I don't think your friend in the Village killed himself. That wasn't a suicide. It was made to look like suicide."

Trevelle scrunched up his face and shook his head, as if the full horror of what had happened had just crashed through.

"I didn't see any sign of computers or hard drives," Reznick said. "Maybe it was an ordinary break-in, but that seems unlikely. Maybe they dressed like maintenance guys to gain access. Whatever happened—they took all the electronic equipment."

"Then they hanged him? Seriously?"

Reznick nodded. "From the look of the body, it happened around the same time that crew in the masks turned up at your place. That crew probably would have shot you, just like they did Fernandez. Different MO, same result."

Trevelle stared at the dazzling lights of the oncoming cars in the tunnel. "I don't want to be part of this. I want this to be over."

"So what do you suggest? You head back to sunny Miami? Does that sound like a good idea to you? Well, does it?"

Trevelle shook his head.

"Get your shit together, son." Reznick headed through the tunnel and got onto I-95 South, glancing repeatedly in his mirror.

"What's wrong?" Trevelle asked.

"Just making sure we're not being followed."

"And are we?"

"No. OK, my friend, you want some advice?"

Trevelle nodded.

"You need to go to the FBI with what you know. After everything, that would be the smart move."

"I don't know."

"What don't you know?"

"They know I stole government secrets in the past, accessed classified NSA documents, and just about everything else—probably more than Snowden. I think they'd throw the book at me. I think I'd never see the light of day again."

Reznick knew Trevelle had a point. "Listen, you've spoken to Martha Meyerstein when you've helped me in the past, haven't you?"

"Sure."

"She's a straight shooter. I trust her. You need to talk to her. I can tell her your concerns. We can get you a great lawyer. Maybe you spend a year or two wearing an ankle monitor, I don't know, but it's better than being dead."

"If it means going to prison, I'd rather take my chances."

"Well, you need to get this figured out. And fast."

Trevelle sighed. "Where are we going?"

"We need to keep moving. We don't know who these people are—the masked guys in Miami, the people who hanged your friend in New York. We don't know where they are or if they've tracked you to New York. These guys aren't going to play games if they find you."

Trevelle stared straight ahead as if mentally working through everything that had happened.

Reznick changed lanes and accelerated.

"Where are we going?"

"I think DC would be good."

"DC? Why DC? Ah . . . the woman lives there. Dyer."

Reznick nodded. "And the FBI HQ is there."

"It's like you're telling me to jump from the frying pan into the goddamn fire."

"I want you to think long and hard about talking to the FBI. You've got time. Will you at least consider it?"

Trevelle nodded. "Yeah, I will. I'm just shaken up. Not thinking straight."

"In the meantime, we've got a four-hour journey ahead of us, almost certainly longer at this time of day. I need to know more about this file. The memo from this private security company."

"I don't want to talk about it."

Reznick sighed. "Well, I do. We need to understand what we're dealing with. The footage you showed me inside your warehouse, that's not some home invasion crew. Forensic gloves, masks, the methodical way they went about their business."

Trevelle nodded, tears in his eyes.

"Think about it. The people who sent that team don't want the contents of that file becoming public knowledge. They don't know if you decrypted it or if you told anyone about it, but they're willing to take out anyone who might have even seen it. They probably took your computers and phones to forensically examine them to see if you sent the file to anyone else."

Reznick glanced again in the mirror. "Are the surveillance cameras still working in your house?"

Trevelle shook his head. "By the time I was on my way out of Miami, the feed had stopped working."

"Right, so they've ripped the cameras out, deactivated them, taken it all. And I'll guarantee, they will have ripped your place apart, right down to its bare bones. And they'll have people working to try and find you. Teams of people."

"Who are they?"

Reznick shrugged. "Based on the memo and what we could hear on the video? Foreign contractors, sent in by this US geosecurity specialist company. And if they're caught, it's nothing to do with the government."

"I know this sort of stuff happens."

"That's right."

"Jesus. Poor David." Trevelle glanced at a road sign. "You know, I never knew if that was his real name." He turned to Reznick. "Are you going to turn me in to the Feds in DC?"

Reznick thought long and hard before he answered. "No, I'm not."

"But you work for the FBI?"

"I'm a consultant. But I don't work for them. I don't take orders from them."

"Please don't hand me in. I'm terrified. If I had to spend time in jail, I swear, I'd kill myself."

"Relax, I'm not going to turn you in. But I want you to at least consider letting me approach Martha Meyerstein on your behalf."

"How did you go from black ops to toeing the line for the Feds? They've spied on innocent Americans since the Hoover days, you know."

Reznick chuckled. "Believe me, I had my doubts about them too. But there are good people there. I know them. They can save lives. They can save your life."

Trevelle pulled out a can of Red Bull from his jacket pocket, cracked it open, and took a few gulps.

Reznick said, "Your friend David had a lot of that lying around his apartment."

"He lived on it."

"Listen, I'm sorry your friend is gone."

"Friends. Plural."

"Right. Sorry. But you need to get your head together. I can help you. But you need to help yourself."

Trevelle closed his eyes and started breathing fast.

"Take deep breaths. Nice and slow."

Trevelle did as he was told. His breathing slowly calmed. When he opened his eyes, he said, "We need to warn Rosalind Dyer."

Reznick nodded. "Let's not get ahead of ourselves. We need to be careful how we go about this. She might be under surveillance. Close physical surveillance as well as electronic."

"I don't care. I have to warn her. I can't let another person die."

"Let's get to DC," Reznick said. "And we can figure things out on the way."

Six

Martha Meyerstein was sitting behind her desk on the seventh floor of the FBI's Hoover Building in Washington, DC, immersed in reading a domestic terrorism intelligence briefing, when her phone rang.

"Ma'am," her assistant said, "the switchboard says a detective in New York wants to speak to you."

"Did he give a name?"

"It's a she. Detective Isabella Acosta, Nineteenth Precinct, NYPD."

Meyerstein thought the name sounded familiar. "Put her through." During the few clicks it took for the call to connect, Meyerstein remembered where she knew the detective from.

"Martha Meyerstein speaking. Isabella, right?"

"Hey, nice to speak to you again."

Meyerstein sat forward. Acosta had been instrumental in bringing a psychotic UN diplomat involved in human trafficking to justice. The same guy who had nearly killed Reznick's daughter on the streets of Manhattan. "Everything OK?"

"Got something for you. I thought you'd want to know."

"What happened?"

"Jon Reznick reports to you, right?"

Meyerstein wondered where the conversation was going to go. "That's correct."

"I don't know what the hell is going on, but I'm hearing from one of my friends downtown, a captain in charge of the Sixth Precinct, that they found some kid hanged in his apartment in Greenwich Village. There are signs it wasn't a suicide, and they have two suspects. One of them, matching Reznick's description, was seen breaking a window and entering the property."

Meyerstein took a moment to gather her thoughts. "That doesn't make sense."

"I didn't believe it either. But Reznick is involved or has gotten caught up in whatever this is. And the NYPD are going to be in touch about this real soon."

Meyerstein leaned back in her chair. "Goddamn. What else do I need to know?"

"They have the two of them on video. They think the guy he's with, a young black male, is ex-NSA. Trevelle Williams."

Meyerstein scribbled down the name. Trouble with Reznick was the last thing she needed right now. "This all sounds pretty out of left field. How confident is the NYPD in the identifications?"

"Look, I know this probably isn't the sort of thing you want to hear. And to be honest, I can't imagine what Reznick might be up to. But it doesn't look good for him, know what I'm saying?"

"I'm telling you right now, Isabella, and you know this as well as I do—Jon Reznick had nothing to do with the death of this young man."

"Trust me, I agree. The problem is we have eyewitnesses who saw him breaking into the apartment, and a woman in the building opposite even filmed it. She thought it looked suspicious. And when she saw the glass getting broken, she called the cops."

Meyerstein felt a migraine coming on. "Isabella, I appreciate the heads-up. I owe you one."

She ended the call, feeling an immense sense of foreboding for what lay ahead.

Seven

It was late in the afternoon, thirty miles north of DC, as Reznick turned off the freeway and drove to the outskirts of a nondescript small town.

"Where are we going?" Trevelle said.

Reznick drove on. "Just a little stop. But not for long."

"Why?"

"Relax, kid."

"I don't want to relax. I'm scared. Two of my goddamn friends are dead."

"You wanna try and keep it together?"

Trevelle got quiet for a few moments.

Reznick saw a food truck at a roadside stop.

"Are you hungry?" Reznick asked.

"Hungry? I feel sick. Are you serious?"

"Well, I'm hungry. I need to eat."

Trevelle shrugged. "Then I guess you've got to eat, man."

Reznick pulled up beside an eighteen-wheeler with Arkansas plates and got out, stretching his legs. He walked around to the other side of the SUV and opened Trevelle's door. "Everyone needs to eat."

"I said I'm not hungry."

Reznick cocked his head. "We all need to eat."

Trevelle sighed as he climbed out of the vehicle. "Sure, whatever. Fries."

Reznick walked over to the food truck. He bought a burger and Coke for himself, fries and two cans of Red Bull for the kid. They leaned against the SUV. Trevelle downed most of the first Red Bull, then said, "I don't feel too good."

Reznick stared at the fries. "They look good."

Trevelle began to eat listlessly, chewing slowly.

"Feeling better?"

"Not really."

"It'll pass."

"I don't think it will. I don't think I'll ever get over this."

"You need to try and compartmentalize your feelings more," Reznick said.

"Compartmentalize my feelings? What the hell does that mean?"

"You need to leave the bad memories and push them aside. If you let them take over your head, you will drown in self-pity. Shit happens all the time. I know it's not easy. But you need to just, you know, not let it throw you so badly."

"I'm pathetic, I know."

"You're not pathetic. You're in shock. Was it your mother who died? Father? Sister?"

"No."

"These were friends. Close friends. But that's all they were."

Trevelle munched on the fries for a minute before he spoke. "My parents don't talk to me."

"Why not?"

"My dad was in the army."

"Was he?"

"Yeah, I was born in Germany. Army brat. He always thought I was soft. I preferred geeking out on my computers to playing sports. He hated that."

Reznick wondered if the kid's father was a hardline disciplinarian and had driven Trevelle to retreat into himself. He thought back to when he was growing up. His dad, a no-nonsense Vietnam vet, had been tough on him. He had learned to deal with it. The powder-keg atmosphere. The aggression. The verbal abuse. Even as a child, he could see his father was suffering his own personal hell. Just another simmering, frustrated, borderline-alcoholic veteran with undiagnosed post-traumatic stress disorder. But he knew other kids, maybe more sensitive ones like Trevelle, wouldn't be able to live with such malevolence in the home. "Hey, for what it's worth, I'd be proud if you were my son."

Trevelle blinked away tears. "Christ, one minute you're telling me I need to compartmentalize my feelings, the next you're saying nice things about me. You're giving me whiplash, man. Makes me anxious."

Reznick smiled. "Don't be. I don't bite. Well, not much."

Trevelle wiped away his tears with the back of his sleeve.

"Feeling better?" Reznick said.

"A little, thanks."

They threw out their trash. Reznick turned and looked at the passing vehicles on the nearby highway. "Less than an hour till DC."

Trevelle gulped down some more Red Bull. "OK."

"We need to decide what the plan is when we get there."

"It would be a mistake to call Rosalind Dyer, or even text her. I'm talking about from a technical point of view. Cell phone security, I mean."

Reznick nodded.

"I think we've got to assume her cell phone has been compromised. I'm assuming it's a government-issue encrypted cell phone. If the guys after her are halfway competent, they'll be listening in. If we call her, it might even put her at greater risk."

"I think we're all at risk from now on."

"Man, you really know how to scare me. What is it with you?"

Reznick clasped the kid's shoulder. "I'm trying to help you stay alive."

"Point taken. Sorry, my nerves are shredded."

Reznick glanced behind them, toward the heavyset truckers drinking coffee and talking, shooting the breeze near the food truck. He was starting to formulate a plan to get them into DC without being traced. Despite Trevelle's confidence in his signal jammer and the newer encryption he'd installed on their phones, Reznick didn't want to take any chances. "Wait here."

"Why?"

"Just stand there. Don't move."

Reznick walked over to the truckers and approached the biggest guy in the middle. The guy wore an oil-stained plaid shirt and a faded Cardinals ball cap. "Any of you guys headed into DC?"

The big guy pushed up the rim of his cap with his thumb. "Yeah, I'm dropping off my load at a hospital. You want a ride?"

"If you don't mind."

"That your Beamer?"

"Rental. Guy's picking it up in an hour. But I was hoping to catch a lift into town. I'm starting a new job first thing."

The guy finished the rest of his coffee. "You got it."

"Appreciate that, thanks. I'll tell my friend."

Reznick walked over to Trevelle. He kept his voice low. "Come on, we've got a ride."

"What? What's wrong with the car?"

"I used my credit card to rent it. If these guys are able to connect you to me, they might already be looking for us. License plate readers fitted to cop cars, road signs, and bridges mean citizens can be tracked and identified. We need to stay off the radar as long as we can."

An hour later, the trucker pulled up at a motel just a block from a downtown hospital in Washington, DC.

Reznick said, "Appreciate this, buddy."

"It's still America," the guy said. "We got to look out for each other."

Reznick smiled. "Damn straight."

Trevelle got out first.

Then Reznick jumped down from the cab and slammed the door shut. He slung his backpack over his shoulder. They picked up keys from the motel reception desk, Trevelle having already checked in online and paid using Dash cryptocurrency. He and the kid were shown to a dingy double room. Damp stains on the wall. The smell of nicotine hung heavy. Cigarette burns on the beige carpet.

Reznick tipped the guy ten bucks but was careful to lock the door behind them. He looked around. "This is interesting."

"What a dump."

"It's out of sight. Quit whining."

Trevelle looked around, his face screwed up as if he was revolted by the place.

"It's not the Plaza, I'll give you that," Reznick said.

"The Plaza? Gimme a break. This place gives me the creeps."

"It's just temporary."

Trevelle shook his head. He hung his backpack over a chair and began to pace the room.

"Chill out, son."

"How can I chill out? This is batshit crazy, what's happening."

"Don't flip out on me, not now."

Trevelle kept pacing. "Flip out on you? I'm seriously out of my comfort zone right now."

Reznick let the kid get it off his chest. He could see there was no point trying to reason with him. He needed to vent.

"I feel like I'm in the middle of a nightmare. Except I'm not waking up. I feel sick. I want my life to go back to the way it was."

Reznick said nothing.

"Do you understand me?"

"I understand what you're saying."

"I'm fucking scared."

"And that's why you need to focus."

"Focus?" Trevelle rubbed his hands over his face, as if trying to wake up from a bad dream. He sat down on the edge of the bed. "Maybe it's not worth it, trying to warn this woman. What do I care if she gets killed?"

"Let me make the call to the FBI."

"And they'll squirrel me away to some fucking secure unit. Claim I've been spying for Russia or some bullshit."

"But you're not."

"I know that. You know that. But the Feds will only see me as a national security risk."

"Well, you are, aren't you?"

Trevelle closed his eyes tight. "That's not really helping."

"Martha Meyerstein is smart. She'll figure something out."

"What are you going to say to her?"

"I'll tell it to her straight. She'll want to know what we know. Show me the memo again. The one you showed me on the High Line."

Trevelle took out his laptop and tapped some keys, then turned the screen toward Reznick.

Reznick nodded as he scanned the document again. "It's written in the language of compartmentalized, highly classified intelligence. The use of the phrase *VRK*. Very restricted knowledge. It is above top-secret intelligence. It means these contractors working for Geostrategy Solutions probably have a military or intelligence background, perhaps at a senior level."

"David told me the company has links to the Pentagon and the CIA."

It made sense. "The FBI can pull some strings, find out which government agency hired them. Get them to realize you're no threat to their operation and back off."

"But what about this poor woman? Rosalind Dyer. I'm assuming she doesn't know she's at risk. Aren't we going to warn her?"

"Why do you care so much about a woman you've never met that you're willing to put your life on the line? Why don't you just walk away? Disappear until this is all resolved?"

Trevelle looked thoughtful for a few moments. "I was a nervous kid. Never liked confrontation—because of my father." Reznick nodded. "But other kids could tell I was weak, so I was bullied at most of the schools I attended. And I was always too scared to stand up for myself. Or for anyone else. If I saw someone getting beaten up, I usually just walked away."

"Being scared is nothing to be ashamed of. Happens to us all, trust me."

"I guess what I'm trying to say is that sometimes there comes a point when you need to face your fears, come what may. Does that make sense?"

Reznick leaned over and patted Trevelle on the back. "You're alright, kid. I was just playing devil's advocate."

"Thanks. But, so, Rosalind Dyer, what're we gonna do?"

"You're damn right we're going to warn her. Whoever contracted Geostrategy Solutions is unlikely to back off from the decision to neutralize her now. Why she's such a threat to them, though, we don't know." Reznick began to consider the options. It wasn't just Rosalind Dyer he was thinking about. He had to think about how the Feds were going to read his actions. He didn't want to hand over the kid, even if it was for Trevelle's own safekeeping and well-being. He understood the kid's deep-rooted concerns. But would Meyerstein be able to get past how the kid had gotten the information about a government-sponsored operation to kill an American citizen? Would she be willing to focus on establishing if Rosalind Dyer was at genuine risk, and if so, from whom? Or would that be secondary to throwing the book at Trevelle?

By agreeing to help Trevelle, he'd made an implicit promise to protect him till the end of this. But his number one concern was to find Rosalind Dyer and warn her of the imminent risk she faced. Perhaps get her to a place of safety.

Reznick scanned the memo one more time. The document referred to foreign associates who were going to carry out the threat. The language was hardly subtle. But because the memo had been encrypted, whoever had written it must have assumed that they could use such language. It was careless in the extreme. Arrogant, even.

"Help me out here," he said to Trevelle. "I'm assuming the European hackers uncovered this memo after targeting Geostrategy Solutions, knowing they had links to the Pentagon and the CIA, right?"

"No question about it. Leftist and libertarian and free speech activist hackers—whichever way the Euro group leans—are ideologically opposed to what they see as deep-state actors. This file would have been like hitting the jackpot for them. They probably sent it to David expecting that if it were anything juicy, he'd share it with WikiLeaks. That would embarrass and humiliate the deep staters and globalists, call them what you will."

"So why not just release the files now?"

"It's possible. But in the circumstances, the people behind this might just get desperate."

"You mean make her disappear, that kind of thing?"

"Exactly. It might make them panic. The best way is for us to use our heads. So caution is key."

The more Reznick thought about it, the more he feared he and the kid were about to get dragged deeper into a giant mess. A random European hacker group claiming they had this information wouldn't carry a lot of credibility. But WikiLeaks would. Hanging Trevelle's friend David was a convenient way to eliminate that threat and send a message to anyone else who might contemplate releasing the file.

Reznick realized he needed to get the kid working. Keep him busy. For both their sakes. He handed the laptop back to Trevelle. "I'd like to know where Rosalind Dyer is. Location. At this moment. Can you do that?"

Trevelle shrugged. "Might take a while."

Reznick stared long and hard at him. "You want to warn her, right?"

Trevelle nodded.

"Then here's the deal: if you manage to locate Rosalind Dyer, and if we manage to speak to her, and if we somehow convince her that what we know is correct and she is fully aware of the impending threat, then you speak with the Feds? That's the deal."

Trevelle hesitated for a moment, then nodded. "Deal."

Eight

Thirty miles west of Washington, DC, in the affluent town of Fairfax, Virginia, Rosalind Dyer was kneeling at a gravesite. She felt the late-afternoon sun warm her skin as it bathed the granite and alabaster headstones all around her in a golden glow. She carefully arranged the bunch of white lilies she had brought in the brass vase. Then she touched the name newly carved into the grave marker and bowed her head.

She said a silent prayer for a man she had never met. A man who'd died three weeks earlier. His name was Andrew Boyd. He was an accountant. And the latest in a string of strange, seemingly accidental deaths. They were part of what she'd become increasingly certain was a cover-up on a grand scale. And she was the only one who'd made the connection: these were murders made to look like accidents. Andrew Boyd had been the seventh person to die under suspicious circumstances.

The more she thought about it, the more she believed it was inevitable that she would be next. It wasn't a matter of if, but when. She had only confided in her husband how she felt. She warned him of the consequences of her actions. He reassured her to put her trust in God and the laws of the land. But she knew they would come for her. They would get to her.

Rosalind's mind flashed back to the day of Andrew Boyd's funeral. She had watched from the back of the crowd of mourners as the rain poured down incessantly. Like the heavens had opened up and were spilling their tears for all to see. The man's eldest son had stood sobbing as he held one of the cords, lowering his father's coffin in the newly dug grave.

Andrew's widow, Catherine, had not cried. She had just stood and stared, holding her other children's hands, as if in mortal shock. It was a crushing blow for Catherine. But she had stood, head held high, as the red soil became sodden beneath her feet.

Rosalind closed her eyes now, one hand on the headstone in front of her. She wondered how Catherine Boyd was going to cope with bringing up their four children alone. Her husband and the family's main breadwinner snatched from them. Rosalind knew they lived in a comfortable old Colonial less than a mile from the cemetery. Andrew had almost certainly provided for them after his death. But Rosalind couldn't help thinking of the void that would be left in their lives without him. The sports practices he would miss; the homework he wouldn't be there to help with; the hikes, like those they'd taken on the numerous beautiful trails in rural Virginia—the ones he'd had pictures of hanging in his office—that would never happen again.

Rosalind had read every newspaper report of the drowning accident. They said he had died of a heart attack in the water. But no one could understand it. Andrew had aced all his physicals. Perfect health. He ran. He went to the gym. Everyone was shocked. Everyone, that is, apart from Rosalind.

Andrew Boyd knew too much. As did the other six who were now dead.

Rosalind wondered how she would die. She prayed it wouldn't be painful. She wanted it to be quick.

Lost in her thoughts, she had the sudden sensation that she wasn't alone. She turned around, looking out over the vast cemetery. But there was no one there.

Rosalind drove back to DC, her thoughts scrambled after the visit to Andrew's grave. She headed to her favorite coffee shop and got a latte and a granola bar. She let herself relax and enjoy the sustenance and the familiar suburban chatter. She noticed most of the other patrons were women with their kids. She looked like them in many ways. She was forty-eight years old and happily married to a lovely man, Travis. She attended church and once a year met up with other women who had served in the Army Reserve twenty years earlier. She had fallen in love with Travis when he transferred to her high school. He hadn't shown off, like a lot of the boys in her class. He was steady, dependable. And she liked that about him. Her gaze wandered around to the other women in the coffee shop. How she envied them. Their humdrum existence was something she craved. But she knew that was no longer an option.

She wasn't seeing nearly enough of her three teenage children. Her two daughters were fifteen, identical twins. Her son, Edward, was a nervous seventeen-year-old with a penchant for wearing black. Edward, in particular, needed his mother. He was more sensitive than his opinionated and self-confident sisters. Quieter and a bit of a loner. And she knew he liked to confide in her about his school, about his lack of friends, about why his sisters laughed at his taste in music, why they thought he was so "lame" still being on Facebook and a million other things. And she needed to be there to listen to her daughters when they talked about boyfriends or girl stuff. Instead she had become engulfed in her investigation and the voluminous background research she had undertaken. And of course, thinking about the closed-door hearing.

Seventy-two hours away.

She was scheduled to appear before Congress as a government whistle-blower. Technically she had protection under the law. But she was under no illusions as to the enormity of what she was doing or facing. For decades, the Department of Defense had managed to sidetrack investigations into its systemic financial mismanagement. Audits that had taken thirty years to come to fruition were, time and time again, caught up in accounting black holes. Fraud, overruns, misappropriation, kickbacks, the list went on and on.

There had been endless accountants and auditors who had come and gone over the years. All had been broken down by the system. Pensioned off. Bought off. But she was going to bring the truth to light—alone, if she had to.

Rosalind couldn't envision exactly how events would unfold. She wondered if *they* would get to her first, before she appeared at the committee hearing. Or maybe the threat was all in her head.

But she didn't think so. She had heard numerous stories about whistle-blowers who had testified before congressional committees and been accused of being everything from vindictive crazies to unhinged troublemakers. She would have to be measured in what she said. If she were only planning to tell them about the systemic problem of mismanagement of budgets, spiraling costs, and kickbacks on billion-dollar defense contracts, she didn't think anyone would bother assassinating her.

But there was something else.

The secret investigation she had begun in the last few weeks. The seven accidental deaths.

Rosalind's gaze was drawn to a woman watching Fox News on her iPad. The station was airing a committee hearing in the same building she'd be in soon. The man speaking was wearing a uniform. The name on the screen was unmistakable. Chairman of the Joint Chiefs of Staff Franklin Ross. The most senior figure at the Pentagon. The man she had ascertained was taking the biggest kickbacks. She'd uncovered two secret accounts. One in his wife's name, one in his. One was in Switzerland, the other in the Caymans.

Rosalind turned away as her mood began to dip. She felt alone and isolated. She was the only one who knew that every accountant who'd gone before her, who'd learned what she knew, was now dead. She hadn't even confided in her lawyer. She felt bad for not letting him know. But she figured that he had enough to worry about with everything that had happened in the main investigation over the last eighteen months.

But the seeds of doubt were growing within her. Was she doing the right thing? Would it be better to just let it all go? Pretend she didn't know what she knew? Should she tell her lawyer about the parallel investigation she had launched, ask him to go public if anything happened to her? Or would telling him put him in danger too?

She stifled a yawn. Her lack of sleep over the last few weeks was making it more difficult to concentrate. She felt more nervous about the upcoming hearing than she had expected. Normally she was a highly competent public speaker. But she had begun to feel strangely unsure of herself.

Even her husband, loyal to the core, had once or twice asked her if she was sure she was making the right decision by testifying. She detected his doubts. Sensed them. And that worried her.

Her lawyer had, only the previous day, mentioned coming to "an agreement" with the DOD for a financial settlement, in exchange for her silence. The suggestion had unnerved her. A lot. Had her lawyer already been approached? Had they threatened him? If she told him what she knew about the murders, would he share that information with lawyers on the opposite side? And then what?

The thing was, she was already in too deep. She couldn't backtrack now and be able to face herself in the morning. But even if she could, she wasn't in the mood for compromise. Perhaps she should be. It would give her an easier life, that was for sure. But integrity was important to her. Besides, it wasn't in her nature to conceal such things.

Rosalind's gaze again wandered around the coffee shop. She wondered who these other women were. What did they do in DC? Did they work for the government? Were they stay-at-home moms? Recently, she had begun to think of leaving her government job, with its pension and great health benefits, and striking out into the private sector. She had already been approached by a couple of Washington think tanks who had offered pretty crazy money. It would mean less stress and a chance to explore her interests. But she, slightly reluctantly, had passed, believing her work was not yet complete. She wasn't brought up to just walk away.

Her work defined her. As a special agent within the Defense Criminal Investigative Service, she reported directly to the assistant inspector general responsible for investigative operations. She had the highest level of security clearance. Most of her job was routine. But the frightening financial irregularities she had unearthed led right to the heart of the Pentagon.

The more she thought about it, the more enraged she got at the appalling waste of public money involved. Hundreds of millions of dollars in slush funds. Secret bank accounts. Dirty money. Kickbacks and corruption. Cronyism. Her parents had instilled in her the value of hard work, self-reliance, and also integrity. Her mother had prided herself on being thrifty. Saving every extra cent in an old cookie tin for her children or special occasions. She didn't believe in being wasteful. Rosalind wondered how the people she was investigating in the highest echelons of the US military could live with themselves. While the brave men and women of the American military were on the ground in all corners of the globe, putting their necks on the line for their country and for freedom, some bastards higher up the chain, who were already handsomely paid and rewarded, had their noses in the trough. It was disgusting. What would be the end result? Troops having to make do with older equipment. Fewer boots on the ground. Less hardware to defend the country. That wasn't the America she knew or believed in.

For what shall it profit a man, if he shall gain the whole world, and lose his own soul? Her father had quoted those words to her from the Bible.

Rosalind couldn't in all conscience just sweep aside what she'd found. That wasn't her way.

Her cell phone rang, snapping her out of her thoughts.

Rosalind reached into her handbag and took out her phone. She wondered if it was her husband, calling to say he was home from running errands with the kids. But when she checked the caller ID, she saw it was her lawyer.

"Hey, Rosalind, you OK to talk?" he said.

"Sure, go right ahead."

"How are you feeling?"

Rosalind kept her voice low. "Anxious. But I'm ready."

"I'd like you to come over to my office."

"Right now?"

"Sometime today or tomorrow morning would be great. I need to go over some of the audit documents and a couple of aspects of your report."

"Let me get back to you on that."

"Hell of a lot of paperwork I've still got to get through before the hearing."

"Tell me about it. I've waded through it all for the past eighteen months. I think if I have to read another auditor's report into accounting irregularities, I'm going to scream."

The lawyer sighed. "There's something else I want to talk about, Rosalind. Something I really need you to think about."

"What's that?"

"What we talked about yesterday."

"I said no to the settlement."

"You did. But even at this eleventh hour, it's not too late."

Rosalind was annoyed that he seemed to be trying to get her to bail on her own investigation. "My mind is made up."

"I understand. But I'm saying this as a friend and not just as your lawyer. Things are going to be rough."

"I know that."

"But do you really? Rosalind, they're going to come after you in the press. There will be leaks from the Pentagon. You know how it works. They're going to blacken your name. And I'm telling you, there will be even more pressure over the next forty-eight hours for you not to testify."

Rosalind sensed he was taking the long road around to get to his point. "What do you mean, 'even more pressure'?"

He sighed. "I talk with their lawyers regularly. I mean every day. That's what lawyers do, right?"

Rosalind wondered if this confirmed she'd been right to be careful about sharing details of her secret investigation. "I'm not sure I understand?"

"It's not just their in-house attorneys—who are very good—anymore. They also now have a powerhouse DC firm on retainer."

"Since when?"

"Since three days ago."

"I'm sorry, what? Why didn't you tell me then?"

"I needed to get the lay of the land first."

Rosalind ran a hand through her hair. "So this hardball law firm is going to rough me up, is that what you're saying?"

He hesitated. "Four of the company's partners are working solely on the legal strategy to neutralize the threat you pose."

"Legal strategy? So you believe that this is not going to be a straightforward closed session?" Rosalind asked.

"The closed session is the least of your problems. They're going to come after you in court, try to prosecute you for revealing classified information. They're going to claim the whistle-blower law doesn't shield you. They want to destroy you."

Rosalind leaned back in her seat and shook her head, struggling to take it all in. It was the last thing she wanted to hear. "Seriously?"

"It gets worse. They are prepared to utterly destroy you, professionally and personally. Drag you through the dirt."

"Personally? I'm sorry, in what way and how are they going to destroy me personally?"

"They hired private investigators, and they have been compiling their own details about not only you, but your husband as well."

"My husband?" Rosalind realized her voice had risen, and she forced herself to speak calmly. "What the hell do they expect to find? We live decent lives."

"They wouldn't show all their cards to me, but they mentioned everything from dope smoking in college to ongoing mental health issues."

"Meaning my clinical depression? The panic attacks? Heart palpitations? What has that got to do with my testimony?"

"Don't you get it? The price you pay is that your reputation is going to be destroyed. Rumors—even false ones—will be leaked to every newspaper and cable TV channel in America. Those rumors will follow you, and your kids, forever. They're even going to portray you as politically motivated, wanting to bring down the President."

"Bring down the President? I voted for him. Are you kidding me?"

"Sadly not. This is going to be a slow-motion, orchestrated takedown."

"What about my findings? The committee will still want to hear about those, won't they?"

"They will. But this firm has also hired some expensive forensic accountants of their own, and they have a report which is going to conclude that it wasn't one or two people responsible, but just antiquated accounting practices and software. And as for the kickbacks, they're going to say that that money was wrongly allocated. They have people, dozens of them, who will swear you are naive, politically motivated, and unstable."

"I don't believe it."

"Rosalind, you need to wake up and smell the coffee. They're working solely on how they are going to manage this situation. But I thought it was important that you fully comprehend what you're facing."

Rosalind was shaken by the news. She felt tearful, ready to break down. But she gathered herself, determined not to start blubbering on the phone.

"They're going to trash your investigation and destroy your reputation. And they're also, as if that wasn't enough, lobbying most of the committee to ensure your findings never make their way to the public. For you, Rosalind, this is a lose-lose scenario."

"Shit."

His next words were quiet. "There's more."

She laughed bitterly. "How could there be more?"

"They're going to come after your government pension, your benefits. They'll try to strip you and your family of all of that."

"They can't do that."

"But they'll try. They've made it clear they're going to play hardball and put you on the defensive all the way. You could spend years of your life dealing with lawsuits and other fallout."

Rosalind sipped her milky coffee and cleared her throat. "I don't know what to say apart from I'm shocked."

"Look, I know your motivation. And I know this is about principles. And ethics. And what is right. And I agree with all of that. But, and hear me out, I worry this could get ugly."

Rosalind felt herself begin to tear up a bit, throat tightening.

"I know the strain it's put on you, your marriage, and those around you. But that will be nothing compared to what's ahead of us."

Rosalind sighed and shook her head. "Frank, I thought you were in my corner."

"You know I am. And I will be there with you each and every hour in front of the committee."

"You think I'm crazy for wanting to do this, don't you?"

"No, I don't think you're crazy. I believe you, I believe you have more than enough evidence that something is seriously wrong. But . . . I don't want this to come out the wrong way, Rosalind."

"Speak your mind."

"I've got a real bad feeling about this. You have no idea how rough this is going to get. I'm talking not only about these new lawyers, but the chair and members of the committee. They've been getting lobbied directly by the Pentagon. They'll have been promised the moon if they dismiss your report. I fear they'll take the bait and use the hearing to put the spotlight on your competence instead."

"Do you think I should just give up on this? Are you saying I should just walk away?"

"I'm saying I don't want you to get hurt. I know you're tough. And you can look after yourself. But is this really worth it? The impact on your family. Your career. Your mental health?"

"I can handle myself."

"I know you can. But . . ."

Rosalind's gaze wandered around the coffee shop. "I want to do the right thing. My father was in the military. I was in the military. And he always taught me to do the right thing, no matter what."

Frank was quiet, letting her work through her thoughts. And those thoughts took her to the calls she'd been receiving late at night for the last month. Calls that, like the murders, she'd told only her husband about. She would wake up from a deep sleep and pick up her bedside phone. But it was only dead air.

"Frank, listen to me," she said, steeling her resolve. "I know more. There have been people killed. Who all died in suspicious circumstances. I have files. Names."

"And you're telling me this now? Are you kidding me?"

"I have the names of accountants. Auditors. Good people. And there is a thread."

"What kind of thread?"

"They were all involved in investigating the financial systems of the Pentagon, among others. And they all died in strange circumstances. Drownings. Suicide. Electrocution. All appear to be accidents."

"Jesus, Rosalind, this is crazy."

"I'm not crazy. In seventy-two hours, I'm going to testify. I'm doing the right thing for the right reasons."

"Tell me more about the names."

"I'll send over what I have."

"This is late in the game to be throwing this at me. It's playing into their hands, don't you see it? They will paint you as a lunatic. What you're saying is crazy."

"I know it is. But it's true, that's what's so terrifying."

Frank sighed long and hard, as if he had given it his best shot.

"You don't believe me, do you?"

"I'm your lawyer. But I'm also your friend."

"You want me to back out of this, don't you?"

"Even at the eleventh hour, there is still time. You need to fully realize that when you walk through the doors into that hearing room, there is no turning back. And it's going to be the dirtiest fight you've ever seen."

"I appreciate that. But my father taught me how to fight dirty. And I'm ready to fight."

Nine

Reznick crouched low in the front seat of the new SUV they'd rented, binoculars scanning the inside of the coffee shop. The woman sitting alone, an attractive fortysomething, matched the photo they had of Rosalind Dyer. "I think this is her," he said. "Black T-shirt, jeans."

Trevelle was checking his cell phone to confirm the GPS location of the woman's cell phone. "She hasn't moved in forty minutes. She likes her coffee, that's for sure."

Reznick saw the woman finally get up from her seat and put on her coat. "Got a visual. This is her. She's on the move."

"You wanna do the talking?"

"Leave it to me." Reznick waited until Dyer had stepped out of the coffee shop before he dialed her number. The woman had gotten about ten yards farther down the street, diagonally opposite from them, when she stopped. She reached into her coat pocket and took out her cell phone.

"Yes, who's this?" Her voice was hesitant.

"Don't be alarmed, Rosalind. You don't know me. But we really need to talk. Urgently."

"I'm sorry, who is this?"

"My name's Reznick. Jon Reznick. I think you're in danger, ma'am. We need to talk."

The woman looked around as if she sensed she was being watched. "Are you the creep that's been calling me in the middle of the night? Is that how you get your kicks?"

"Definitely not. Now you need to listen to me."

"Excuse me?"

"Rosalind, you need to listen to me right now. This is not a game. I'm the guy who wants to save your life. So listen to what I have to say."

"No, you listen. Don't think you can intimidate me. It won't work. So I'm going to hang up and call the cops."

"Do not hang up. You hang up, I can't help you. We believe you are at risk."

Rosalind was looking around. "You said we . . . who is 'we'? Who are you, for that matter? Is this some sort of joke?"

"This is no joke. Do you see the black Chevy across the street? Turn around, ninety degrees clockwise."

The woman turned and stared across the street toward the car.

"Do you see it? Do you see us?"

"Yes."

"White guy and black guy. I'm the white guy. The guy beside me is a computer-whiz kid who was passed sensitive information. It's related to you. We know everything about you. And we want to help. But you need to trust us."

The woman looked dazed.

"I know who you are, Mrs. Dyer. We know who you work for. And I want to get you and the computer nerd with me to safety."

"Who the hell are you?"

"I told you. My name is Jon Reznick. And I believe you're in danger. That's why I'm here."

"Are you insane? What if you're just trying to lure me into your car so you can murder me?"

"Rosalind, I've worked special operations around the world. So, no, I'm not insane. The kid here has worked with me before. He's ex-NSA."

"Sorry, I'm not buying it."

"Think about this, Rosalind. If I intended to cause you harm, would I have called to warn you?"

The woman stayed silent for a few moments. The wind blew her hair into her face, and she smoothed it down behind her left ear.

"How do I know I can trust you?"

"You don't. But we need to talk."

"So talk."

"I work on a consultancy basis for the FBI. But they are not involved in this. At least not so far. Where do you want to meet? And we'll be there. A place of your choosing."

"To say what, exactly?"

"I'll tell you everything we know."

"Which is what, exactly?"

Reznick sighed. "There are people who want to assassinate you."

From across the distance, Rosalind Dyer's eyes met his. "I know."

Ten

Later that night, Max Charles sat quietly as the three men took their seats in his office. He looked across the shiny mahogany table at his director of operations, Steve Lopez. Sitting on either side of Lopez were the firm's associates, Carl Franklin and Don Darcy—both former Special Forces operatives who advised on such matters.

Charles glanced at the summary of recent events in front of him before fixing his gaze on Lopez. The man had been a close adviser since Charles had left the Agency. Lopez wore a dark-gray suit, white shirt, and navy tie. He had crew-cut brown hair and unfathomable black eyes that always made it seem as if he was lost in his own thoughts.

"Today, Steve," Charles said, "I will get answers. I will not shout. And I will not scream. But I will get answers."

Next to Lopez, Franklin and Darcy shifted in their seats.

"I've never known a chain of events to spiral out of control like this, let alone one that brings potential heat from the Feds or the cops. Something has gone very wrong. So, my first question to you, Steve, is, am I right?"

Lopez cleared his throat. "Things have gone very wrong."

"Why is that?"

"It's complicated. But we're on it."

"I didn't ask if you were on it, Steve. I asked you if I am right that this is going very wrong."

"It's not a great situation, I agree."

"It's a fucking mess. I don't like mess. You know that, right?"

Lopez nodded, face impassive.

"I like tidy. We had a plan. But the plan went to shit, and I need to know why."

Lopez said, "Max, we are confident we will get on top of this."

Charles stared at him. "Our clients at the Pentagon and the Agency always get what they want. No questions asked. They're not interested in whether we're encountering problems. It's our job to predict and handle the unforeseen stuff. That's why we get paid so well."

Lopez nodded but stayed quiet this time.

"I distinctly remember I asked for this problem to be shut down. To be taken care of. And yet, here we are, playing catch-up." He looked at Franklin and Darcy. "Maybe I just don't seem to understand the intricacies of this particular operation. Maybe I'm getting too fucking old. Someone speak to me!"

Lopez sighed as his gaze fixed on Charles. "First, yes, it's an ongoing problem, but we will deal with this, Max. Second, I'm taking full responsibility."

Charles sat forward and gripped the armrests of his chair. "How did this file—this classified file—get into the fucking cloud at some facility in Rotterdam, when it was supposed to be locked down on our dedicated server upstate?"

Darcy said, "Our systems guy, who I know very well, said the access occurred via Tor, which, as you know, anonymously routes internet traffic. Nevertheless, our guys were able to trace the breach to a group of hackers that operates in Europe—Germany and the Netherlands, mostly. They accessed it but didn't decrypt it, and they passed it on to a guy down in the Village."

Charles spread his hands. "So how did it get from our secure server to Tor? How did it go from our dedicated server to the cloud and to Europe? I'm assuming that we're using military-grade advanced firewalls and systems?"

Darcy nodded and winced. "This is where it gets fucking unbelievable."

"I'm listening."

"It was a bit of social engineering—"

"In plain English!"

"Basically, our head of cybersecurity at the Ithaca facility was approached by a girl in a bar. She stole his cell phone."

Charles shook his head. "Are you kidding me? What a dumb fuck."

Darcy shrugged. "He must have said just enough to make her think his job was interesting. We're pretty certain she knows the guys in Europe. The phone gave them access to a limited number of files and passwords, and the sequence of events spiraled from there. The good news is that, thanks to a few back doors established by the NSA, we were able to get in and remotely delete every copy of the file from their cloud server and local systems."

Charles got up from his seat and began to pace the room. This crisis had resulted in not only an operation being compromised but also the threat of the problem expanding beyond their control. They needed to get a firm grip on the situation. "Have we retrieved everything from the guy's apartment in the Village?"

Franklin cleared his throat. "Yes, it's been taken care of. I'm satisfied the New York side of things has been shut down. But this Miami kid . . ."

"The NSA guy?"

"Ex-NSA. Trevelle Williams. We briefly had a bead on him when he stopped by the hacker's place downtown. But he's on the run again. And guess what?"

Charles looked at him.

"Reznick is with the kid."

"You've got to be kidding me. Jon Reznick? Fuck."

Franklin nodded. "NYPD have eyewitnesses who saw Reznick climbing into the hacker's apartment."

Charles shook his head. He knew all about Jon Reznick. He knew he had worked on CIA black ops a decade earlier. The guy's reputation was legendary. But it was Reznick's more recent contacts with the FBI that worried him. Charlies needed to think about that side of things.

"Reznick must've seen the body," Franklin said. "He's not stupid. He'll know what's really going on."

Charles poured himself a glass of water from the jug on the table. He gulped it down, sating his thirst. "Where are they now?"

Darcy glanced at Franklin, and they both nodded. "We believe DC."

Charles threw the glass against the wall. It shattered, dripping water onto the carpet. His men didn't flinch until he roared, "I've heard enough! Find them. Now!"

Eleven

The red-brick house was located on a tree-lined street adjacent to the Bethesda Presbyterian Church.

Reznick and Trevelle walked up the path and knocked on the front door. Reznick turned and looked at the kid. "You OK?" he said.

Trevelle just shrugged. "I'm OK. Maybe a bit nervous."

"You're gonna be fine."

The door opened, and a ruddy-faced fiftysomething man ushered them in, smiling broadly.

Reznick introduced himself, then said, "We're here to speak to Rosalind Dyer."

"She's inside waiting for you," he said. "I'm her pastor."

Reznick shook hands with him, as did Trevelle. "Appreciate you being so accommodating, sir. I hope we're not putting you out at this late hour."

"Not at all. I'm all about bringing people together. All I ask is that we treat each other with respect and civility in my house."

Reznick nodded. "Won't be a problem."

They followed the pastor down a hallway and into a softly lit drawing room. Pencil etchings of the church and some watercolors of DC hung on the walls.

Rosalind Dyer was sitting at a table by the window.

The pastor said, "Gentlemen, Rosalind reached out to me. She is a member of our church. And she wanted to meet you gentlemen in a place of sanctuary so she would feel comfortable."

Reznick smiled. "That's perfectly understandable, sir. I appreciate you facilitating this meeting."

The pastor said, "You gentlemen need some sandwiches? Coffee?"

Trevelle said, "That would be great, thank you."

Reznick nodded. "If you don't mind. I'm starving."

The pastor pointed to seats opposite where Dyer was sitting. "Take a load off. And I'll get the food and drinks."

Reznick stepped forward first and approached Dyer. He reached out and shook her hand. "Very nice to meet you, though I'm sorry about the circumstances."

"Hi."

Reznick introduced Trevelle, and they both sat down at the table across from her. "If it makes you feel better, Trevelle is struggling to take all this in too. A lot of stuff is going on."

Dyer shifted in her seat as if uneasy and untrusting as she looked at Reznick. "This is all very strange," she said.

Reznick nodded. "Yeah, you can say that again."

"So," she said, "if you don't mind, I'd like to start again, face-to-face. What's your name?"

"My name is Jon Reznick."

"And who do you work with?"

"I'm a former Delta operator, subsequently employed by the US government on intelligence operations at home and abroad, but recently I've found myself in a consultant role at the FBI. On a case-by-case basis."

Dyer fixed her gaze on him as if scrutinizing his motives. "Case-by-case basis, huh?"

Reznick shifted in his seat.

"Your name is familiar to me. I've done some checking of my own."

"You have?"

Dyer nodded. "I remember reading a report about you being involved in finding Martha Meyerstein after she was abducted."

"That's correct. I was involved in that."

"I think you were more than involved. You rescued her."

"A lot of people were involved."

The pastor returned with a tray of sandwiches and iced tea and placed it in the center of the table. "It's a bit hectic today. Wife's out of town."

"Thank you very much," Reznick said.

"If you need anything, I'll be next door," the pastor said, then quietly closed the door behind him.

Dyer still stared at Reznick long and hard, then her gaze lingered on Trevelle. "I'm a very good judge of character," she said. "The fact that I'm sitting down with two strangers in my pastor's front room at nearly midnight should tell you that I trust you. But I wanted to meet in a neutral environment, without prying eyes and ears. The pastor is someone I trust. He's a good man."

"Do you mind if we get down to business?" Reznick asked. "We've got something to show you."

"Sure."

Trevelle took his laptop out of his backpack and placed it on the table. He booted it up and logged on to a virtual private network in Iceland. He pulled up the encrypted document, typed in a couple of passwords, and the document appeared, fully decrypted, on the screen.

"This was sent to me," Trevelle said. "I used to work for the NSA." He glanced at Reznick. "I've also worked with Jon on a couple of investigations. Anyway, this document was passed to me by a friend in New York, who received it from hacktivists in Europe." He turned the screen so Rosalind could read it for herself.

Dyer scanned the memo quickly. Then she reread it. The color seemed to drain from her face. "That's my name."

Trevelle nodded, giving her time to digest the information.

"They're really going to kill me?"

Reznick picked up a ham sandwich and wolfed it down.

"This might be fake," she said. "Have you considered that?"

Reznick nodded. "But here's the thing. I don't believe it is."

"You want to give me your rationale?"

"I'm going to lay out how this started, first of all. That alright?"

"Go right ahead," Dyer said.

"Trevelle is a very, very talented cybersecurity expert. He's a hacker these days, and he's helped me out on various things in the past. I trust him. But anyway, he contacted me, saying he was scared. I'd never heard him like that before. Something spooked him. Bad."

Trevelle leaned over, turned the laptop toward him, and tapped on the keys. Then he turned the laptop toward Rosalind again. "This is why I contacted Jon in the first place. I must warn you, this is seriously disturbing."

Dyer stared at the video footage as the masked men with flashlights looked around the warehouse in Miami.

"That is my home," Trevelle said. "I was watching this remotely in real time from a diner about five miles away. I'm a creature of habit. Somehow these men knew that I usually get up at three in the morning and head down to South Beach. They knew I'd be gone. And they were waiting for me to come back. At the same time this was happening, I got a message from a friend of mine in New York. It was a reminder. Asking me to decrypt a classified file he didn't have time to look over."

Dyer watched the video until the summary execution. To her credit, she didn't flinch or look away. "That's disgusting. Who's the guy they killed?"

"A friend of mine who was visiting. I don't think these guys knew he would be there."

"I'm sorry for your loss," Dyer said.

"There's more," Reznick said. "They also killed the guy who sent him the file."

Dyer closed her eyes.

Reznick pointed to the screen. "That document we showed you names you. You just watched masked men enter Trevelle's home after he received the document and kill someone, and the guy who sent him the document ended up on the end of a noose. All of that tells me the chances are high not only that the document is authentic but that you are in grave danger."

Dyer rubbed her hands over her face as if she wanted to wake up from a bad dream. "This is horrible. Sickening."

"I know," Trevelle said. "But I think you have a right to know what we know. So you can make an informed decision about what you want to do."

Dyer said, "And you guys came all this way to warn me?"

Reznick leaned forward. "Correct. Now, Rosalind, we need to focus. It's clear to me that both you and Trevelle are in real danger. I'm probably on their radar, too, by now. My advice would be for both of you to contact the FBI. You mentioned Martha Meyerstein earlier. I report to her. And she will protect you and Trevelle, I give you my word."

"Jon, there's a lot you don't know."

Reznick watched her. "What do you mean?"

"There's an . . . investigation I've been working on. I think the events you've described . . . the . . . the hit—put out on me—are all because of my work."

Reznick and Trevelle glanced at each other. "You work for the Defense Criminal Investigative Service, right?"

Dyer nodded.

"Tell me a bit, if you can, about this investigation. We've shared what we know, after all."

Dyer sighed and closed her eyes tight, as if wanting it all to go away. "Look, I'm glad you've brought this to my attention. But I have a pretty good idea what this is all about. I'm not going to drag someone else into this."

Reznick sat forward. "Rosalind, we're already in it. We're too far along not to get dragged in further. Listen, you need to realize that this is no drill. No bullshit. Someone wants to take you out. And soon."

Dyer's gaze lingered on him for a few moments. "They want to intimidate me."

Trevelle glanced nervously at Reznick. "You know these people?"

Dyer was quiet as she mulled something over. She eventually spoke, her voice a whisper. "There has been a campaign against me. There have been calls to my house. Silent calls in the middle of the night. Threats made to my lawyer."

"What about?" Trevelle asked.

Dyer shook her head. "I don't know what to think anymore. I'm numb."

"It would be helpful if you could tell us what this is about," Reznick said. "That way I can better advise you. I'm guessing you know something. Something important. Maybe to do with national security."

"You know I work for the DCIS as a special agent. You know what that means?"

"Investigating defense contractors, missing millions, slush funds, right?"

"Exactly. I examine a lot of balance sheets. And in the last three or four years, I've been tasked to review budgets and financial projections, for the Pentagon, mostly—some special projects, special operations, sensitive stuff."

"What's this about, specifically?" Reznick asked.

"Specifically, in less than seventy-two hours, Mr. Reznick, I'm going to testify at a closed session of the Senate Armed Services Committee."

"And whoever you're going to testify about wants to silence you?"

"Got it."

"What exactly are you going to say?"

"I can't say. Or rather, I'd prefer not to say."

"I don't want names. Just an idea of what you're going to be talking about."

Dyer sighed. "I don't know if I trust you enough. Yet."

Reznick's gaze was drawn to the street outside. A navy Lincoln Navigator crawled down the street and parked diagonally opposite the church, farther down the road.

Dyer moved her seat back away from the window. "What is it?"

Reznick reached into his backpack and took out his binoculars. He saw two men wearing suits, white shirts, and ties, one speaking into a cell phone. He couldn't be sure. But he thought they looked like undercover Feds. "I think we've got company."

Trevelle said, "They look like Feds. Don't you work for them?"

"Trust me, if they've come after us, their intentions aren't to shoot the breeze with me or anyone."

Dyer looked at him. "They're here for me, aren't they?"

"They're here for all of us. We need to move."

Twelve

It was just after midnight, and Meyerstein was staring out of her seventh-floor office window in the FBI's Hoover Building. She was about to give a briefing to the Director about Reznick. And she was worried. The death of the man in New York City and Reznick's possible involvement shone a harsh spotlight—and not only on the fact that Reznick was operating without oversight. It would also reflect on her decision to use Reznick within the FBI, as and when she saw fit.

Her team had hurriedly compiled a dossier and timeline as they struggled to catch up with the chain of events that was unfolding. But she knew from experience that nothing Jon Reznick was involved in was ever straightforward.

Her phone rang and Meyerstein picked up.

"You ready, Martha?" asked the somber voice of Bill O'Donoghue, director of the FBI.

"Yes, sir, on my way." She picked up the dossier and timeline from her desk, headed out of her office and down the corridor, and knocked on his door.

Meyerstein waited for a few moments. She knocked again.

A voice inside shouted, "Yes."

Meyerstein walked in and handed over the dossier and timeline. "Here it is, sir, as promised."

"Pull up a chair."

"Thank you."

O'Donoghue picked up the dossier and took a few minutes to read it. Occasionally, he scribbled some notes on a pad. His brow furrowed deeper and deeper, as if his mood was darkening the more he read. He leaned back in his seat and shook his head. "Do you know who I just spoke to on the phone?"

Meyerstein shook her head.

"The President's national security adviser. He'd been tipped off by someone inside the Pentagon."

"I'm sorry, sir. I agree, this isn't good."

"Isn't good? Is Reznick for real? Has he lost his mind? I'm due to give a press conference in a few days about the importance of the FBI and ensuring the fair and proper rules and regulations that govern us. I'm going to be stressing the importance of working within the law. Stressing the importance of our country's Constitution and legal framework. And now this? Some crazy running around getting involved in all manner of criminality. Can you imagine the fallout if the *New York Times* or CNN or whoever learns that Reznick has been working for us?"

Meyerstein sat quietly, not wishing to fire him up even further.

"Serious question, Martha. Has Jon Reznick gone clinically insane? Has he lost his goddamn mind?"

"Reznick has not lost his mind, sir. For what it's worth, the situation appears far more complicated than the national security adviser or the Pentagon is letting on."

"Do you know anything about this Rosalind Dyer?"

"I do, sir. I drafted the briefing."

"How did we find out Dyer was involved? How did we get her name?"

"NSA. Reznick's voice was identified when he called her cell phone. She is a highly respected special agent with the DCIS, albeit under investigation at this moment."

"Rosalind Dyer is believed to have stolen classified documents. No one is above the law."

"Yes, and I know the law well. She could face up to five years' imprisonment if found guilty. I get that. And we must investigate. But my reading of the situation is that she'll be seeking immunity under the Whistleblower Protection Act. So I think it's a bit more nuanced than simply whether she has removed or retained classified material."

O'Donoghue shook his head. "I don't want to hear about nuanced. The Pentagon believes she is going to give up government secrets pertaining to national security. And their lawyers are scrambling, trying to get an arrest warrant, without the media hearing about this."

"I believe she's scheduled to appear at a closed session of the Senate Armed Services Committee."

O'Donoghue pinched the bridge of his nose. "And the thing is, will she reveal, either deliberately or inadvertently through cross-examination by members of the committee, that Jon Reznick is helping her? Have you thought of that?"

Meyerstein shook her head. "It's not something I've contemplated."

"Can you just imagine if they find out that the FBI uses the services of Jon Reznick? Do you know how that would look?"

"I understand what you're saying, sir."

"Do you, Martha? Do you know the pressure we're under these days? And then this? We will be annihilated if this gets out. And trust me, it will get out. Some media-hungry congressperson won't be able to resist getting on their white horse and portraying us as enemies to the forces of democracy, openness, and Christ knows what else."

"This is a situation that needs to be managed, sir."

"Managed? Reznick is running around out of control."

"I don't accept that, sir."

"You don't accept that? Do you want me to give you a recap of all the times Reznick has run amok? Breaking into that diplomat's apartment in Manhattan after his daughter was put in a coma? And that's just the beginning."

"Bill, I think when you're dealing with someone like Jon Reznick, we have to accept that there are going to be times when he pushes the envelope."

"He doesn't push the envelope, Martha. He scrunches it up and sets it on fire. He doesn't do rules. We're the goddamn FBI!"

Meyerstein sighed. She had tried for years to contain Reznick's excesses. And O'Donoghue didn't even know the full extent of his take-no-prisoners attitude. Reznick was a trained assassin, after all. The Director didn't know about the MS-13 gangbanger he'd shot in cold blood, despite the man's surrender while Reznick rescued the girlfriend of a compromised FBI special agent. Meyerstein had spoken to the SWAT team leader who had witnessed the killing, and he'd agreed not to mention it in his report. She'd plunged headfirst down a slippery slope into illegality. She knew it. But something deep inside her admired Reznick. Maybe even more than admired.

"What are we going to do with Reznick? I mean, this is indefensible."

Meyerstein shifted in her seat. "Bill, let's leave him out of this for now."

"I don't want to leave him out of it, Martha. The guy's nuts."

"With respect, he is highly intelligent and very principled. Stubbornly so. Yes, he seems to go out of his way to find trouble, but in this situation we need to know more about why he's involved. Let's establish some more facts before we come to a conclusion."

O'Donoghue sighed. "That's a circular argument. You're always defending him, no matter how indefensible his actions, while I sit here wondering what the hell is going on."

They shared a wry smile at that.

Getting back to business, Meyerstein said, "You read the timeline?"

"I did."

"Time of death for the body found in the attic of the apartment is still to be established, but the preliminary analysis is that the guy was dead long before Reznick broke in."

O'Donoghue tapped his fingers on his desk. "So what the hell was he doing there?"

"The ex-NSA hacker he was seen with, Trevelle Williams—I've spoken to him on the phone before, during at least one investigation. And that was a situation pertaining to national security."

O'Donoghue pointed to her. "You see, that's my point. Ex-NSA hacker? Why isn't he in jail? The FBI now relies on hackers to help us with investigations pertaining to national security? Are you kidding me?"

"Do you remember that former Delta friend of Reznick's who was rescued from that hospital facility in upstate New York? It was Trevelle who got Reznick in."

"Illegally."

"Look, this is a complicated situation."

"This just gets more goddamn murky. Hackers, hangings, and now a DCIS investigator wanted for stealing government secrets? It's preposterous!" O'Donoghue picked up the timeline again and studied it. "Why haven't they all been hauled in for questioning?"

"We were able to trace the three of them to the house of a local pastor. The team we sent in were obviously identified by Reznick, who knows countersurveillance, tradecraft, whatever."

"So what the hell happened?"

"When our guys knocked on the door, they were long gone."

O'Donoghue shook his head. "Gone? We look like amateurs."

"To be fair, sir, they were waiting for backup before they approached the house. And that was all the window of opportunity Reznick needed. They slipped out the back of the house without anyone seeing them."

O'Donoghue tossed the timeline onto his desk. "How much longer can we tolerate this, Martha? I get cold sweats every time I hear Reznick's goddamn name."

"Reznick isn't helping anyone's blood pressure, I agree. Look, Bill, hear me out. I want to establish what exactly happened, what the connection is between Dyer, Williams, and Reznick. I can assure you, Bill, there's more to this than meets the eye. I just need time."

"Time's running out. And just so you know, Martha, we'll find Rosalind Dyer. And she'll be arrested. And so will Reznick."

Thirteen

Reznick was sitting alone in a stolen Chevy Suburban on a dark street in Bethesda. He checked his watch. It was just past two a.m.

Suddenly, headlights appeared out of the darkness farther down the tree-lined street. A car pulled up outside a smart Colonial house. Reznick flashed his headlights. Once. Twice. Three times.

Meyerstein got out of her car, turned, and looked directly across the street. She began to cross the road.

Reznick wound down his window.

Meyerstein stared at him. "I've been expecting you."

"Sorry I didn't call ahead."

"Are you serious?"

"I know, it's all gotten a bit crazy."

"No kidding. Do you mind explaining what the hell is going on, Jon? And I don't mean you turning up at my home unannounced. Do you know you're a wanted man?"

Reznick held up his palms.

"This is my house, Jon! Where I live, goddamn it! It's the middle of the night!"

"I know, it's not the way I should do things, I get that. It's not good protocol, I know all that."

"Seriously, whatever is going on, you need to drop it."

Reznick stayed quiet, not wishing to enrage her further. He needed her on his side at all costs.

Meyerstein scrutinized his face. "You haven't shaved. You have bags under your eyes. You look terrible."

"What can I tell you?" he said. "Sleep deprivation does that to a man."

"You could help yourself by cutting down on all that Dexedrine."

"You're probably right. Anyway, it's nice to see you, by the way. You look nice."

"I feel like shit if you must know." She looked around. "The neighbors will be wondering what the hell is going on. I wouldn't be surprised if a few are already calling the cops."

"Two minutes of your time, that's all."

Meyerstein looked around once more, then walked around the car, slid into the passenger seat, and quietly shut the door. "This is most irregular."

"What can I say? I'm an irregular guy."

Meyerstein didn't smile. "I'm not in the mood, Jon."

"Was that the Feds you had on my tail outside the church earlier?"

"I can't comment on that, Jon."

"They need to brush up on their surveillance methods. They stood out like a car full of sore thumbs."

Meyerstein cleared her throat but said nothing. "Do you want to tell me what this is all about?"

Reznick reached under his seat, pulled out a file, and handed it to her.

"What's this?"

"Remember the hacker in Miami? Trevelle Williams? You spoke to him once, maybe a couple of years ago. Martha, don't act as if you don't know anything about him."

"This is the guy you're running around New York with? And now DC?"

"That guy came to me with that information. It was passed to him from a friend of his, another hacker in New York."

Meyerstein sighed. "Don't tell me, you discovered the body."

"How the hell do you know about that?"

"Isabella Acosta gave me the heads-up."

"Isabella, huh? Good for her."

"This is not good, Jon. No matter how you look at this. Not good."

"Just so you know, someone got to that guy before we got there. Almost certainly the same guys who were looking around Trevelle's home in Miami." Reznick pulled out his cell phone. "Take a look at this footage. A warning, it's pretty graphic." He played the footage of the masked men and the point-blank killing of the bespectacled Fernandez.

Meyerstein stared at the footage. "This is not a home invasion crew, that's for sure."

"Absolutely right. Thank you. These are pros, Martha. This was in Miami. Were these mercenaries from there? Who knows. They took Trevelle's computers and hard drives. And they're looking for him. I'm trying to protect him."

"You need to bring him in."

"Look at it from his point of view. The kid is scared. He's ex-NSA, he's a hacker, he's convinced he won't see daylight again if he gives himself up."

"I'll do all I can, I promise. But as it stands, you're in a sticky situation. The NYPD is looking to question you about the death of the guy in the Village. You're a wanted man. But more importantly, Rosalind Dyer is wanted by the FBI."

There wasn't time for him to ask her how the FBI had learned about Dyer or what charges they were planning to press.

But it confirmed for him that Dyer was right—someone in the government was very afraid about what she was going to testify about. Arrest her or kill her—they'd do whatever they could to silence her.

"Read the file," Reznick said. "You'll see a decrypted version of a memo that was passed from a hacktivist group in Europe to the dead guy in New York, who passed it to Trevelle. And I just showed you how they didn't hesitate to kill Trevelle's friend when they were looking for him. The kid is seriously spooked. But the memo they accessed—"

"Do you mean stole?"

"Whatever, the memo needs to be read to be believed. They— whoever in our government has hired this private firm—want to neutralize Rosalind Dyer, an American, on American soil, using a foreign intelligence service. That's what this is all about. This is what we've got our hands on."

Meyerstein looked at her watch. "I don't have time for this now."

"What do you mean you don't have time? You need to make time for this. I'm asking for a favor. A big favor. Just check it out."

Meyerstein sighed. "None of this negates the fact that Rosalind Dyer is believed to have stolen classified government documents."

Reznick shook his head. "That file you're holding also contains some rather interesting documents that Rosalind Dyer is alleged to have stolen. Swiss bank accounts linked to members of the Joint Chiefs of Staff. It's outrageous, and she's doing the right thing by trying to expose it."

"Jon, you're overstepping. You're allowing this to become personal. You're becoming emotionally attached."

"Yes," he said, "I am. The kid came to me for help. I owe him. He's helped me out in the past. He helped you in the past too."

"When?"

"When I used him to find out more about the Russian mob who kidnapped you, remember that? There's numerous other investigations his hacking skills have helped with as well. Besides, he doesn't have anyone else. He can't go to you guys or the cops. Neither can Rosalind."

Meyerstein said nothing.

"What the hell am I supposed to do? Let the kid get killed? And what about Rosalind? Don't you get it? People are going to kill Rosalind Dyer to keep their bad behavior hidden. Some of the reasons why are in that file. And that's why I'm reaching out to you, someone I trust within the FBI."

Meyerstein hesitated slightly before she answered, and when she did, she wouldn't meet Reznick's eyes. "I can't comment, Jon. It sounds like quite a conspiracy theory, and I'd like to help. But that's not possible in this case."

"A woman's life is at risk."

Now she did look at him. "Maybe. But it's complicated on my end too. We're investigating Dyer for theft of classified documents. We have to uphold the law."

"Martha, doesn't the fact that there's a plot to silence her make you question how legitimate the FBI's investigation is? You're being used. I can't in all good conscience just ignore the threat to her life. And neither should you."

"I don't operate according to my conscience. I operate according to the laws of this country."

"Those laws are being broken."

"This is not your fight."

"It is now."

Meyerstein said nothing.

"Read just a piece of what's in that file. The people we've entrusted to run our military are defrauding American taxpayers for their own personal gain. It's appalling."

Meyerstein stared out the windshield, down the street. "O'Donoghue wants me to cut the cord with you. To terminate our working relationship. Situations like this just give him more ammunition. It can't go on. It's not going to end well."

"What are you going to do?"

"I don't know. But it's not the first time I've come under pressure because of your actions, let me tell you."

"What do you want to do, Martha?"

"You're not making it easy for me, Jon. You never do."

"I'm not trying to making things difficult for you. But I swear, your guys are off base on this."

"Be that as it may, the Director isn't a fan of yours. He is uneasy about your methods, Jon. And there's only so long I can protect your role."

"How about you? Are you uneasy about me?"

Meyerstein sighed. "Am I uneasy about you? I think it's important to have your capabilities available to us. I think it's important that you feel you can reach out to me like you're doing now."

"I agree. Martha, for me, it's a privilege to try and serve in any way I can. I know I'm unconventional. Frankly, I don't give a damn what the rest of them think. I'm only concerned what you think. I don't want to embarrass you or the FBI. So if you do want to cut the cord, just say it and I'll be out of here. And I know it won't be personal."

"I don't want that, Jon. Not at all. But I feel . . . I feel conflicted about us."

"In what way?"

"What you do makes me uneasy. The methods you use. And I know when you turn up, trouble won't be far behind. But I like being with you. I want to be with you a helluva lot more than I am. There, I've said it. Does that make sense?"

Reznick nodded. The truth was he felt exactly the same. He just couldn't express those same feelings. He felt uncomfortable even broaching the subject of their personal relationship. He didn't emote. He was like his father that way. Unless it was anger. He had no problem showing his anger. His feelings were something private to him. Buried deep within him. It was just the way he was. His father showed little emotion to Reznick growing up. And so he had become just like him.

"What I'm trying to say, Jon, is that you mean a lot to me. But you also infuriate me. But what can I say, I miss you. A lot."

"I miss you, too, for what it's worth."

Meyerstein smiled. "That's nice to know."

"I'm sorry for turning up like this."

"Don't be sorry. I'm glad you're here." Meyerstein cleared her throat. "Let's get back to business. Rosalind Dyer. Jon, I'm not sure you know the full story."

"As God is my witness, this woman, Rosalind Dyer, is telling the truth. I believe her, and I believe in her. She's a true American patriot. She just wants to see justice done."

"What about the law? Does she believe in the law?"

"I hear what you're saying. She's a whistle-blower. But we need people to speak out. My father was the one who first told me about Daniel Ellsberg. You heard of him?"

Meyerstein nodded. "He leaked the Pentagon Papers. Do you think it's patriotic to leak classified information?"

"In that case, yes. The American people didn't know about the illegal bombing of Laos and Cambodia. Should they have been kept in the dark?"

"Are you saying what she's doing is the same thing?"

"Not at all. But I'm saying we have a history in America. Where people stand up for what they believe is right. Is true. Freedom of speech. What does the Constitution say?"

"Jon, I understand deflection, trust me. But Rosalind Dyer has responsibilities. If she unearthed information during an investigation, she needed to deal with it via the appropriate channels. DCIS has very, very strict guidelines about what can and cannot be shared and with who. You should know that better than anyone. It's about national security."

"National security? Gimme a break. That's what they said about Daniel Ellsberg leaking those classified files. What about the public's right to know what's being done with their money? Who's on her side?"

"I don't want to get into a long-drawn-out argument right now. She needs to turn herself in. Can you help convince her to do that?"

"No can do, Martha."

"You're making this difficult for me, Jon."

"Read the file. Dyer knows a lot. A lot more than she's letting on. And people want to silence her. Forever. Whether you think she deserves to be in jail or not, she doesn't deserve to be murdered."

Meyerstein bowed her head for a moment. Then she got out of the car, taking the file with her, crossed the quiet suburban road, and walked up the path to her home.

She never looked back.

Fourteen

Rosalind Dyer descended the stairs of the Bethesda metro with a backpack full of clothes and headed to the bathroom, as Reznick had advised her. She changed in one of the stalls and put on a wig, glasses, sweatpants, and an Adidas top and sneakers. She stepped onto the platform and hopped on a train. Six stops later, she arrived at Shady Grove, the last stop on the line. She looked around. An SUV flashed its lights in the distance.

Dyer walked over to the SUV, knowing her movements weren't being tracked. Trevelle had already jammed the surveillance cameras in and around the station.

Reznick was behind the wheel, Trevelle sitting in back, scanning his cell phone.

Dyer climbed in the passenger seat and took off the wig and glasses. "Don't you think this is overreacting, Jon?" she said.

"Just a precaution. The FBI is on our tails. And you've got a crew trying to kill you. We need to be sharp."

Trevelle handed her a new phone.

"What's this?" she said.

"Your government-issue phone can't be trusted."

Dyer looked at him as if he'd lost his mind. "I think you guys are being paranoid. This is crazy."

Reznick pulled away slowly. "Under the circumstances, Rosalind, it's better to be safe than sorry. How do you think the FBI was able to find us? It was through your phone."

"I've been so busy thinking about the hearing, I never thought about such basics."

"The new phone will keep you off the grid, at least for now."

"Speaking of which, tell me about your meeting with the assistant director?"

"It was short. To the point. I passed on what I know and tried to lay out the fundamentals."

"Was she sympathetic?"

"Not exactly. But she's a good person. And I trust her. She'll take a look at the file. But there's no promises or guarantees."

"Jon, I need to give evidence to the committee. I need to do this. There's too much I've uncovered. I can't go into hiding."

Trevelle piped up from the back seat. "Aren't you scared? I know I am."

"Yeah, of course I'm scared," she said. "But I just can't walk away from this."

"Walking away from this would be a smart move," Reznick said.

Dyer laughed. "Whose side are you on?"

"I'm playing devil's advocate. The smart move is to say fuck it and move on. Get safe."

"There's too much water under the bridge. I can't just stop now. I owe it to my position, what I believe in, my honor. It's called integrity."

"Ideals and honor are all well and good," Reznick said, "but they don't beat staying alive, trust me."

Dyer sighed. "Expediency was never my thing."

"Mine either."

"I think you're more scared than you're letting on," Trevelle said.

Dyer smiled and turned around to look at him. "You got me. Look, of course I'm scared. I wish I wasn't. I wish to hell I didn't know what I know. But I can't unmake the past. So I need to testify."

Reznick drove on, the car's headlights bathing the road in a ghostly glow. "Can't you testify to the committee via videoconferencing? You'd be safe, and the committee would get to hear and see you."

"I asked for that. But it was refused."

"Seriously?"

"The chair was fine with it, but the rest of the committee—and it was all men—told my lawyer that it wasn't an option. They wanted to speak to me in person, scrutinize the evidence I've compiled, and talk through the report I'm going to submit. I think they were concerned that I would be coached."

Reznick nodded. "Let me get this straight. The kickbacks and corruption you've uncovered—are we talking military high echelons? Is this what we're really talking about?"

"I'm talking Joint Chiefs of Staff, two of them, who left a paper trail leading to a slush fund and secret accounts in Switzerland, Panama, the Caymans, and the British Virgin Islands. Compiling the evidence has taken over my life. So, before you ask, I can't cut and run on this. There's too much at stake. Too much invested in this."

"And you've tried to raise this with your superiors?"

"On numerous occasions. The inspector general has gotten involved. He read my preliminary report. Meanwhile, I'm on paid leave while they conduct an internal investigation into *my* actions."

"You don't sound convinced that they'll do the right thing."

"I think they've just been hoping this thing goes away. They want me out of the way. But I don't scare easy. My father was in the military. I was in the Army Reserve. My brother served in Afghanistan."

Reznick nodded. "Army?"

"Rangers."

"Impressive."

"He's been my rock. My faith. As has my husband. My brother will be coming to watch me testify."

"Good for him."

Dyer sighed. "He's in a wheelchair thanks to an IED. Both legs, below the knee, just gone."

Reznick's mind flashed on searing images. Two Delta operators screaming and crying, blood and lower limbs scattered obscenely among the molten metal and fragments of the bomb. He'd visited both men at the Walter Reed Army Medical Center, not far from where they were now. It still hurt him to think of their injuries and the courage they'd shown throughout their rehabilitation. He didn't know if he would have been so resilient.

His father had had a deep-set fear that Reznick would be maimed. Lose a limb. He remembered the first time he came back from Iraq, his father on the front porch, American flag flying from the second-floor window. The house he'd built with his own hands and imagination after he had come back from Vietnam. His father stood, as if to attention, head held high, tears flowing down his face.

Reznick had hugged his father for the first time in years. His father had sobbed hard, hugged him tight, as if not wanting to let him go. Relieved his son was in one piece and that he'd made it home. Except Reznick had felt a disconnect when he returned home. Not only with his family and friends, but with life. It was like life was going on all around him, and he didn't feel part of anything. It was like that for years.

"Jon, did you hear what I said?" Dyer's voice snapped Reznick out of his thoughts.

"Sorry, I didn't catch that."

"I was just saying to Trevelle, I'm not the sort of person who's going to go quietly. I won't be intimidated. And I will not cave under pressure."

Reznick sighed, dark worries filling his mind. He wondered if Dyer had really thought this through. He admired her courage. Her integrity. But stuff like that meant nothing if people were determined to kill you.

Trevelle leaned forward. "Who do you think is responsible for this contract on your life? I mean, it's gone through this Manhattan global security company, but it didn't start there. That's got to be authorized at a high level, beyond classified."

Dyer said, "I would guess that it originated from within the Pentagon. The CIA, maybe even the DCIS. No one wants gossip about defense contract kickbacks going public and making them look bad, especially when two joint chiefs would take the fall. They protect their own."

Trevelle said, "Yeah, but there's no proof the Pentagon is pulling strings."

She nodded. "It's true, the order didn't start with the private security company. I would bet that this is a Pentagon SAR."

"What's that?" Trevelle asked.

"SAR stands for special access required. Special access programs, they're sometimes referred to. They're black projects, with only a select few having access to the highly classified details. This private company is probably one the Pentagon contracts for these sorts of projects."

Reznick said, "I've worked on quite a few special access programs. Mostly unacknowledged. They're called USAPs, right?"

Dyer nodded. "But there's a subset of unacknowledged special access programs, known to some as waived SAPs, that are exempt from most reporting requirements."

Trevelle said, "Hang on, you guys, back up. Do you mean including not reporting the operation to the legislative branch?"

"Correct," Dyer said. "How Orwellian is that?"

"That's fucking outrageous," Trevelle said. "So a handful of people within, say, the Pentagon, they're operating with impunity, without legal oversight?"

"Pretty much. And it's only the chair of intelligence or the defense committee who needs to be told—and sometimes even then it's only verbal notification. It's really sketchy."

Trevelle whistled. "That's crazy. I don't like that shit."

Dyer shook her head. "Sometimes, a military needs such protocols. But without democratic oversight, or cursory oversight at best, it allows a handful of individuals to run illegal operations without anyone being the wiser. And this is the end result. But we're only scraping the surface."

They fell silent as Reznick took the exit for another highway. Eventually, he said, "Let's get back to basics. It's important not to lose sight of your safety. Don't get me wrong, I want you to testify and do the right thing. But not if it costs you your life."

"I've got to complete this journey, Jon. No matter what." Dyer examined the new cell phone Trevelle had given her. "Am I OK to use this now?"

"Go right ahead. You won't be tracked. I promise."

"Who are you going to call?" Reznick asked.

"My husband. He'll be worried."

"Give him a call. But be careful, they might be listening in on his end. So don't give him any information about where you are."

Dyer dialed and put the phone on speaker. She waited for a few moments before it was answered. "Hi, honey, it's me."

"Rosalind, where the heck are you? I've been worried sick. You said you were just running out for coffee and to do a few errands. It's the middle of the night. Are you alright?"

"I know. I'm sorry. Listen to me, I'm safe. But things have escalated."

The sound of one of her three children yelling in the background could be heard. "Yeah, here too."

"What do you mean?"

"The FBI is here. Have been for the last hour. They say you stole classified documents, federal property. They're here to arrest you."

Fifteen

Reznick drove for countless miles through the darkness into rural Maryland. He had begun to formulate a plan. The fact of the matter was that there were no good options. And he wondered if going on the run with Dyer and Trevelle had been a smart move.

The more he thought about it, the more he realized that he should have drawn a line in the sand and insisted the Feds get involved. But he couldn't in good conscience hand over Trevelle or Dyer if it meant they would lose their liberty. They weren't bad people. The reality was they were both principled in their own ways. He admired them both. Maybe that was it.

Reznick pushed those thoughts to one side. He had made a decision. And he was going to stick with it, no matter what. But first, the top priority was to get Dyer and Trevelle to a secure place. Out of sight. At least until Dyer testified.

He did feel deeply conflicted after his conversation with Meyerstein. But what Dyer had unearthed, the venal corruption among the highest American military leaders, sickened him. Siphoning off public money for personal gain? It was the troops, like his Delta partners, who suffered. Who died needlessly because money that should have been going to equipment and operational readiness was diverted for someone's personal gain. And the people around the world who relied on America to protect them in times of crisis suffered too.

Dyer's story needed to be told. She needed to be protected. Bottom line? He couldn't just walk away.

Reznick admired people like Dyer. People who weren't afraid to go against the grain. To do the right thing in the face of pressure and against insurmountable odds. And even knowing that people were out to kill her, to prevent her from telling her story before the committee, still Dyer wouldn't buckle. He liked that about her. A lot. She would not be crushed.

The car's headlights landed on a deer ahead in the road, snapping Reznick back to reality. He slowed down. The animal just stared at him from the middle of the road, as if wondering why someone or something was encroaching on its territory. The beast didn't flinch.

Reznick stopped the car a few yards from the deer.

"Well, I'll be darned," Dyer said. "It's not moving."

Reznick waited patiently; he didn't want to startle the animal. A few seconds later, the deer trotted gracefully off into the trees by the side of the road. Reznick pulled away slowly. His thoughts focused again, not on the people in the car with him, on his responsibility to them, but on Lauren, his daughter. He had responsibilities to her too. What if something happened to him and she was left alone? What then?

And then it dawned on him. Meyerstein was right: he was not acting rationally. He was being driven by his own morality. Instead of his head, it was his heart, his beating heart and soul, that was dictating how he should act. It was how his father would have acted. Do the right thing and to hell with the consequences. But by doing so, was Reznick planting the seeds for his own downfall and others' as well?

No good options.

Reznick was facing a major dilemma. He knew Dyer was determined to testify. But the people sent by the private security firm would be pulling out all the stops to track her down.

He wondered who he could trust, if anyone. He trusted Meyerstein. But the FBI was under huge pressure to find Dyer. How far could he expect Meyerstein to veer from the oaths she was beholden to?

Dyer dabbed her eyes as she sat in the passenger seat. "I can't believe I'm out here in the middle of nowhere. What am I doing?"

"We'll find you a place that's secure. But we need to hurry."

"Know what I can't believe, Jon?"

"What?"

"I can't wrap my head around the fact that all of this has happened simply because of my investigation. That people have been killed. It's more than just the hacker guy in New York."

"What the hell are you talking about?"

Rosalind told them about her parallel investigation into the suspicious deaths of auditors and accountants who had been involved in the oversight of government finances, especially within the Pentagon.

"Who knows about that?" Reznick said.

"My husband and my lawyer. That's it. But I intend to tell all in front of the committee, closed session or not. I fear there will be a price to pay."

Reznick nodded. "Sometimes there's a price to pay for doing the right thing. But the road less traveled is never easy. Making your own choices. Setting off on a new trail. Never goddamn easy, you understand?"

"I do. But I'm starting to doubt myself. I wish I hadn't started this whole goddamn thing. My lawyer says money, perhaps a multimillion-dollar settlement, is on the table if I drop out of the investigation and decline to appear before the committee. But I've come this far. I won't be bought off. That's not my way."

"Then stick to your guns."

"What about my family? They're the ones who will have to pick up the pieces. The FBI views *me* as the criminal."

"Have a bit of faith," Reznick said. "I think the Feds, once they know the full story, might come around to your way of thinking."

Dyer shook her head. "I had no idea it would come to this. Look at me, a fugitive. I don't know if my heart is really in this now."

Trevelle said, "I believe in you."

"Your friend died because of me. What about that?"

"You didn't kill him, Rosalind."

Reznick sighed. "You need to be strong. Dig deep. Are you brave enough to head out on a new path? Strike out on your own?"

"Yes. But what about my husband?"

"What about him?"

"My husband has high blood pressure. This could kill him. I should've thought of that."

"Don't be so hard on yourself."

"And what if they can't find me and decide to go after my husband? Or even my kids! What if they threaten or hurt my family? How could I have been so goddamn stupid?"

Reznick shook his head. "We need to focus on you. Hour by hour. Until this is over. And our top priority is that we need to keep you out of sight until the hearing."

Dyer nodded. "I feel so isolated."

Reznick said, "There's a guy I know. Lives about ten miles from here. We'll go there. He'll take care of us."

Trevelle said, "Can you trust him?"

"He was in Delta. He's a good guy. It's been a while, but he's pretty solid."

Dyer nodded. "So the plan is just to stay overnight, to lie low until the committee hearing?"

"You OK with that?"

"Fine. Let's do it."

Reznick glanced in the rearview mirror at Trevelle. "What about you?"

"I'm cool with that, Mr. R."

"Fair enough. Let me make a call."

Reznick pulled out his cell phone and called a number from the contact list he maintained of other ex-Delta operatives. Guys like him. Guys he knew he could turn to in a jam.

It rang four times before a gruff voice answered. "Yeah, who's this?"

"Mr. Kazinsky, you remember me?"

There was silence for a few moments. "Nobody calls me Mr. Kazinsky. Apart from . . . Reznick?"

"You got it first time, Ed."

"Jon fucking Reznick, no way, man. How the hell are you?"

"I'm in a bit of a tight spot, and I'm looking for help."

"When?"

"Right here and now. A place for me and two others to stay. I need to get out of sight for a day or so, and then we'll be gone."

More silence. "Where the hell are you?"

Reznick checked the satnav map. "Three miles south of Gaithersburg."

"You got to be kidding me. Seriously?"

"I'm within range, brother. Can you help me out?"

"For you, man, anything. So, you want to find Huntmaster Drive. Big lamp at the end of the drive. That's me."

"We're not disturbing you or your family?"

"I got no family, man. They're gone. But hey, fuck 'em, right?"

Ed Kazinsky had arms like lamb shanks. Veins bulging from his neck. He opened the front door wearing a pale-blue button-down shirt and dark jeans, and he had blue eyes that seemed to linger too long, as if constantly sizing up whoever he was looking at. He looked like he kept himself in shape. He spoke in a quiet voice, almost humble. He invited them into his house and showed them around.

It was clear to Reznick, or anyone for that matter, that Kazinsky had a serious penchant for guns. On one wall was a wood-paneled, glass-front display containing rare handguns, long rifles, semiautomatics, and Civil War muskets.

Reznick's thing for guns was more functional. He was happy as long as his 9mm Beretta was close to him. But Kazinsky was something else. Clearly a collector. Maybe even an obsessive gun nut.

Kazinsky showed them into a cavernous living room. He put another log on the roaring fire, bathing the room in a dark-orange glow. He brought out some blankets and gave them some drinks and food.

Dyer said, "Thank you for helping us out. This is a beautiful house."

Kazinsky just nodded. "Part owned by the banks and my ex-wife."

Reznick smiled. "Still a nice place, man."

Kazinsky was looking around the room as if unable to relax. He seemed ill at ease in strangers' company. It wasn't long before he showed Trevelle to a bedroom upstairs, already made up for guests, log fire on, and Rosalind to a neat bedroom down the hall, with a bathroom en suite.

Reznick waited until his ex-Delta brother returned to the living room and sat in front of the roaring fire. It was just like old times. They talked, mostly, as he did with all his ex-Delta buddies, of the old days. Training. Operations. Iraq. Fallujah. And inevitably, the dark side of special operations. The loneliness, depressions, marriage breakdowns, and jail time.

He listened as Kazinsky talked about a business failure that had cost him tens of thousands.

Reznick detected a sadness in Kazinsky's demeanor. The way his shoulders were slightly hunched, eyes more downcast than he remembered, as if life had been tough on him.

Kazinsky poured himself and Reznick each a single malt scotch. He handed Reznick his glass of the amber liquid and raised his own. "To old friends," he said.

Reznick took a sip of the whiskey, letting it warm his belly. "Yeah, old friends." He relished the smoke-and-honey aftertaste of the neat malt. "That's seriously nice. Clean."

"It's like velvet, isn't it? Eighteen years to mature. Took me a lot longer, Jon, let me tell you—to mature, that is—but what the hell."

Reznick smiled. He noticed a slight tremor in Kazinsky's hand. "You OK, Ed? Saw just a slight shake there."

"It's nothing to worry about. I'm on a beta-blocker. I've seen better days, that's for sure. "

"What's the drug for?"

"The beta-blocker? Early-onset Parkinson's. Had a heightened anxiety problem and the medication seems to help the tremor."

Reznick nodded. He sensed a terrible emptiness about Kazinsky that he didn't remember from before. "What's the problem, man? You don't seem yourself."

"Wife fucked off and left me, that's the long and short of it. Fucking bitch."

"Sorry about that. Not easy. Not easy at all."

"Ran off with some young bodybuilder she met online. You believe that?"

Reznick said nothing.

"She thought I'd changed. People change though, right? I've changed."

Reznick stared at his former Delta colleague. "We all change. I'm not the same crazy guy I was when I was twenty. Life catches up to us all. Takes its toll."

Kazinsky finished his whiskey and put down the empty glass on the wooden table beside him. He looked at the crackling fire and sighed.

"What about your friends and family?" Reznick asked.

"I don't go out much."

"That's fine. Not illegal in this country. Yet."

Kazinsky didn't even crack a smile. "I don't like what I see with the world. You know what I mean?"

Reznick sensed him getting unduly morbid. "You know, it's easy to just cut yourself off from the world. I should know better than most."

Kazinsky nodded empathetically. "Sorry, Jon, I just get a bit down. I lost a lot of money in my business dealings. Wife left. And it all kind of started getting fucked up."

Reznick decided to change the tone. "Well, I for one am grateful for your hospitality. At such short notice."

Kazinsky got up and poured out another scotch for himself and Reznick. "What the hell was I supposed to do? I try and help, God knows I do. But it ain't easy. I guess I miss a lot of the camaraderie. I'm lost. I don't see people from one day to the next. One week to the next. I just sit. And stare at the walls."

"That's not healthy, Ed."

"Tell me about it. I'm also on an antidepressant."

Reznick could see it all made sense. Events had conspired to change the man. "Do you still work?"

"There might be something in a few months, could be lucrative, but nothing so far."

"Want me to try and ask around? I know a few of the guys, mostly security consultants advising corporate clients, that kind of thing. You're well placed with your knowledge to get in there. You remember a guy named Brad Jameson?"

"Sure."

"He's based out of New York. I've met him from time to time. He's always asking me if I want work. He would jump at the chance to employ you."

Kazinsky was quiet for a few moments.

"What do you think, Ed?"

"I've spoken to a few people about that kind of thing, so I'm going to see how that works out for me. Few irons in the fire."

Reznick continued, "Ed, listen to me. I've got your phone number. How about if I put in a personal word for you if things don't work out? Hell, I'll talk to Brad right now if you want. Get you on your feet in no time."

"Appreciate that, Jon. That would be good. Yeah, maybe something to think about."

"Just let me know, and I'll put in the calls."

Kazinsky stared into his glass again as if lost in his thoughts.

Reznick took a sip of his scotch and put down his tumbler. His cell phone rang and he groaned. "You mind if I take this?"

"Go right ahead, man."

Reznick got up and walked across the room before he took out his phone. He recognized Meyerstein's number.

"Jon, we're trying to pinpoint your location," she said. "We need to know where you are."

"Hold on, Martha." He covered the mouthpiece and looked across at Kazinsky. "Sorry, Ed, it's a private call. You mind?"

Kazinsky got to his feet and grinned. "Don't sweat it." He left the room, shutting the door behind him.

"Sorry, Martha. So, have you read the file I showed you?"

"Yes, I have."

"And?"

"We're investigating this as we speak. You have my word, a team is looking into this. Dyer's preliminary report on the corruption was sent to the inspector general, but nothing seems to have happened. They just sat on it. Buried it."

"Are you kidding me?"

"Sadly, no."

"You've read over it, right? Her file. The extracts from her investigation that I gave you."

"I've looked at it."

"And?"

"It's compelling. I've written to the inspector general asking for an explanation."

"Good, that's something to build on. Thank you."

"I know it's frustrating. But in the meantime, Jon, she needs to hand herself in. I hope she'll be exonerated, but if not, she needs to face the music."

"I've suggested that myself. But she's concerned not only about keeping herself and her family safe but also about ensuring she has her chance to testify to the committee."

Meyerstein was silent.

"You need to put yourself in her shoes."

"I'm not in her shoes, Jon."

"Martha, she's worried she'll be sent to jail for a very, very long time."

"There is a live warrant for her arrest. Whether I believe her investigation is justified or not is frankly irrelevant."

"How?"

"It's not up to me to decide. The law should run its course. We'll find her, Jon. And I can't have you interfering when we do. That's not who we are."

Reznick wondered what he needed to do to get Meyerstein to listen to him. "Martha, I feel like I'm banging my head against a brick wall. Rosalind just wants to testify. That's all. Then she'll turn herself in, and you can talk to her."

"Why don't you put her on the phone now?"

"Why?"

Meyerstein sighed. "Jon, I just want to talk to her."

"Hold on." Reznick headed out of the room and into the hall and called out Rosalind's name. She came downstairs from her room and followed him into the living room. "It's the FBI. Martha Meyerstein. She'd like to talk. She won't be able to track you. So you've got nothing to fear on that front."

Rosalind bit her lower lip. "What do you think?"

Reznick shrugged. "Your call."

"Fine."

Reznick turned the phone on speaker mode and placed it on the table.

"Rosalind Dyer speaking."

"Rosalind, this is Martha Meyerstein, assistant director of the FBI. There is a warrant out for your arrest. And we're going to find you."

Dyer sighed. "I didn't want to cause any trouble."

"You have to understand how this looks from our point of view. And from the point of view of the DCIS. You stole classified files. Data. There are so many charges, it's hard to even list them. It's treason, that's what they're saying."

"Ma'am, you've got to believe me. You need to see the bigger picture."

"Then you need to give yourself up. Right now."

"And if I don't?"

"Then God knows where that leaves us."

Sixteen

It was the dead of night as Max Charles looked out of the Gulfstream, down onto the lights of DC. He began to contemplate the meeting that lay ahead. A meeting with the man who was pulling the strings. It would be interesting. The man he was meeting was a multibillionaire, according to *Forbes*. The guy had made his money in oil, Manhattan real estate, and the funding of tech start-ups. And the man was Charles's firm's most lucrative client, racking up tens of millions of dollars in fees in the last eighteen months alone. Geostrategy Solutions provided geopolitical strategies for the man's Nigerian oil interests, greasing the wheels that needed to be greased, eliminating union and political threats to the economic interests of his client. But it wasn't just in sub-Saharan Africa that Charles's client operated.

He was pulling strings in America, unseen.

The client, John Fisk, was a close friend of presidents, chairmen of the Joint Chiefs of Staff, Pentagon big shots, and a host of politicians. He funded numerous campaigns through a myriad of firms. Some based in Bermuda, some in the Caymans, and many run by trusts, unaccountable and untraceable to even forensic accountants.

It was a web of companies whose interests included oil drilling, mining in South Africa, and mineral extraction in the Ukraine, but their owner's influence was wielded through slush funds for American politicians and multimillion-dollar deals with private security companies like Charles's, which provided advisory services in various countries that included, if required, regime change. Fisk was also the brains behind the Commission, a shadowy organization that still existed in a different guise, drawing up plans to eliminate US politicians who got in his way.

The Gulfstream descended as they approached Dulles. Charles disembarked and got into the back of a waiting SUV. Then he was whisked to a sprawling gated estate not far from McLean, Virginia.

Charles was shown into the library, where Fisk was already waiting. Fisk, despite the late hour, wore a gray suit, black shoes, and a pale-blue shirt.

"How was the flight?" Fisk asked, making small talk.

"It was comfortable, thank you."

"Can't stand airports. Waiting in line. People coughing, spluttering, spreading their fucking germs. Their kids wheezing. TB in the air. Being in such close proximity to people. Disgusting."

Charles smiled. The man was a notorious germophobe. He was also phobic about what he ate. Railed about chlorinated chicken in America. "I gather you didn't bring me down here to discuss airport hygiene, important though that is."

Fisk gave a rueful smile. "Do you know why I do what I do?"

"You care about this country."

Fisk walked across to the floor-to-ceiling windows and stared out over his floodlit estate of tennis courts and a nine-hole golf course. "Absolutely correct. I care passionately about how we're drifting away from the path that has brought us such exceptional success, progress, and preeminence in the world. I love this country. I've lived long. But I look around this land, Max, and all I see are people who don't understand what it takes to keep this country where it needs to be. We lead the world. But we only lead the world because we control the world. We decide the rules."

Charles smiled. "Correct. You know better than anyone, John. America's military needs the freedom to protect this great nation, without oversight. People don't need to know how they are protected. As long as they are protected and the nation's interests are protected, the Pentagon and the CIA should be allowed to operate as they see fit. What the hell is it to politicians anyway?"

Fisk sat down in his seat and looked across at Charles. "How long have we known each other, Max?"

"Can't be far off thirty-five years. Maybe more."

"It's nearly forty years. And I've come to value your judgment, your insights on my companies, and your counsel on national security matters. I respect and admire how the CIA operates. Your work over many years within the Agency continued the great work of men like Dulles."

Charles nodded.

"Max, help me out here. I don't understand what's happened with this DCIS woman."

"Rosalind Dyer?"

Fisk nodded. "Our plan seems to have morphed into something more disturbing. Visible on the surface. That's not how we do things. I had expected the whole thing would have been settled long before now. I've got to be frank, Max, I expected her to be dead already. That's what I had been led to believe."

Charles sighed. "That was the plan. It's a mess . . . A friend of mine in MI6 in London has a word for this: *clusterfuck*."

Fisk stared at Charles. "How did this happen?"

"A memo authorizing the team we hired to neutralize her got out. We've spent the past few days chasing down anyone who might have seen it."

"A memo that should only have been seen by your people?"

"Correct. When we were drawing up plans, I said that we shouldn't leave a digital trail. Four people knew about the assignment, and it shouldn't have gone beyond that."

"Who drew up the protocol?"

"Brigadier General Felix Spalding. Special adviser at the Pentagon."

"Did you speak to him ahead of the operation?"

"We're both members of the same gym in New York. We talked it over. I thought it was settled. I stressed verbal authorization only. But I guess something got lost in translation. He sent a memo, encrypted, to one of my guys, laying it all out."

Fisk tilted his head back for a few moments as if deep in thought. "He's a weak link."

"He's a good man, but I agree, it didn't have to be formalized."

"What are we going to do about him?"

Charles felt the temperature in the room turn cold. He knew what Fisk meant.

"So we've got Spalding and three others who know about the plan to neutralize Dyer."

Charles nodded. "Four people aside from us and the team we hired to carry it out."

"What happens if this document makes it into the mainstream? What if this document is picked up by the *Post* or the *Times*? What happens then?"

"We would have a major problem on our hands."

"That's correct. Spalding could give evidence against you. And I can't have that."

Charles had known Spalding for years. He'd come out of Fort Bragg and worked Special Forces. Charles knew his family. His wife. They were good people. But a cold wind was blowing, chilling him to the bone. "I don't think it'll come to that."

"But it might."

Charles was quiet for a few moments, not wishing to initiate what he knew was going to come next.

"Dead men tell no tales, Max. You should know that better than anyone."

Even for Charles, this was going to be a tough one to stomach. "Just so I'm clear, you want him taken care of?"

"Yeah, he's got to be. Is that a problem?"

Charles sighed. "Not a problem. I'll take care of it."

"Soon. But for now, we need to focus on Rosalind Dyer first and then deal with him. How does that sound?"

Charles made a mental note. "Got it."

"Dyer. You told me in our early discussions that she had heart palpitations five years ago. And we agreed, albeit informally, that this was a perfect way to point to the cause of death if we were going to induce her having a heart attack while in jail."

"We didn't envision the chain of events that have since unfolded. And that was before she had agreed to testify before the committee. I had expected her to be arrested within the last twenty-four hours—that's the info I was given from inside the State Department. But the FBI have been dragging their heels, and we hadn't foreseen that she would drop off the grid like this."

"There's a lot we haven't foreseen. And now she's running around with Mr. Reznick and some hacker? That's careless on your part, Max, allowing this to develop."

"I don't dispute any of this. It's a one-in-a-million series of events that have come together. We've also got the added problem of Assistant Director Meyerstein being in touch with Reznick. But I've got a plan in place to keep her quiet."

"I'm not worried about her. I'm worried that Dyer is going to testify. And this could jeopardize the military-industrial nexus. We have plans in place with friendly nations abroad. Plans for foreign wars. Regime changes around the globe. Color revolutions in Africa. Plans years in the making that could all be jeopardized if the Pentagon gets drawn into this. Not to mention Rosalind Dyer seems to have made a few inquiries about the unexplained deaths of Pentagon auditors. The optics are not good. You know what I'm talking about?"

Charles nodded. He understood what Fisk was saying. "She is proving to be a serious threat to our clients, our friends, and their companies. But I know what you expect, John."

"She cannot testify, Max. I can't stress this enough. But we need a plan. Plan A seems to have blown up."

"I've got a plan B, don't worry."

"You do?"

"I have people working on this as we speak. Trust me. There's more than one way to neutralize someone."

Seventeen

Reznick and Kazinsky were nursing another single malt each as they talked some more into the wee hours. The log fire was crackling, the smell of burning woodchips and shavings filling the house.

"You miss Delta, Jon?"

"I think about it."

"But do you miss it?"

"Not so much. I miss the people. I think about the guys I was with. The friendship. It's a brotherhood. Of course, I'm going to miss that. It was tight-knit. Real tight. Yeah, I miss that, I guess. What about you?"

Kazinsky took a sip of his scotch and shook his head. "Seems like a long time ago, that's for sure."

"That it was."

"I kinda went downhill when I left. I couldn't sleep. Flashbacks. I forgot who I was. I got meaner. Deniable operations making me wake up in the night. It went on for years."

"I've been there. I know. It takes its toll."

"No one else knows what it's like. Not a goddamn soul." He scrunched up his face.

"You find it tough, still?"

Kazinsky nodded.

"There's stuff we see and do that you don't want to ever think about. But we have to try and keep it somewhere deep in the mind, locked away."

"I can't do that. I've tried to. Sometimes I close my eyes and I see the eyes of an Afghan farmer, an old, old guy, skeletal thin, pleading for his life, before I killed him. Remember Kandahar?"

"Hard to forget."

"I thought he was going for his gun. Then I remember the blood on the walls of the home. A family lived there."

Reznick nodded.

"No one knows what it's like unless you're there. In hundred and ten heat, blinded by thirst, anger, I went out of my mind for days, weeks, I don't know."

Reznick said nothing. He knew those same feelings. The alienation. The loathing. The rage.

"Best friend Ron Farley, SEAL Team Six for a few years, then he began working for the Agency in Baghdad. You know what he did when he got home?"

Reznick shook his head.

"He went to his neighborhood bar in Jackson. He drank himself crazy. Then he went home and killed his wife and dog before turning the gun on himself."

"Fuck."

"I'm no angel. I know what I am. What I've done. And when I came home, for a while, I went a bit wild. I'm not proud of what I did."

"What do you mean?"

"You know . . . had a spell inside a correctional facility."

"What for?"

"Held a gun to a guy's head in a bowling alley. He owed a friend of mine money."

Reznick grimaced.

"Worked for the mob at one point. I was screwed up. Hung out with a Hell's Angels crew. They were nuts. I was nuts. I was drinking. I went off the rails for about five years."

"Looks like you're back on your feet now. Beautiful house. How did you get all this?"

Kazinsky gave a rueful smile. "No one to enjoy it with."

"You'll be OK." Reznick looked around the living room. "High ceilings. Big space."

"Massive basement too. You should see the wine cellar. You wouldn't fucking believe it. You believe that? A kid from the shit end of Pensacola, with a house like this?"

Reznick nodded.

"But I'm cash poor."

"Still a nice house, man."

"You know how I got it? Well, part of it. The rest, as I said, is owned by the fucking bank and my ex-wife. But I'll get it back in full. Anyway, interesting story. Once I got myself straightened out, I was providing security advice for a Wall Street guy and his family. Started off as personal protection. And then it evolved into advising him on protecting his business interests. At home and abroad. Scouting locations. And he paid very well, and he also gave me some handy stock market hints. Bought some high-tech start-up stocks in Silicon Valley for a few dollars a pop. And within three years, their price had blown up to a hundred and forty dollars a share. It was crazy. And I made more than a couple million bucks like that. But it's all gone with the divorce."

Reznick looked around the huge room. "So you still working for the Wall Street guy?"

"Off and on. He actually put me in touch with a guy he knows, used to be a Navy SEAL, and he got me a gig with a security firm in New York. Consulting work."

"Interesting."

"They're very demanding. But it's putting my kids through college."

Reznick was keen to get Kazinsky on to a lighter subject. "So how are your kids?"

"My oldest, Jimmy, is at Boston College, studying drama."

"He's going to be an actor? You're kidding me."

Kazinsky grinned. "Who fucking knew? He's talented. And he hates guns."

Reznick nodded. "Good for him."

"What about your daughter? Lauren, isn't it?"

"She's finishing up at college in Vermont, but she's talking about working for the FBI."

"Wow, now that's interesting."

"I do some stuff for them, off and on."

Kazinsky's brows rose. "You advise them? The FBI?"

"On one or two issues or investigations. Happened purely by accident."

"The Feds? Jesus."

"A bit of this and that."

"I heard you were working for the Agency at one point."

Reznick shrugged. "I've worked for a few people."

Kazinsky lowered his voice to a whisper. "So what's the story with the woman and the kid? You helping them out?"

Reznick took a couple of minutes to lay it out. He concluded by saying, "This is confidential. I trust you, Ed. That goes without saying."

Kazinsky knocked back his drink and put his glass down on the coffee table in front of him. "Jon, you've got to trust. If you haven't got trust, what have you got?"

"I just wanted you to understand this is a delicate situation. And we'll be out of your face within the next twenty-four hours, probably less."

"Stay as long as you need. I know how stuff works. It's messy."

"Appreciate that."

Kazinsky stared into his half-empty glass.

"You want me to call in some favors and get some work for you?"

"If I don't know them, I don't want to know, Jon."

"Perfectly understandable." Reznick stifled a yawn. "Need some shut-eye," he said. "You mind if I crash out?"

"Not at all. I think the hacker dude is sound asleep. And Rosalind is in the adjacent room. And don't worry, I showed her the key to lock her door."

Reznick got up and hugged his old buddy tight. "Ed, I owe you one."

"If you need me, I'll be at my computer here, just buying and selling shares."

Reznick shook his head. "I never would've figured you for a Wall Street guy, Ed."

"Neither would I! I'm from fucking Pensacola. The only person to do anything with their life from Pensacola that I knew was Weegie Thompson, who ended up playing for the Steelers."

"Now that was a seriously good player."

"Damn straight, bro. Good to see you again. And get some sleep. You look like shit!"

The log fire in the bedroom was crackling, the orange glow bathing the bedroom. Reznick was curled up in a sleeping bag on one side of the room, eschewing the comfort of the bed; Trevelle was wrapped up in blankets in front of the fire. Reznick felt himself drifting away. Eyes getting heavier. He felt himself floating. Drifting on dark, oily waters. The sound of breathing. Deep breathing. Growing shallower. Whispers in the breeze. He sensed he was being watched from the shore. Shadows moving. He felt himself moving. And then he realized the river was taking him downstream. He tried to move, but nothing. Tried to grab a branch by the shore. He just floated by. Only the rustle of the palm leaves in the desert wind. The dust, sticking in his throat like grit.

Then a blinding sun. Sun-bleached shacks. Sounds of screaming. The sound of a bullet fizzing past. He sensed he was back. Back in Fallujah. The stench of death in his nostrils. Decomposing corpses being eaten by rabid dogs. Children playing in the ruins of the city. Snipers taking potshots at them. Tortured bodies in ditches. Eyes drilled out by psychotic gangs. The midday sun blinding. Unbearable heat. One hundred and twenty degrees in the shade. Merciless. Bloated bodies floating in the Euphrates. Downstream. He watched as if in a dream.

He turned and saw a faceless American soldier floating past, eyes dead. Someone's son.

Dark whispers were carried on the wind. Like a night terror. Someone was there.

Reznick woke bolt upright, Trevelle's cell phone light in his face. "What the—"

Trevelle pressed his finger to his mouth for Reznick to be quiet. He whispered, "Your friend just sent a message."

"What?"

Trevelle showed him the WhatsApp message sent three minutes before. Reznick scanned the message. It read: *You interested in the whereabouts of Rosalind Dyer? I can tell you where she is for $250k, no questions asked.*

It took a few moments for Reznick's head to clear away the whiskey fuzziness. The reply read: *Money in your account, friend. Where is target?*

The response read: *My home address, sound asleep. I've deactivated the alarms.*

Reznick rubbed the sleep out of his eyes as he gathered his thoughts. "How the hell did you do that?"

"A spyware I'm developing. Downloaded remotely to his phone without him knowing, then anytime he messages or calls, I see it. In my business, it's important to know who you're dealing with. Now I know. The people he's communicating with are in Denmark. But they're clearly using a VPN to mask their true location."

Reznick took a few moments to get his bearings. "I can't believe that. Never in a million years."

"What are you going to do?" Trevelle whispered.

Reznick grabbed his gun and headed for the bedroom door.

Eighteen

Reznick crept downstairs and into the living room. He saw Kazinsky sitting at his desk with his back to the room, computer on. A strange blue glow from the monitor bathed the room in an ethereal glow. He walked up behind Kazinsky and pressed the 9mm Beretta to the back of Kazinsky's head. "Not a fucking move."

Kazinsky sat still. "Man, what's going on?"

"Don't play dumb with me. Who did you contact?"

"What are you talking about? I'm emailing my ex-wife."

"Don't lie to me, Ed. I saw the message you sent."

Kazinsky stared at the screen.

"You need to start talking or it's over. Right here and now, man."

"Jon, I have no idea what you're talking about. I let you into my house. And this is how you repay me?"

"Cut the bullshit. The kid with me is a computer genius. And he just intercepted your message selling us out. You want me to show you?"

Kazinsky went quiet.

Reznick pressed the gun tight into his scalp. "You feel that cold metal on your skin? Well, do you? I don't fuck around. You know I don't make idle threats."

"OK, I can explain."

"I'm on a short fuse. One wrong move, you die."

"I want to . . . try and explain."

Reznick took a couple of steps back, gun trained on his old Delta buddy. "Explain you selling out one of your own? Seriously? Is that how fucking desperate you are?"

Kazinsky slowly turned around in his chair, hands still on his head. "That's exactly how desperate I am. Jon, please, man, I'm in deep."

"What do you mean?"

"I owe my ex-wife hundreds of thousands. I haven't got a cent. I'm broke. I helped my son on a production he was working on with a friend. It went bust. And all my savings with it. Now my ex-wife is wondering why I haven't sent her part of the divorce settlement. The reason is, I have nothing but this old house that now I have to sell to pay her the share I owe. I'll be living in a shack in the woods before long."

"Sad stories don't do it for me these days, Ed. I've had my fill of sad stories. You want to hear a sad story? You want to hear about how my wife's body was never found on 9/11? Pulverized to dust, that's what happened to her. So spare me the fucking sad stories."

"I need the money. The firm I know, they have offices all over. DC, New York, L.A. They've been trying to get some work for me, but nothing's really working out. I thought this would be a way for me to get back on my feet."

"By selling me out? And the kid and Rosalind?"

"You don't know how fucking desperate I am. I'm at the end of my rope." Kazinsky began to sob like a child. "I want to kill myself. You have no idea."

"Who exactly did you message?"

Kazinsky bowed his head.

"We'll find out soon enough."

"Jon, please, look at me! Look at me! I'm a bum. That's what my father called me. That's what my ex-wife called me. I drink too much. I fooled around with other women when I was married. I'm a mess. I'm nothing. You understand that?"

"That's all very interesting. But I asked you a question. I won't ask a second time. Who did you message?"

"He works for Geostrategy Solutions. In New York."

The firm's name crashed through Reznick's head like a brick.

"He knew you and I had worked together. He said if I heard from you, looking for help, to give them a call."

"Who are they sending? What's the guy's name?"

Kazinsky said nothing.

Reznick stepped forward and pressed the gun tight to his former friend's forehead. "You will tell me, Ed, so help me God."

Kazinsky sighed. "I have no idea, Jon, swear to God. I'm sorry. I'm sorry I sold you out. Please don't hurt me, man."

Reznick felt a cold anger clawing at his insides. A surge of adrenaline spiked his heart rate. He smashed his fist hard into the side of Kazinsky's neck, right into the carotid artery. His ex-Delta buddy slumped forward, unconscious.

Reznick lifted him up and dragged him to a storage room. He locked him inside and put the key in his pocket. He switched off the computer, the lights, and plunged the house into darkness. His senses were switched on. He needed to get himself, Trevelle, and Rosalind as far away from the house as possible. He didn't know how long they had. Maybe an hour, maybe less.

He headed upstairs.

Trevelle's face was lit up with a white glow from his cell phone.

"Here's what's going to happen. Are you listening?" Reznick said.

"What did you do to him? You didn't kill him, did you?"

"No, he's just incapacitated for a little while. But we need to move."

"Man, I'm scared. Really batshit scared."

Reznick hauled Trevelle to his feet. "You can do this. Do you hear me?"

"Sure, I think so."

Reznick went next door and knocked hard on Rosalind's door. "Rosalind, we need to get out of here!"

A few moments later the door unlocked, and Rosalind peered out, bleary-eyed. "What?"

"People are on their way. I don't know who. But you and Trevelle need to get out of sight."

"What about you?"

"Let me deal with this."

A few minutes later, Reznick, Rosalind, and Trevelle had gathered up their gear and headed downstairs. They were standing in the hallway.

"Do you mind telling me what the hell happened?" Rosalind demanded.

Trevelle quickly explained to Rosalind how he had intercepted the message from Kazinsky. "There are people coming to kill you. Probably all of us."

Rosalind looked surprisingly composed. "So we need to move."

Trevelle began to shake. "Yeah, but where? What are we going to do? Where are we going to go?"

"You and Rosalind are going down to the basement," Reznick said. "Get out of sight while I try and come up with a plan."

Trevelle shook his head. "Sorry, man, I can't."

"What do you mean you can't?"

"I'm claustrophobic."

"What?"

"I can't go down there! I hate confined spaces. Basements. No windows. I hate being locked in."

Reznick grabbed him by the arm. "Listen to me, you need to shape up. And focus. This is not just about you."

"I swear to God, Jon, if you lock me in there, I'll start screaming. I'll panic. I have a deep fear of confined spaces."

Reznick had envisioned heading up to the highest room in the house with a sniper rifle from Kazinsky's collection and taking down any attackers as they headed toward the house. "This is not the time, my friend. I need you to help me help you."

"I'm sorry. I can't do it. Please, don't lock me in. I was locked in a closet when I was a child. I can't deal with that again."

Rosalind looked at Reznick. "You need a plan B. There must be another way."

Reznick had heard enough. He smashed open the glass cabinet holding Kazinsky's rack of rifles. He took down a sniper rifle with attached night vision sights and a sound suppressor. He found ammo in a liquor cabinet.

He turned to Trevelle. "Check your phone. Have you got a fix on any approaching vehicles?"

Trevelle pulled up a program that got him entry into Kazinsky's home surveillance system, showing the driveway, front, and rear of the house. "Negative. All quiet so far."

"Keep away from the windows. Do you hear me?"

Reznick bounded up the stairs to the second floor and crawled to the far window. He took out his binoculars from his backpack and focused on the driveway entrance about a half mile away.

A few minutes later, a silhouetted vehicle, lights off, crawled into view, slowing to a stop at the bottom of the driveway, partially concealed by huge oaks.

His mind was racing. He couldn't believe they were here already. Had they been nearby? Was it chance? No matter, they were here now. "Think, goddamn it."

He wondered whether he should lay down some fire. Disable the vehicle. Then pick them off one by one. He checked the silhouetted vehicle again. It was parked opposite some huge trees. Maybe they were waiting for backup. That would make sense.

One team to block access to the driveway while the other does the hit.

He figured they had a window of opportunity to escape. But it wouldn't last long. They had to move.

Reznick went back downstairs to tell Dyer and Trevelle the grim news. "So, we've got a problem."

Trevelle shook his head. "Oh man, fuck, seriously?"

"It might be nothing. But if they're waiting for a second team, and if either of the teams is the Miami team or similarly equipped, we'll have a fight on our hands."

Dyer went to the downstairs window and peered through the blinds. "They're still there."

"We've got to hope that they're working under the false assumption that we don't know they're coming."

Trevelle nodded. "We've got to use that head start."

Reznick said, "Let's get going."

"Hang on," Rosalind said. "I'm not sure this is the best strategy. Why don't we call the cops?"

"Too late for that. My view? Best strategy in the circumstances is to move. And quickly."

The three of them headed down into Kazinsky's basement and through a creaking door into a garage. Inside was a Toyota Hilux pickup. He spotted a key fob hanging from a rusty nail on the wall. Reznick grabbed it and climbed into the driver's seat. He saw it was keyless. A stroke of luck, finally. He started up the engine. It purred to life. "In the back, heads down."

"Where are we going?" Trevelle asked.

Reznick edged the vehicle forward, and the garage doors automatically opened.

Trevelle said, "I can't see a thing."

Reznick's eyes gradually began to adjust to the darkness. He could make out a dirt road at the rear of the property that led to woods. The GPS showed a forest trail leading from the rear of the location due south.

Dyer was crouched down in the back seat. "I'm scared, Jon."

Reznick didn't answer. He just drove the truck out of the garage and accelerated down the dirt road, headed for the opening in the trees.

Nineteen

It was the dead of night, and Meyerstein was sitting at her kitchen breakfast bar, unable to sleep. She sipped her cup of Earl Grey tea. Her cell phone rang, and she answered quickly.

"Assistant Director, sorry to call you at this time, but it's urgent." The voice belonged to Jenny Reilly, an up-and-coming FBI analyst.

Meyerstein was mentoring Reilly, who worked in the 24/7 Strategic Information and Operations Center based on the fifth floor of the Hoover Building. "What've you got? Have we found Reznick?"

"No, sorry."

Meyerstein sighed. "So why the call?"

"Routine police patrol outside Gaithersburg, Maryland. Four people, on vacation from Central America. Only one could speak English, apparently. Loaded to the teeth with weaponry."

"Is this connected to Reznick or Rosalind Dyer?"

"We believe both. We think these guys were tracking down Dyer, in particular. We believe Dyer and Reznick were hiding out in a house nearby, with a friend of Reznick's from his Delta days. These four guys said they were hunters. And liked shooting."

"They've come a long way to do some shooting."

"Police checked the SUV. Destination in the GPS was a house owned by Edward Kazinsky. Turns out he's a former Delta operator like Reznick."

Meyerstein began mentally mapping out what had happened. "So Reznick was there."

"One hundred percent."

"How can you be so sure?"

"Cops got into the house and Kazinsky was inside, alive. He was locked in a closet and says Reznick is with Rosalind Dyer and a black kid."

"That must be the hacker, Trevelle Williams."

"Correct, ma'am."

"Jenny, I want this out to every agent. Let all field offices know."

"The thing is, ma'am, they've dropped off the grid again. Not a trace of them. Digital or otherwise."

"Get on it. We need to find Reznick and Dyer before it's too late."

Twenty

The headlights of the Toyota pierced the darkness surrounding the bone-dry dirt road as they powered through the forest of trees, clouds of dust behind them.

"Where the hell are we?" Trevelle asked.

Reznick glanced at the GPS. "Two miles and we'll come to a proper road."

"Then what?"

"Leave that to me."

"What does that even mean?"

"It means we need to keep moving."

Reznick drove on past some old wooden shacks. "Hold on!" he said as they plunged through a stream in the woods and back onto the dirt road. A minute later, the headlights picked out the asphalt. He felt himself relax. "OK, we're back in civilization."

He was driving down a minor road in rural Maryland. Not a car in sight.

"What now?" Trevelle asked.

Reznick looked again at the GPS, which had gone blank. He wondered if the wiring had gotten dislodged on the rutted dirt road. "Shit. Damn thing died on us. Trevelle, help me out."

Trevelle took out his cell phone. "Yeah, got it. We're two miles from Rockville. Straight ahead on this road. Then what?"

"My plan is to leave Kazinsky's truck and get another ride."

"Do you mean steal a ride?" Dyer said.

"Got it," Reznick replied.

"What about a diner? Usually cars in and around diners."

"Cops will be out looking for us," Reznick said. "Is there anywhere else that might be open twenty-four seven that has parking?"

"In this part of the world, I don't think twenty-four seven is even a thing."

Trevelle tapped furiously on his cell phone. "God bless Google Maps. Harris Teeter, south of Rockville. Supermarket. Straight ahead."

Reznick drove on for a few hundred yards. He took a hard right turn and pulled into the near-empty parking lot, right next to a minivan. The lights of the supermarket bathed parts of the parking lot, but it was deathly quiet, no sign of anyone. "Let's get inside, get a cup of coffee. Refuel. But ideally we need to get away from here, find a place to hide out. Just for twenty-four hours. Any ideas?"

Trevelle said, "I don't know, maybe."

"What do you mean, maybe?"

"I have a friend, she lives in Potomac. That's close, isn't it?"

"Real close," Dyer said.

"She's cool. But I don't know if she'll do this. It's a big ask."

"You wanna try?" Reznick said. "We need as much help as we can get. But she needs to be trustworthy. Do you trust her?"

"Hell yes, I trust her. Very much."

"Does she have a car?" Reznick asked.

"Her parents have a car."

"I'm going to ask you again," Reznick said. "Can we really trust her? I thought I could trust Kazinsky. I was wrong."

"I'm telling you, we can absolutely trust her. She's cool. Ridiculously cool. She smokes some weed. But if you're OK with that, she'll be fine with you."

"Send her an encrypted message."

"And say what?"

"Tell her you need an urgent favor."

Twenty-One

Thirty minutes later, Rosalind spotted a mud-splattered white Chevrolet Suburban driving into the parking lot. A young woman was driving, smoking a joint, waving through the window at them. She wondered if the girl should be behind the wheel but decided to let it slide. Her main concern was getting out of sight. "Interesting."

Reznick turned to Trevelle. "Is this her?"

Trevelle grinned. "Oh yeah. She's great."

"Is she stoned?" Reznick said.

"Probably."

The young woman rolled down her window. She was in her late twenties and had high cheekbones and long brown hair. She had a nose ring in her right nostril. "Trevelle, what the hell's going on, man?"

"Fifi, it's a long story. I know it's late and this is all pretty weird. And I know I'm expecting a big favor, but you mind if my friends get a lift too?"

"Plenty of room. Jump in, guys."

Rosalind slid in the back seat beside Reznick. Trevelle sat up front.

Fifi turned around and offered the joint to Dyer. "You want some grass?"

"I'm good, thanks."

Fifi shrugged. "Not a problem." She looked at Trevelle. "Man, I haven't seen you since . . . forever!"

Trevelle turned around and rolled his eyes. "We left the NSA on the same day. Fifi's a lot of fun."

Fifi laughed and drove off. "Lot of fun. Were the NSA pissed or what?"

"Mighty pissed," Trevelle said.

Rosalind interrupted the love-in. "I appreciate you helping us out."

"Don't sweat it, hon," she said.

"Fifi, we're looking for a place to disappear until tomorrow," Trevelle told her.

"Disappear? I love it. Are you guys fugitives from the government?"

Trevelle laughed. "That's exactly what we are."

"Then I'm 100 percent your guy."

"Got any suggestions?"

"Let me think. Oh yeah, I've got a suggestion. So as long as you guys haven't murdered anyone or aren't planning to kill anyone, I'm cool with it."

Reznick said, "Appreciate that. And no, we haven't murdered anyone. At least not yet."

Fifi burst out laughing. "You guys are crazy. I love it! Well, here's the thing. My parents are out of town. They have a cool place in Georgetown. I have the keys. Skiing in Europe or some such shit."

Rosalind leaned forward. "And they won't mind?"

"Probably. But if you're just staying for a day or two, no problem. They won't be back for another week. You mind telling me what this is all about?"

Rosalind said, "It's complicated. And we're going to need your discretion."

"Whatever." Fifi negotiated a few tight bends before she found a straight bit of road, just outside town. "OK," she said, taking a long drag of the joint, "we're finally on the move."

"I owe you one," Trevelle told her.

"Damn right you do."

Fifi and Trevelle struck up an animated conversation, oblivious to the two adults in the back seat. They talked about South Beach, why she hadn't visited him for six months, Fifi setting up a new cybersecurity consulting firm with two former NSA staffers, marijuana laws in Colorado, and why the President should be certified.

Rosalind zoned out and wound down her window, grateful for the cool night air rushing in. "That better?"

Reznick cleared his throat and did the same. "Smart move." He looked at her. "How are you feeling? It's crazy, right? Out of your comfort zone."

Rosalind nodded, but she felt a million miles away. "You could say that."

"Are you going to be OK?"

"I thought my lawyer would've called by now. He said he was going to call me by midnight at the latest. Just to give me an update. But I haven't gotten a text or anything."

"He doesn't have the number of the new cell phone Trevelle gave you."

Rosalind scrunched up her eyes. "Of course."

"Give him a call," Reznick said. "Your phone can't be traced."

Rosalind sighed. "By the time I get in front of the committee, I'm going to be a physical wreck."

"You'll be fine. Give that lawyer of yours a call. He might be able to give you the latest picture."

"I'm scared I'll wake him."

"Under the circumstances, he'll want to know you're alright."

"True. When I spoke to him yesterday, he warned me they were going to come after me. Said he had been approached by a powerful law firm working alongside the Pentagon lawyers, telling him they were going to, metaphorically speaking, kill me."

"It's lawyer talk. I hope you told him to go fuck himself."

Rosalind laughed. "Yeah, maybe I should have." She got quiet for a few moments. "You must think it's silly, getting frightened by all this."

"No one likes to be threatened. Sometimes it's easier to walk away. And sometimes that's the smart move. But sometimes, just sometimes, you've got to stand your ground and fight."

Rosalind took out her phone. "Well, here goes." She called her lawyer's cell phone number. It began to ring. The call was answered on the third ring.

"Who's this?"

It was a man's voice that she didn't recognize. She wondered if she had the wrong number. "I'm looking to speak to Frank Leivitz. I'm sorry, who am I talking to?"

"Frank's not available. Who's this?"

Rosalind thought the man sounded evasive. "Tell him Rosalind Dyer wants to talk. Do you know when I can speak to him? It's urgent."

"Hard to say."

"I'm sorry, who exactly am I speaking to?"

A beat. "About Frank . . . it's probably best that you know."

Rosalind wondered why the guy was being so cryptic. Why was he answering her lawyer's cell phone in the middle of the night? Who the hell was he? She felt her stomach tighten. She sensed something was wrong. Very wrong. "Know what?"

"You won't be seeing Frank again."

"What are you talking about? Who the hell are you?"

"You should probably turn on your TV."

"What?"

"Just do it."

"Why?"

"Just do it. You're next on our list."

Rosalind ended the call. She began to hyperventilate, gasping for lungfuls of the air rushing through the window. "I don't feel well."

"What's wrong?" Reznick asked.

Rosalind tried the best she could to explain the call.

Trevelle pulled out his iPad and opened up CNN, tilted the screen so Rosalind and Reznick could see.

The female reporter said, "Breaking news this hour. A man believed to be top Washington, DC, defense attorney Frank Leivitz was found dead outside his downtown apartment a couple of hours ago. Sources say he was being investigated for corruption. Mr. Leivitz was seen on his balcony by a neighbor before apparently falling to his death."

Twenty-Two

The SUV slowed down as Reznick scanned the pristine, tree-lined street in Georgetown. The vehicle approached the electronic gates, which opened automatically, and they drove down into an underground parking bay.

Reznick waited until they were out of sight. He clicked open his seat belt as Dyer, still in shock after learning of her lawyer's sudden death, didn't move from the back seat. "Time to move, Rosalind," he said sharply.

She sat frozen, as if in a trance.

"I said, it's time to move, Rosalind."

Her head turned slowly, and she stared blankly at him.

"Rosalind, you need to get back in the game or it's all over."

"What the hell is happening, Jon?"

Reznick leaned over and unbuckled her seat belt for her. "Know one thing. They're playing for keeps. They're trying to unnerve you."

"He was a good man. A friend."

Reznick got out of the car and walked around to Dyer's side and opened the door. He reached out. "Take my hand, time to move. It's OK, you're going to be fine."

Dyer did as she was told. It looked to Reznick as if she wasn't taking it all in. Maybe she was shutting down, perhaps a coping mechanism to deal with the acute shock she had to be suffering.

"Take my hand."

Dyer gripped his hand tightly.

Reznick waited until Trevelle and Fifi went inside. Then he escorted Dyer slowly into the house, knowing she was in a fragile state. He locked the doors behind them.

Fifi led the way, and they followed her up some winding stairs and into a second-floor living room. Modern art on the whitewashed brick. Huge TV on one wall.

"Keep the blinds drawn," Reznick ordered. "Get the fire lit. And can I have some blankets for Rosalind?"

Fifi got the living room warm and cozy. "I'm so sorry. That's crazy."

Dyer wrapped the blanket around herself. "He was the sweetest man."

Fifi sat down beside Rosalind and wrapped an arm around her. "We're here for you. I want to help in any way I can."

"Frank was so smart. He promised me he would be with me every step of the way."

Reznick sat down on the sofa opposite. He leaned forward. "It's tough, I know."

Dyer nodded. "He would never kill himself. Never. He was a family man. A great one. You'd have to be crazy to do that or even consider that. He wasn't crazy. Not depressed either. I just don't buy it. Someone killed him, didn't they? The guy who picked up his phone, right?"

Reznick nodded. "Your lawyer believed in you and what you were trying to do, right?"

Dyer closed her eyes for a moment. "Yeah, very much. He was very pro-privacy, anti-state surveillance. He was an old hippie. But now . . . he's gone. I just can't believe it. It's too much."

Reznick stared into the fire as his mind began to consider the options for Rosalind. "I'm very sorry."

"He thought I was brave, doing what I was doing. But he was wrong. He was the one who was brave. He didn't have to take on my case."

Reznick shook his head. "But he did. So, Rosalind, I know it's not easy to broach this subject, especially right now, but we need to reassess what you're going to do in light of everything that's happened."

"What do you mean?"

"I've seen enough. I know how this is going to play out. And it's not going to be good."

"Don't you think I know that?"

"I don't know if you do. So I want you to listen carefully to what I have to say."

Dyer nodded. "Of course."

"I strongly recommend, based on the terrible death of your lawyer, that both you and Trevelle allow yourselves to be taken into secure custody by the FBI until this is over. It is imperative for your safety."

Dyer sat and stared into the fire as though she were contemplating her fate.

"Did you hear what I said, Rosalind?" Reznick said.

Dyer nodded.

Trevelle sat down on the floor in front of the fire. "My main concern was to warn you, Rosalind, of this threat. I did tell Jon before that I would consider a safe house or whatever until this blows over." He turned and looked at Reznick. "I'm scared, man.

I'm not afraid to admit that. But I think I'd need assurances from the FBI before I went into custody. I hope you understand that."

Reznick nodded. "Leave that to me." He looked again at Dyer, a blanket wrapped around her. "Your call, Rosalind. I can pick up the phone and get you to safety in a matter of minutes. Sometimes, the smart thing is to head for cover."

Dyer shook her head. "Then it would all be in vain. They would win. My efforts, my lawyer's efforts. He paid for it with his life. He wanted me to back off, to take the settlement. But when I refused, he said he'd support me all the way."

"What about your husband? And your kids? What about the impact on them? Just say the word and I can get your family taken into protective custody."

Dyer sighed. "Jon, there are no indications that they are at risk. What if the FBI uses my family as a bargaining chip?"

"Rosalind, trust me, the people who are targeting you could get to you through your family. Have you ever considered that?"

"It's making me sick thinking they could be in danger. There is no easy decision. But my mind is made up. I'm going to testify tomorrow. Come what may."

"No matter what?" Reznick said. "No matter the consequences? What about your family?"

"I love them. But I need to do this. I wouldn't be able to live with myself if I didn't see this through."

"Well, I'm with you," Trevelle said.

Fifi smiled at Rosalind, holding her hand. "I really admire what you're doing. If I can help you in any other way, just let me know."

Dyer said, "You've been very kind. All of you."

Reznick knew at that moment there was no turning back. For Rosalind. Trevelle. Or for him. He admired Rosalind's courage. But he knew it was a high-risk strategy to testify, come what may. "If that's your final word, Rosalind, I just want you to know, this ain't over. Whoever wants you out of the way is still out there."

Dyer nodded.

Reznick stared at Trevelle. "You understand the consequences of this?"

"It means we're all under threat. And Fifi."

Fifi shrugged. "Hey, I ain't leaving."

"This isn't your fight, Fifi. So if you want to bail, you need to let us know now. We'll find some other digs."

"Like I said, I ain't leaving. I don't bail on friends. I've never bailed on anyone. Apart from the NSA. Right, Trevelle?"

Trevelle sat quietly, not responding.

"I want to help," Fifi said. "I'm in."

Rosalind dabbed her eyes. "Thank you. You're very kind. All of you."

Reznick looked around at the faces of the three. "OK, so, if you're not going to go to the Feds, and Fifi is still on board, we need a plan. I want to go on the offensive. We can't wait and react to events. Any suggestions?"

Fifi said, "I know IT better than anyone other than Trevelle. Cybersecurity, systems, hacking, cloud penetration analysis, whatever."

Reznick's mind was racing ahead. He snapped his fingers as an idea began to form in his head. He looked at the two computer kids. "So, I want to know, how good are you guys? Is it all talk, or can you walk the walk?"

"What do you mean?" Trevelle said.

"Hacking. Accessing information. You both worked for the NSA. I'm assuming you know math and all sorts of advanced coding and hacking techniques."

Fifi nodded. "Why do you need to know?"

Reznick sighed. "Honestly? The bad guys are still after us. But if we found out more about them, we might be better placed to protect ourselves. Maybe keep one step ahead of them. And it might help us to know what to do next."

Fifi shrugged. "Got it. What do you want?"

"Let's take a few steps back. That call Rosalind made to her lawyer. Who answered?"

Rosalind said, "I don't know who that was."

"I want to pinpoint where that person was or is."

Dyer closed her eyes, as if the mention of her lawyer had dredged up the bad memories again.

"Who was that guy? Who knows? Possibly the guy who killed Rosalind's lawyer. Or maybe he knows who did. It's one of those two. So my question is, can we access that guy's location?"

Trevelle looked at Fifi. "What do you think? Access via telecom companies?"

Fifi nodded.

Reznick looked across at Dyer, who looked washed-out, drained of life. "Rosalind, get out your cell phone and tell me, exactly, what time you called that guy."

Dyer took her cell phone from her pocket and scrolled through her calls. "It was six thirty-two a.m. and finished at six thirty-four a.m."

Reznick pointed at Trevelle and then Fifi. "Talk to me. Both of you."

Trevelle said, "Hybrid positioning system."

"What's that?" Reznick said. "I've heard of GPS."

Fifi said, "I've got an app I've been developing over the last eighteen months. It's pretty cool. Early stages of development. I've been testing it out."

"So how does it work?" Reznick said.

"It uses various positioning technologies. We start with the Global Positioning System, that's the backbone, but we throw into the mix cell tower signals, wireless internet signals, Bluetooth, and IP addresses, and I'll get you a fix on the cell phone's location."

"Do it!" Reznick said.

Fifi went upstairs, brought down a laptop bag, and took out a MacBook Air. She entered the cell phone number of the lawyer. Then her software began scanning millions of cell phone company and telecom records.

A few moments later, a Google Map with a small red arrow appeared on the screen.

"When Rosalind called," Fifi said, "her lawyer's cell phone was at a business park in Arlington, Virginia. Within ten yards of there anyway. Looks like the call was taken from inside a company called Strategic Security. Fourth floor."

Reznick clenched his fists. "That would make sense. And that's also the current location of the phone?"

Fifi nodded. She looked at Trevelle. "You want to check for yourself?"

"I trust you. Great work. Bank on that location, Jon."

Reznick's mind began to prepare how he was going to respond to the information and location. "How far away is Arlington from here?"

Fifi shrugged. "If you drive, with a bit of luck, you could be there in fifteen minutes."

Twenty-Three

It was a nondescript business park on the outskirts of Arlington. The building was bathed in floodlights. Reznick pulled up in Fifi's car about two hundred yards away, with a line of sight to the glass lobby. He trained the binoculars on the office. A yawning, uniformed security guard was reading a hardcover book. Reznick ran through some scenarios in his head. He wanted to get inside. But he knew they'd ask for ID, maybe even biometric identification.

He wondered if Trevelle or Fifi might be able to gain access to their systems, allowing Reznick to get in.

Then again, it might also tip off those inside that their security had been breached or was about to be breached. Could he risk it?

Reznick pulled out his cell phone and called Trevelle.

"Hey, Mr. R., you OK?"

"I'm fine. Everything OK there?"

"We're good. All secure."

"What about Rosalind?"

"Sleeping soundly, thank God."

"Trevelle, I need a favor."

"Shoot."

"I'm at the address. I need to double-check. Is the cell phone Fifi pinpointed still at the same address? I need to be 100 percent sure."

"Gimme a second." The sound of tapping keys on a laptop. "Affirmative, exact same spot."

"Copy that. Now that we've got a fix on the ex-lawyer's cell phone, are there any other electronic devices in that office within range? It's important we have an idea what we're dealing with."

"Mmm . . . let's see." More tapping. "Got an iMac desktop. And that's it."

"Can you activate the microphone on the desktop and the cell phone? I want to determine who's there."

A few more taps. "Two male voices. Both speaking a language I can't understand . . . can't make out the accent." Trevelle sighed as he tapped more keys. "So . . . ah, interesting."

"What?"

"Uber pickup coming in thirteen minutes."

"Under whose name?"

"Carlos Sanchez. Don't know if that's a real name or what. But taxi for two, I see."

Reznick's mind was racing ahead. "Interesting. Great work. Now, where is the Uber taking them?"

"It appears to be headed to . . . 115 Second Avenue Northeast, Washington, DC. Capitol Hill."

Reznick's brain was making connections fast. "Take note of that address, keep it encrypted."

"You want anything else?"

"Yeah, how many units in the building they're going to?"

A few more taps. "I make . . . sixteen co-op apartments. High end."

"Very good work, man. Thanks."

"When you coming back?"

"Just hang in there. Maybe a couple of hours, hard to say."

"Stay safe, Jon."

"You too." Reznick ended the call. He entered the address Trevelle had given him into the GPS and headed straight there. The location was a four-story Beaux Arts building across the street from the Supreme Court. He imagined the area would be favored by politicians, staffers, judges, and lawyers who worked on Capitol Hill. He saw a police car in the distance, cruising past.

He drove down the road, doubled back, and parked just over a block and a half away from the building's entrance. Good line of sight, but not too close. He didn't want to attract attention.

Reznick switched off the engine, then cut the lights. He opened up his backpack and took out a camera with a long telephoto lens he had borrowed from Fifi. Watching and waiting until the two men arrived in their Uber.

Twenty minutes later, two men wearing dark suits were dropped off outside the apartment building.

Reznick photographed the two short-haired Latino men as they surreptitiously glanced around. Tough-looking fuckers. He switched on the camera's built-in Wi-Fi and emailed the photos to Trevelle.

Then he called him. "Find out who these guys are. Quick."

"Why?"

"I think they've been hired to kill Rosalind."

Twenty-Four

The sun was edging above the horizon, bathing the low-rise apartment buildings in a burnt orange glow, when the two men finally reemerged.

Reznick had popped two Dexedrine to keep him awake and was hyperalert. He slunk down low. He wondered where they were headed. Had they received a tip-off about where Rosalind was? Was that it? Whose apartment did they just visit? Was that relevant to what they were doing? Was it a safe house for them?

The more he thought about it, the more convinced he was that they were part of a kill team, sent to the city to neutralize Rosalind Dyer. He could tell by the way they carried themselves that these were no poseurs in sharp suits protecting VIPs. These were tough motherfuckers, make no mistake. They reminded Reznick of Brazilian military personnel that he had trained in Central America a decade earlier.

The men drove off.

Reznick messaged Trevelle to keep track of the men's movements, deactivate the alarms, and pinpoint which level the apartment was on. He also told Trevelle not to answer the door for anyone. Not under any circumstances. And he told him to keep away from the windows.

A short while later, Trevelle messaged to confirm the men had been in the top-floor apartment and all alarms to the building had been deactivated.

Reznick was sorely tempted to follow the men. However, he was also curious about the apartment. He picked up his backpack, got out of the car, locked the doors, and crossed the street.

Then he casually walked up to the entrance door and took out the tension wrench in his pocket.

Reznick got to work on the dead bolt keyhole. It had been a little while. He was maybe a bit rusty. He turned the wrench using a bit of pressure, making sure the lock pin didn't fall back. Then he inserted a pick into the top of the keyhole.

He felt the pick push the pins up and used the tension wrench to keep them up. He listened for the sign. A clicking. There it was. A second later, the dead bolt opened.

Reznick removed the tension wrench and pick. He pushed open the door. He climbed the stairs to the top level. He knew the alarm inside had been deactivated. The lock on the apartment was an old Yale lock.

He pulled out the pick, inserted it, and had the lock open within a few moments. He turned the handle and went inside, then locked the door from the inside.

Reznick headed down the hallway. Expensive Brazilian dark-wood floors. The smell of men's cologne still in the air. The first bedroom was empty. Mirrored closets, blinds drawn. He checked inside the closets. Nothing.

He headed through to the living room. Blinds again drawn. The whole place seemed to be empty. Unfurnished.

He wondered what the guys were doing in an unfurnished apartment. Were they just killing time? Or was there another reason?

Reznick headed through to another bedroom just off the living room. A rug on the floor. He moved it aside, pulled out the flashlight from his backpack, and examined the floor. He saw telltale scrapes on the dark wood. He kneeled down and pulled off a Swiss Army knife attached to his belt. He used one of the blades to pry up a floorboard.

He lifted it up and placed it carefully on the rug.

He shone the flashlight down through the opening. Black metal glistened. He peered inside. The smell of grease. He could make out what looked like a sniper rifle. He leaned in closer. Tucked in beside the rifle were hundreds of rounds of ammo and a foldable tripod.

What are those guys up to?

Reznick took out his cell phone. He snapped a photo of the contents and sent it to Trevelle for safekeeping. He pulled out the rifle, ammo, and tripod. He stripped down the rifle and placed it inside his backpack, alongside the ammo and tripod. He carefully replaced the floorboard and put the rug back on top.

Was this a safe house? Then again, maybe it was going to be used as an integral part of an operation. The question was, what was the real purpose of the apartment? Was it purely storage? A gathering point before the operation? Or a vantage point for a hit?

Reznick looked around. He went out into the hallway. Adjacent was another empty bedroom, blinds drawn. He peered out through the wooden slats and saw it overlooked the front entrance to the apartment block.

He crouched down, pulled open the blinds.

Reznick took out his binoculars and surveyed the scene. He scanned the buildings about a hundred fifty yards diagonally down the street from his position. The binoculars picked out a plaque on the entrance of an imposing building. He felt his heart rate quicken. "Son of a bitch."

It was the Hart Senate Office Building. The location where Rosalind was set to testify in just twenty-four hours.

Twenty-Five

Trevelle was sitting at the kitchen table in Fifi's parents' place, running cutting-edge facial recognition software on his MacBook. A notification flashed on the screen. He had a match to the photo Reznick had sent. The two men he was checking both came up as Guatemalan citizens. What was that all about?

Trevelle turned around and cocked his head toward Fifi. "Check this out."

She looked over his shoulder. "You kidding me? So why Guatemala? What's the connection?"

"Reznick believes they've been hired to kill Rosalind. And now we've got a match from a database."

"Nice work, Trevelle."

Trevelle called Reznick's cell phone number and conveyed the names of the Guatemalan suspects he had photographed.

"That is interesting," Reznick said.

"I'm assuming these guys are military contractors."

"No question."

"So what do you want me to do with this information?"

"Send those images, encrypted, to Martha Meyerstein, you got that?" Reznick said.

"What will I say?"

"Say Jon Reznick wants her to look into these two guys. He believes they are Guatemalan citizens. And they may be linked in some way to the Rosalind Dyer case."

Trevelle said, "I don't understand how they fit into it. Who sent them? Geostrategy Solutions?"

"Almost certainly. Just send the images and what we know to Meyerstein. Gotta go."

Trevelle ended the call and sent the encrypted images and a short message to Meyerstein. He looked at Fifi. "I think we're onto something."

Fifi studied the faces on the screen. "Who do you think they are?"

"Killers."

"Mercenaries?"

Trevelle shrugged. "Probably. It's not my area of expertise, obviously. This whole thing freaks me out."

"I'm guessing they're not in this country on diplomatic visas."

Trevelle felt himself smile.

"What?"

"Just you. You say funny things. But, you know, you're a good person. I just wanted to say that. For helping us out like this. It's above and beyond the call of duty."

"I'm not doing nothing you wouldn't have done for me."

"I know, but I really appreciate you helping me out on this. You're really sticking your neck out for me. And Rosalind."

Fifi sat down at the opposite end of the table, mug of coffee cupped in her hands. "I thought I had finished with all that bullshit when I quit the NSA. Shit, maybe we need to set up a support group."

Trevelle smiled. He missed the day-to-day interaction with former NSA friends, staffers, and contractors. It felt good to be with an old friend, albeit in terrible circumstances.

"I feel so sorry for Rosalind," Fifi said. "She's doing the right thing. But now she's the one who's being threatened. It's insanity. I can only guess how scared she must be."

Trevelle nodded.

"She's definitely going to testify tomorrow," Fifi said.

"How can you be so sure?"

"She told me. No ifs, ands, or buts. Despite what happened to her lawyer."

"Tough choice."

"So, are the Feds really going to arrest her and stop her from giving evidence if they find her before then?"

"She's a whistle-blower. We know what happens to NSA whistle-blowers. It never ends well. That's the reality. The FBI has already raided her home. They believe she stole classified documents. National security concerns. It's way out of control."

"That's bullshit. They throw that at everyone."

"I know. It's the stick they use every time."

Fifi drank the rest of her coffee and put down the empty mug. She rubbed her face as she yawned. "Do you want some coffee? Toast?"

"Love that."

"I'll check if Rosalind wants anything too." Fifi headed to the living room. She came back a few moments later. "She's sleeping on the sofa," she whispered. "Don't want to disturb her."

Trevelle nodded. "She needs to rest." His cell phone vibrated, and he groaned. He didn't recognize the number. "Yeah?"

"Trevelle?" A woman's voice.

"Who's this?"

"Martha Meyerstein, FBI. You might remember, we've spoken before."

Trevelle signaled to Fifi, and he put the cell phone on speaker. "Yes, we have."

Meyerstein sighed. "The pictures you sent. I want to talk about them."

"Yeah, good quality, huh?"

"Were they taken by Jon?"

"Yes, I can confirm that."

"And who else has seen them?"

Trevelle looked at Fifi. "Just me."

"Look, you're aware that the FBI is currently investigating the theft of classified material, Trevelle."

"I'd rather not get drawn into that."

"Trevelle, if you are aiding or abetting criminal acts, you will be in trouble. And we'll find you. You're going to get dragged into this whether you like it or not."

"Ma'am, you should know me by now. I have helped the FBI and Jon Reznick on various investigations he has been involved in. I have never compromised national security. Quite the contrary, I would argue."

Meyerstein was silent for a few moments.

"Ma'am, can I ask you a question?"

"Depends what it is."

"Did Jon show you the footage of my friend being shot dead in cold blood?"

Meyerstein said nothing.

"Someone wants to silence not only me, but ultimately Rosalind Dyer. And that's why we're taking such extreme measures. The whole thing is a mess. My friend Fernandez was a good guy, and he didn't deserve to die like that."

"Miami-Dade police are investigating. As is the FBI's field office in Miami."

"Anything so far?"

"I can't say any more at this stage. I'm sure you can understand that."

"Ma'am, I'm not going to tell you how to do your job. I will say that we're trying our best to stay alive. I fear for our lives. Can you appreciate that?"

"Wouldn't it be safer if you gave yourself and Mrs. Dyer up?"

Trevelle looked at Fifi, who raised her eyebrows, as if not quite sure what he should do.

"I understand that you're in a scary situation, Trevelle. It must all be overwhelming."

"It is!"

"I get that. And I want to help. I really do."

"I need guarantees."

"I can't do guarantees, you know that. That's not what we do."

"What about if I say I'll hand myself in once Rosalind testifies?"

Meyerstein paused before answering. "Is that a firm offer?"

"Here's the deal. I'll hand myself in after she testifies to the committee. But you guys need to forget about tracking us down and instead focus on finding the people who are trying to kill us. What do you say to that?"

"What about Rosalind?"

"What about her?"

"If you both hand yourselves in, following Rosalind's appearance in front of the committee, I can live with that. We can take you both to a safe house."

"All we ask is that you find the people responsible. I don't think this is over. Not even close."

Twenty-Six

Reznick was preparing to leave the Capitol Hill apartment when his cell phone vibrated in his pocket.

"Jon, it's Trevelle. You got a problem."

Reznick sighed. "Yeah, I'm well aware of that, Trevelle. I'm working on it."

"No, you don't understand. The two guys. They're on their way back."

"What? Now?"

"Affirmative."

"Where the hell are they?"

"Close."

"How close?"

"One minute away. Maybe less. You need to get out of there."

Reznick's mind began to race. He peered through the blinds to the street below. "I don't think I've got enough time."

"So what are you going to do? You can't just wait there for them."

Reznick began to weigh his options. He needed to think rationally. Not emotionally.

"Jon, seriously, you need to move."

Reznick knew that running out of the apartment wasn't a smart move. "Trevelle, do me a favor. You need to activate the alarm system again."

"I'm sorry, what? This ain't the time for games. I'm goddamn serious, Jon."

"Listen to me. Activate the alarm."

"That doesn't make sense?"

"I'm going to stay where I am. I'll figure something out."

"Jon, can't you just get out the back door?"

"Negative. There's no time."

Trevelle sighed down the line. "As long as you know what you're doing, man."

"Trust me, I got this."

"Fair enough. Jon, you have to stay still or you'll set the alarm off."

"Do it right now." Reznick looked around the apartment, trying to find a good place to position himself. "Give me twenty seconds before you activate the alarm."

"Got it. You're on the clock. And take care, man. These guys are maybe thirty seconds away."

Reznick ended the call and went back through to the living room. He lay back on the sofa, feet up, Beretta drawn.

A few moments later, he heard the sound of a car pulling up outside. Then the front door to the building shut. Reznick lay still, not daring to breathe. The sound of his heart beating hard. Time seemed to stop as he lay in wait.

The sound of a key scratching the lock in the door.

The front door creaked open. Voices low.

The alarm beeped into life for a couple of moments before it was deactivated in the hallway.

The men were speaking in Spanish as they walked into the living room holding bags of groceries.

"Freeze, motherfuckers!"

The men turned and stared at him.

Reznick got to his feet, Beretta trained on the bigger of the two. The smaller guy dropped his bag, and Reznick shot him in the knee. The guy fell to the ground, clutching his leg, moaning in agony. Blood seeped onto the hardwood floor.

"Dumb move!" Reznick said.

The bigger guy was shaking his head. "We don't want no trouble."

"Too late."

"Who the hell are you?"

"Nice and easy, big guy. On your knees, bags down, hands on head."

The man complied as his colleague writhed in agony, face screwed up in pain. Cursing and swearing in Spanish.

Reznick stood over the injured man. "Who sent you? Who are you working for?"

The man clenched his teeth. "I don't know what you're talking about. Some crazy fucking mistake, I don't know."

Reznick sighed. "Listen, my friend, here's how it's going to work." He pressed his foot onto the man's bloody knee, exerting pressure.

The man clenched his teeth, eyes shut tight, moaning in agony.

"Simple question, son. Who are you working for?"

"I told you, I don't know."

Reznick pressed harder with his heel. "Maybe I didn't make myself clear. So I'll try again. Tell me what you know, and you will live. That's the best and only offer I have. I need a name! Who sent you?"

The kneecapped man was shivering as he went into shock. "I don't know his name. He calls me. He said this woman knows too much. She knows about the other killings."

"What woman?"

"Rosalind Dyer, the investigator. She knows about all the other killings. That's why they wanted her dead."

Reznick nodded. It tallied with what Dyer had told him. "Did you take part in the other killings?"

"No, sir, I swear."

Reznick knew it was probably a lie. "Tell me about Miami."

"I don't know what you're talking about."

"Were you down in Miami?"

"Absolutely not. We flew in from California."

"Where from?"

"We're both from Bakersfield."

Reznick nodded. "Who did you serve with in the past? And before you waste my time, I know you're from Guatemala."

"Man, we're just doing a job. We need the money. Bad. They pay very, very well. My family needs the money. My daughter, for an operation in America."

"I'll ask one last time. Who did you serve with in the past? I'm assuming you guys didn't just learn how to kill people in the yard behind your favorite cantina."

The man began to nod frantically. "Yes. We did serve. Guatemalan army. G2."

"What the fuck is G2?"

"Military intelligence."

Reznick stared down at the man. He had begun to put together the pieces of the jigsaw. These were indeed, as he'd thought, contractors. Mercenaries. Guns for hire. Assassins for hire. You wanted someone killed, no matter who they were, guys like this would do it. No questions asked. And with plausible deniability for the US government. "So you live in America?"

The man nodded.

"So you left G2. Then what?"

"We get paid. We do what we have to do."

The injured man on the ground suddenly thrust his hand into his pocket.

Reznick instinctively shot him twice in the forehead. A double tap.

The big guy on his knees was shaking bad, eyes wide. "I don't want any trouble."

Reznick trained his gun on the guy's head. "Looks like you've come to the wrong place. Are you going to be as stupid as your friend?"

The man shook his head. "No, man."

"Give me a name. Who hired you? And you can live, which is more than can be said for your friend here."

The man made the sign of the cross. "Luis Molena, so help me God."

"Tell me about Luis Molena."

"He lives here in America. That's all I know."

Reznick kept his gun trained on the man as he rifled through the big guy's jacket pockets with his spare hand. He pulled out a cell phone. "Luis Molena, huh? Passcode?"

"Nine, four, two, eight."

Reznick entered the passcode. He began to scroll through the messages. "A lot of instructions. It appears you were directed to Miami, after all. You involved in the raid on the warehouse, huh?"

The man bowed his head.

"You've been very busy boys."

Reznick scrolled some more. He saw video footage that had been messaged from the cell phone. He pressed play. It showed the men in masks at the Miami warehouse, flashlights on, before they shot Fernandez dead. He replayed the footage and showed the kneeling guy. "Is this a little trophy? This for your amusement, motherfucker?"

The man bowed his head lower.

Reznick pistol-whipped the guy until he passed out. He sent the footage from the other guy's cell phone to Trevelle. Then he called the young hacker and explained where he'd gotten it. "You get that footage?"

"Copy that, Jon. Safely received. That was on their phone? They filmed themselves killing Fernandez?"

"I'm sorry, man. Listen, you need to send that to Martha Meyerstein. Right this minute. I've got two of the people I believe are responsible."

"Are you kidding me?"

"Tell me, how is Rosalind?"

"She just woke up. She's jumpy."

"Listen, I'm going to be back in the next half hour. Things have gotten a bit messy here."

"Messy, what do you mean messy?"

Reznick stared down at the two men lying motionless on the ground. One dead, one unconscious, blood pooling and congealing around his feet. "It doesn't matter."

"It does to me. Did you kill them?"

"You don't need to know."

A silence stretched between them. "Oh man, that's not good. I don't like the sound of that. I don't want blood on my hands."

"It's not on your hands. It's on mine. Sit tight. I'll be back before you know it."

"Do you think there are others out there, Jon?"

"Almost certainly."

"Fuck."

"Listen, I'll see you soon. We need to talk."

"About what?"

"How we're going to get Rosalind safely to the committee tomorrow morning."

Twenty-Seven

Reznick pulled off the dead guy's belt and used it to tie the unconscious guy's ankles together. Tight. Then he used the unconscious guy's belt and pulled his hands behind his back, hog-tying him. The fucker wasn't going anywhere. Not for a while.

The cell phone he'd taken from the other guy started ringing.

Reznick pressed the phone to his ear and took the call. "Yeah?"

A silence before an electronically distorted voice spoke. "Well, this is interesting."

"Who is this?"

"You don't really expect me to tell you that, do you?"

"Identify yourself."

"All in good time. I had hoped one of my operatives would have picked up."

"Not available."

"I warned my men that you were in town. But it appears they didn't heed my warning. One step ahead, Jon. Good for you. You're very resourceful."

"I asked who you are. And why are you using a voice changer to disguise your identity?"

"So many questions. I like that about you, Jon. It shows you're curious. And intelligent. Intelligence is a good thing."

"So are you going to get to the point?"

"I want to talk."

"Don't think we have much to talk about."

"I have to disagree with you there. I want to talk about you, Jon. And about what I can do for you."

"Forget it."

"And in return what you can do for me. I'm a pragmatic man. There's a lot to be said for pragmatism in life. It pays to be accommodating. No matter who you're dealing with. No matter the hand you are dealt."

Reznick sighed as he paced the room. "One of your guys is dead. The other is out of it. Like I said, not much to talk about."

"A minor inconvenience. Listen, here's my point. I've made a few inquiries about you, Jon. And I think you're the sort of man I need."

"Unbelievable."

"I pay very, very well. You won't ever have to worry about money again."

"Not interested."

"I admire your pride. Really, I do. We're from the same sort of background. Blue-collar, working-class Americans. A dying breed. I know a lot about you. And about your father."

"You don't know anything about me. And you sure as hell don't know about my father."

"Afraid you're wrong there. I've even got your father's file in front of me. A tough guy, apparently. Just like you. But you don't want to end up like your father."

Reznick felt a seething rage inside him ready to explode. He knew the guy was fucking with him. But talk about his father was off-limits for anyone. He loved his father. When he looked at him, looked into his eyes, he saw the type of man he really was. Integrity. Honor. A fierce sense of independence. And pride. The man who had returned from Vietnam and built a family home by Penobscot Bay. But also the tough guy who went to work the day after his wife's funeral. A working man. A man who had fought all his life. Who had instilled in Reznick a strong work ethic. What it means to be a man. His father was one of a kind.

"I want to help you, Jon. And I want you to help me."

"Not a chance."

"Don't make the mistake your father made. He died a virtual pauper. An alcoholic. There's no honor in poverty."

Reznick felt as if a knife had been plunged into his chest. He felt the ripples of rage burning deep in his soul. But he knew he shouldn't respond. He should just get the hell out of there. But something within him felt compelled to defend his father's name. He knew the guy was trying to get under his skin. He got that. But he would not put up with any shit talk about his father, and certainly not from someone who didn't know him.

"Don't be like your father, Jon."

"You want me to take the bait, right?"

"Our backgrounds are the same. My father ended up just like yours. Broke. Blind drunk seven days a week."

"My father, if you really knew him, was a true American. He did drink. Too much. Yeah, we didn't have much money. But that was never my motivating factor in life. Maybe for you. Never for me. That's why you and I are different."

"That's how you'll end up, Jon. But I can change that. You're resourceful. You're smart. Hand over that woman, and I'll make you a very, very, very rich man."

The unconscious man was slowly coming to.

Reznick walked over and kicked the guy hard in the head, knocking him out cold again.

"There's a clear choice for you, Jon. A ton of money, in exchange for Rosalind Dyer. Just give her up."

"You said there's a clear choice. What's the other choice?"

"Either hand her over or you'll die along with her. To me it's a slam dunk, Jon. Take the goddamn money. That's your best choice."

Reznick shook his head. "I'll take my chances. No deal."

A deep sigh came down the line. "Bad choice, Jon. Real bad choice. That your final word?"

"Final word."

"Very well. We'll find her. And we'll find you. We'll choose the time and place."

The line went dead.

Twenty-Eight

Max Charles put his cell phone back in his pocket and began pacing the presidential suite at the Four Seasons in DC, his firm's confidant, Malcolm Black, taking notes on a sofa. "The ungrateful dumb fuck!"

"Having Reznick involved in all this really complicates things," Black said. "He's the real deal."

"Yeah, no kidding. What I wouldn't give to have him on our team."

"And he turned you down flat?"

"Not interested."

"I don't like it, Max. Some bad optics."

Charles shot him a look. "What don't you like?"

"Reznick's been turning us inside out from the moment the hacker kid approached him. And now he's taking our operatives out of the game?"

Charles kicked over the trash can full of shredded paper and candy wrappers. "Motherfucker!"

"We'll get them out of there. Don't worry."

"Extraction team en route?"

"They'll be there in fifteen minutes."

Charles felt his blood pressure rising again. "Reznick will be long gone. He's running circles around us. Soon the Feds will be swarming the place. Or the cops. What is so fucking difficult?"

"The good thing is they weren't the team for the hit. We've got the Miami A-team in town now," Black said.

"The location has been compromised. How are they going to take this woman out? It'll take too long to get another apartment, and the hearing is tomorrow. The weapon and ammo will be gone too. I guarantee it."

"Team A is drawing up a plan. We're going to make sure that we take her down. I think this situation might actually offer us a better chance of getting to her now. A new opportunity."

Charles rubbed his face with his hands. "Maybe. What about the B-team?"

"Ideally, we get them out of there, and our extraction guys will have the apartment cleaned within the hour. But the Feds might be able to piece this together."

"Fuck them," Charles said. "And fuck those dumb Guatemalan fucks for getting their asses kicked by Reznick. Serves them right. And fuck the other bastards who got caught by those shitkicker cops in Maryland. But mark my words, this ain't over."

"I know."

"No more fuckups. All I care about is killing Rosalind Dyer."

Twenty-Nine

Reznick drove back to Georgetown, having left the dead Guatemalan and his unconscious sidekick to be picked up by the Feds. He quickly showered and was served a breakfast of pancakes and black coffee by Fifi. "You've gone above and beyond," he said. "Thanks very much."

"Jon . . . ," Fifi said. "Are you . . . ?"

Reznick was wolfing down the pancakes. "What?"

"Trevelle said you kill people. Is that true?"

"I do a lot of stuff. It's not something I really want to talk about."

"Do you think those guys are going to turn up here?"

Reznick shrugged. "I don't know. Like I said before, if you want to bail, or get us out, I understand."

"Sorry to disappoint, but that ain't gonna happen. I stick around."

"OK, appreciate that. But I was thinking it might be wise to move Rosalind anyway."

"Just as a precaution?"

"The capabilities of this crew shouldn't be underestimated. I don't know for sure if I was followed. I'm pretty sure I wasn't. But

I think it's best to move one last time. So you won't have to worry about us."

"I don't mean for her to leave. Or you. Or Trevelle. I'm just glad I can help."

"Hey, relax, I know that. But it's not fair to you either. We'll be out of here soon."

Reznick finished his breakfast and was enjoying his strong coffee. He saw pictures on the kitchen wall of a couple standing in the snow. "That your parents?"

"My mother and stepfather. In Aspen."

"Love Colorado. You get along with him?"

"My stepfather?"

Reznick nodded.

"I think he's getting used to me. This is his place. But he's also got an apartment in New York, a place in Los Angeles, and an estate in Westport, Connecticut. You wouldn't believe the size of that place. Amazing views over Long Island Sound."

Reznick whistled.

Fifi smiled. "He thinks I should start working for hedge funds or whatever it is he does in Connecticut."

"Not your cup of tea? Math and computer guys do well in that industry, I'm told."

Fifi rolled her eyes. "I'd rather scoop out my eyes with a spoon."

Reznick laughed. "Know what you mean. So tell me, how's Rosalind been while I've been away?"

"She's OK, I guess. She slept and seems a bit more rested. Anxious but rested."

Reznick got up from his seat. "Thanks for the pick-me-up. I'm going to talk to her."

"Be my guest."

Reznick headed to the living room. Rosalind was sitting slumped on the sofa, swathed in blankets, watching Fox 5 DC. It was showing interviews with neighbors of her dead lawyer. Reznick picked up the remote control and switched off the TV, then pulled up a chair next to her. "We need to talk."

Dyer turned and stared at him, glassy-eyed. "Where have you been?"

"I had something to deal with."

"I'm not stupid, Jon. Have you been meeting with the FBI?"

"No. I was in touch with them earlier today, though."

Dyer stared at him as if trying to determine if she could trust him. "You're worried I'll hand you over."

"A little."

"I'm a man of my word."

Dyer smiled. "That's good enough for me. You've been very kind to me."

"Forget about me. What about you? You're looking a little better. How are you feeling?"

"Nervous. Kinda scared."

Reznick nodded. "Perfectly natural. I'm glad you had some sleep. You're going to need to be strong, Rosalind. That is, if you're going to go through with this."

Dyer nodded.

"Do you need some more sleep or rest before tomorrow? Do you need some medication to help you sleep?"

Dyer shook her head. "I've had an hour or so, and I've napped. I'll be fine."

Reznick reached out and held her hand. "The guys I just ran into mentioned *other killings*. So it looks like they're aware of this parallel investigation of yours."

Dyer looked dumbstruck. "I don't understand how they could."

"These are very dangerous people we're dealing with. I need to know exactly what you know."

Dyer closed her eyes and sighed. "I wanted to wait and tell the committee."

Reznick smiled at her. "You can do that too."

"I'm tired of it all. I'm scared. Scared of everything."

"Tell me what you know."

"Get me a laptop."

"Why?"

"Just do it."

Reznick went to the kitchen and got the laptop from Fifi. He placed it on the coffee table.

Dyer reached into her pocket and took out a USB flash drive. She leaned over and inserted it into the side of the laptop. A few moments later, it loaded up. The display showed photos of seven men, biographies underneath each.

"What's this?"

"Just over three weeks ago, I made a connection. You see, I've been looking through all the documents from accountants, auditors, and partners in accounting firms who have investigated kickbacks and missing money from Pentagon contracts. Some of it was due to secret accounts, some to outdated accounting systems set up in the 1950s, but there are also structural inefficiencies, corruption, and downright bad practices. The Department of Defense has an annual budget of seven hundred billion dollars. Its real annual budget is in excess of nine hundred billion dollars. And that's not including secret black budgets run by the CIA. The drone programs. Do you know a team of twelve hundred auditors costing four hundred million dollars had to admit defeat a couple of years back, unable to sign off the accounts?"

"That's outrageous," Reznick said.

"There are hundreds of Pentagon accounting silos," Dyer said. "Money vanishes into budget black holes. No one knows where it begins, where it ends. It's a national disgrace."

"I understand that. But who are these seven guys?"

Dyer's next words were barely a whisper. "They're all dead. These seven men are all dead."

Reznick stared at her. "Yeah, but who are they?"

"Accountants. Financial experts. A couple worked for the government, including the Pentagon and the DCIS. Three were auditors who investigated the accounts closely over the last two years, and two were partners from different accounting firms in DC who were assigned to the case. The latest one was Andrew Boyd. I attended his funeral two weeks ago."

Reznick nodded, allowing Dyer the space to tell him what she knew.

"All seven of them died in different situations over the last three years. A major audit started about then. Then they started dying off. One in a car crash, one from a fentanyl overdose, one from a home invasion. Andrew Boyd drowned. One, a former colleague of mine, is missing. One fell from his balcony on vacation in Hawaii, and one shot himself in the head in the woods near his vacation home in South Carolina."

"All made to look like accidents, right?"

"Exactly. There was a stop-start feeling to my investigation, having to chase down this firm, that expert, interview that witness, and there were innumerable delays and dead ends."

"Have you told anyone at the DCIS?"

"My husband. My lawyer."

"Why didn't you speak to the inspector general?"

Dyer gave a wry smile. "I've lost count of the number of whistle-blowers who have been ruined when they go through official channels. It should work, in theory. But it's only playing into the cheaters' hands. I've been conducting this whole thing under the radar. The colleague of mine who went missing? I've spoken to his wife. We're friends. And she's heartbroken. Her husband just vanished. Hasn't been seen in over a year."

Reznick leaned back on the seat. "That's a lot to take in."

"That's why they really want me dead. Maybe they eventually would have killed me like they did the others, but that's why I took the documents that I did. To prevent them from sweeping all this wrongdoing under the rug again until another auditor uncovers it and they kill him or her too. I was almost certain—and knowing what those men said to you, now I am certain—that they knew I was looking into these deaths. And my testimony in the closed session tomorrow gives me the perfect platform from which to expose them."

Reznick looked again at the faces on the laptop.

"I feel like I know each one of them. I need to tell their stories," Dyer said.

"I admire that. I hear exactly what you're saying. But here's the thing. Especially after everything you've just told me, I do think both you and Trevelle would be infinitely safer in the FBI's hands."

"I'm going to take my chances, Jon."

"Is that your final word on it?"

Dyer nodded. "My mind is made up."

"Well, if you're sure, then I will do my best to help make sure you testify tomorrow."

"I don't want you to get into trouble with the Feds over this."

Reznick smiled. "I think it's probably too late for that. They're already on my case."

Trevelle walked into the living room. He saw the faces on the laptop, and Reznick explained the situation. "Shit, you for real?"

Dyer nodded.

"What is it, Trevelle?" Reznick asked.

"Sorry to interrupt, but I forgot to tell you, I spoke to Meyerstein earlier."

"You did?" Reznick said.

"I told her I would hand myself in to them, but only after Rosalind has testified. I want the Feds to catch these crazies. And I don't want to bail on anyone, not now."

Reznick held up his hand so he wouldn't be interrupted. "I need to make a call." He got up from his seat.

Dyer said, "Don't sell me out, Jon."

"Don't worry."

Reznick headed through to the kitchen, where Fifi had on her headphones as she tidied up. He shut the door. He sat down at the kitchen table and called Meyerstein, relaying what had happened at the apartment about an hour earlier.

There was only silence.

"Did you hear what I said? Two bodies. One dead, one tied up. Guatemalans. Ex-military intelligence."

"Is this some sort of joke, Jon?"

Reznick pressed the phone tight to his ear. "Listen to me, I haven't got time to get into a philosophical argument. I'm giving you a heads-up."

"Jon, this is outrageous."

"Did you get the new Miami footage?"

"I thought . . ."

"I said, did you get the new Miami footage?"

Meyerstein sighed. "Yes, I did. It's being analyzed."

"Those guys filmed themselves killing that poor kid."

"But to kill one of them?"

"I didn't start this. These guys are the hunters. Rosalind Dyer and Trevelle are the hunted. And now me too. Listen, do you want to know where these guys are?"

Meyerstein snapped. "Of course I do."

"Get this. There was a sniper rifle and ammo in an upstairs bedroom, line of sight to the Hart Senate Office Building. I took it from there. It's now in my possession. I'm going to send over some footage."

"What?"

Reznick gave her the address. "You'll find them there. You need to get over there now. I didn't want to call the cops."

"I understand."

"These guys were going to be part of a team or were linked to a team that's in DC, here and now, tasked with neutralizing Rosalind Dyer. This is a serious operation they have going down. I got lucky. But that luck can change. These are dangerous people, Martha."

He heard Meyerstein shouting the address to her colleagues.

"I've got a team on the way right now. We'll secure the area." A long silence. "Jon, I'm sorry this is happening."

"So am I."

"But it's important you know. Rosalind needs to get to a secure location. And quick."

"She will. But only after she's testified. That's the deal."

"Jon, I'm begging you, bring Rosalind in! Otherwise, this is not going to end well."

"No can do. There's a plan to kill Rosalind Dyer. The two guys I just handed you won't know what other teams are in town. They're lower down the food chain. Now that the apartment is compromised, they're going to try to get her some other way. Figure it out, Martha. We're running out of time."

Reznick ended the call. He sat and pondered his options as he sent Meyerstein the footage from his cell phone. The clip, taken in the apartment near the Hart Senate Office Building, showed the two hit men, one dead and one unconscious. He was annoyed with himself for not telling her about the sniper rifle and ammo as soon as he left the apartment.

He contemplated the situation as Fifi and Trevelle joined him at the table. They placed their laptops on the big wooden table in front of them.

"What's going on?" Reznick said.

Trevelle tapped away at the keys as he logged on. "I told Fifi about those seven guys."

Fifi said, "She needs to testify. If she doesn't testify, no one will know. It will all get buried in the machine."

"Got a little update for you, Jon," Trevelle continued.

"What kind of update?"

"From the moment the guy with the electronically distorted voice contacted you while you were in the apartment to the moment you ended the call, we were listening in."

"You were?"

"We've been working on identifying his voice."

"You can do that?"

"Reverse engineering. Fifi has some software she developed."

"Why didn't you tell me?"

"You didn't ask. We've managed to strip away the electronic distortion. Anyway, what we found is pretty interesting."

"You got something?"

Fifi nodded. "Oh yeah!"

"So you can identify him?" Reznick said. "Seriously?"

Trevelle said, "Once we stripped away the distortion, which incidentally is ten-year-old technology, we ran his real voice through several databases. And we believe, definitely believe, we know who it is."

"You guys are seriously the most way-out-of-left-field people I know."

Trevelle rolled his eyes. "Jon, you kill people. Now that's left field."

"Point taken."

"The voice, let's focus on that for a moment. You want to prove it beyond a reasonable doubt, you'll need audio forensics experts to look over this clip. But I think we have a pretty good idea who it is."

"Who?"

Trevelle smiled across the table at Reznick. He turned his laptop to show a grainy image of a white guy in shades. "Photo was taken four years ago on Sanibel Island, Florida. This is the guy."

"Who is it?"

"Max Charles, former senior CIA way back in the 1970s. Involved with the Contras, Central American death squads, and the militaries in those countries. Regime change specialist. False flag operations. Assassinations. Works on various CIA front operations, including aid agencies in the Third World."

Reznick stared at the image. "Max Charles. The name seems familiar."

Fifi said, "Let me refresh your memory. He currently runs a shadowy consulting firm in Manhattan. Geostrategy Solutions. Specialists in private security. Geopolitical advisers. Offices right in the middle of Manhattan on Lexington. Know what else?"

Reznick shrugged.

"Max Charles advises the State Department and the Pentagon and has close contacts with MI6 and Mossad. What do you think? This our guy?"

"Now all we need is a link to Guatemala. And don't mention any of this to Rosalind," Reznick said.

The pair of hackers nodded.

"She might freak out. It's important we keep her in the right frame of mind. Besides, there's a lot of moving parts on this. We've got Max Charles, his Guatemalan goons in town, and we've got Rosalind, who is poised to testify, here in DC, tomorrow morning."

Fifi said, "I understand what you're saying. But doesn't she have a right to know about this Max Charles?"

Reznick leaned back in his seat, arms folded. "Fine. You want to tell her? See what she does."

"You think she'll freak out?"

"Fifi, she's supersmart. She already knows she's at risk. And she's rejected any offers to hand herself in and let the FBI take her to safety."

Fifi said, "I guess. What do you want us to do with this information? We can't just sit on it."

"Get the audio of my conversation with Max Charles, stripped of the electronic distortion, and send it to Meyerstein. But also send the original conversation which disguises the voice."

"Right now?"

"Right now. Tell her what you know, that you think this is Max Charles. And let the Feds deal with it."

Thirty

Meyerstein was watching the real-time footage on the big screens in the FBI's fifth-floor Strategic Information and Operations Center. A SWAT team was moving from room to room at the DC apartment where Reznick claimed he had left the Guatemalans. It was stripped bare. Each and every cupboard and closet. Nothing. No one was there. No injured. No dead. And no blood. Not a trace.

Meyerstein felt empty inside. She also felt like a fool. She had instigated the raid on the information Reznick had provided. And there was nothing there.

She slammed her hand hard down on the conference room table, sending papers flying. "Goddamn it, what the hell? Gimme answers, people. What the hell happened?"

A senior analyst, Barry McNulty, said, "They sent in cleaners. Very professional. All my team agree."

Meyerstein turned and looked across at McNulty, who was sitting at the conference table, laptop in front of him. "So quickly?"

"Appears so."

"Why the hell did it take us so long to get there? The SWAT team entered fifty-five minutes after Reznick called. Did they really take that long?"

"Breakdown in the chain of command. We're still trying to figure it out. From what I can tell, the SWAT team was diverted when the hostage rescue team called for immediate backup. A Somali guy on a terrorism watch list started shooting off his gun eight blocks away. So the call was made to go there."

"That was all handled though, right?"

"In hindsight, absolutely."

"I'll deal with that later. For now, tell me about the audio that was sent to us by Trevelle Williams. Max Charles, right?"

McNulty tapped a few keys on his laptop. "Audio forensics have confirmed that he's the one talking. Absolutely no voice morphing. It's him."

Meyerstein's mind flashed up images from her past. The name Max Charles made her blood run cold. "That's the same guy I told you about. He was involved in that Russian crew that abducted me, if you remember. He was pulling the strings for that Russian mobster who lived in New York. He had links to the Ukraine and to Russian oligarchs. After that, he dropped off the grid. No one seemed to know where. Just disappeared. Son of a bitch! Do you remember?"

"How can I forget, ma'am."

"What do our records show?"

"Unconfirmed sightings in Belize, Sudan, and Guatemala, interestingly. Usually flying in and out on a private jet registered to a shell company in the Bahamas owned by an American company that doesn't file returns."

"Great. Well, he's back. I need to know, is he using an alias? Has he been in America without us knowing it? For how long? It boggles the mind."

"I'll check it out."

"And this is definitely the voice of Max Charles?"

"He's known as Max Charles, ma'am, but he was born Thomas McAleese in the Paulus Hook area of Jersey City seventy-eight years ago."

"That's his real name?"

"McAleese, that's right."

"What else do you have on his background?"

"He won a scholarship to Yale. Very bright. And along the way he changed his name to Max Charles. Probably because he wanted to fit in more with the Ivy League crowd at Yale at the time."

Meyerstein sat down in her seat.

"The CIA got tipped off by a professor about his test scores and psychological profile. He was recruited by the Agency. As a young man, he was mentored by Dulles, no less. Allen Dulles."

"I know the type."

"Both Dulles and McAleese, or Max Charles as he was then already known, shared the same Cold War ideology. Virulently anti-socialist, communist, leftist, and saw Ban the Bomb, Campaign for Nuclear Disarmament, and anti-war movements as Moscow-led fronts."

Meyerstein scribbled down the details on a writing pad in front of her. "So where is he now? New York?"

A fresh-faced twentysomething IT guy with glasses put up his hand. "Ma'am, you might not like this."

"What do you mean I might not like this? Like what?"

"Max Charles is here."

"In DC?"

"No, ma'am. Max Charles is in this building as we speak. He's up on the seventh floor with Director O'Donoghue."

Meyerstein's head was swimming as she took the elevator to the seventh floor. She brushed past the desk of the Director's long-serving assistant, who looked up from her desk. "Hi, Martha, you got an appointment?"

"Not today." She walked past the desk.

"He's in a meeting!"

"Too bad." Meyerstein knocked twice on the door and strode into the office.

O'Donoghue was sitting on the sofa and looked surprised to see her. Standing beside the windows, hands behind his back, was a tall, elderly man wearing a gray suit.

The man turned around and gave a thin smile. "Max Charles. Nice to meet you."

Meyerstein shut the door behind her and stared at Charles for longer than she intended. "I'd like to speak to the Director alone."

"Martha, pull up a chair," O'Donoghue said.

"Sir, if it's alright with you, this needs to be private."

O'Donoghue pointed to the chair. "Please, Martha. What's the problem?"

Meyerstein reluctantly pulled up the chair and sat down, adjacent to O'Donoghue. She looked at Charles, who was still standing beside the window, hands behind his back in an imperious manner. "Your name has come up in an investigation I'm currently running," she said. "Max Charles, you said?"

O'Donoghue stared at her.

Meyerstein fixed her gaze on the man standing beside the window. "Your name is Max Charles?"

The man stared at her long and hard.

Meyerstein looked at O'Donoghue, who was now frowning. "Sir, I'm sorry to drop this on you. I wanted to talk about this in private. But it appears Mr. Charles has beaten me to it."

"What are you talking about?" Charles said.

"I'll tell you what I'm talking about. We've analyzed a voice recording that appears to be a match for your voice. You spoke with Jon Reznick, who occasionally consults with us, this morning. You're behind the attempt on Rosalind Dyer's life. What have you got to say for yourself? And what the hell are you doing here? This is outrageous."

Charles looked at O'Donoghue and smiled. "What is this, Bill?"

O'Donoghue said nothing.

Charles looked again at Meyerstein. "Maybe I should explain. I speak to a lot of people. What is this in connection with, this conversation I supposedly had?"

"Your name came up previously in connection with my kidnapping, several years back, as well, you may remember."

"My name? I'm sorry, I think you've made a terrible mistake."

Meyerstein shook her head. "Russian mob? That jog your memory?"

Charles gave her a patronizing smile. "I think you're very much mistaken. Although, you might be getting mixed up with my other work, as I do have a lot of back-channel connections with Russians living in America. For the purposes of opening dialogue between us and Moscow. My services are used by the Pentagon."

"I assume you wouldn't mind answering some questions regarding that investigation?"

"Not at all. Glad to help. I'm due to visit my attorney later today, so I'll mention that we spoke."

"The FBI will be in touch. But we are also investigating serious allegations concerning the testimony tomorrow morning of Rosalind Dyer. Are you involved with people who are attempting to dissuade her from speaking before the Senate Armed Services Committee?"

Charles spread his palms and smiled. "Assistant Director, I think we're at cross-purposes. I believe I know something about what you're getting at."

"You want to tell me?"

Charles sat down on a sofa opposite O'Donoghue. "Bill, I'm sorry this probably sounds a bit crazy. But I'll try and explain what's happened."

O'Donoghue sat stony faced.

Charles looked across at Meyerstein. "Rosalind Dyer . . . That's why I'm here. I'm representing the interests of the United States. I work for the American government."

"In what capacity?"

"As you can imagine, a lot of my work is classified. My company consults for organizations as diverse as the Pentagon, NSA, CIA, and several oil majors. But you probably know that already."

"Indeed I do."

"Geopolitical risks and such. And I liaise with intelligence agencies across the world, including our own."

Meyerstein shifted in her seat. "You aren't working for the CIA?"

"No, I'm not. You might be interested to know that I still have the highest security clearance, though. And it's required because I consult with various governments and businesses around the world."

"Who are you representing in regard to Rosalind Dyer?" Meyerstein asked. "I need a name."

"I'm working for the President's national security adviser, Brad Firskin."

Meyerstein's blood ran cold. She felt as if she'd been hit by a ten-ton truck. "And they're pulling the strings on this little operation you're running?"

"Don't be so dramatic, Martha."

"Don't patronize me. I'm wondering if Brad Firskin, who I know very well, will be interested in what we've found out about your operation. I've got to be honest, it's rather alarming."

"What are you talking about?"

"I'm talking about the leaked document intercepted by hackers that talks about neutralizing Rosalind Dyer."

Charles smiled. "I believe I know what you're referring to. It was an internal draft document. The person who wrote it is no longer working for my company. And his use of inflammatory language is inexcusable and deeply regrettable. I'm guessing that's where the misunderstanding arose. It was a lighthearted but ill-thought-out first-draft memo, as far as I can remember."

"Who drafted it?"

"I'll need to speak to my attorney. But I can get you that information within forty-eight hours, I'd imagine."

"Someone wants Rosalind Dyer dead."

Charles looked at O'Donoghue, who had remained quiet throughout the exchange. "I was just discussing the matter of Rosalind Dyer with Bill. We go way back."

O'Donoghue nodded.

"And I was trying to give some background about my role and my company. I'd like to focus on what Rosalind Dyer is alleged to have done. Serious criminality. Think Edward Snowden. Chelsea Manning. Appalling. She's stolen classified files not only from the Defense Criminal Investigative Service, but also from the Department of Defense. And the Pentagon contacted me accordingly to try and resolve the situation. We're talking about our national interests. And that's why she can't be allowed to give testimony tomorrow."

"I'm not buying it."

Charles shrugged. "It's the truth. You want to know another reason?"

Meyerstein folded her arms. "Try me."

"Rosalind Dyer, if she takes the stand tomorrow, not only will embarrass the government, the United States, and the CIA, but will almost certainly expose herself to the cruel light of day. She will be ridiculed."

"What are you getting at, Max?" O'Donoghue asked.

"Let me explain," Charles said. "And don't get me wrong, Martha, I know what you're probably thinking about me. That I'm an old-school Cold War relic. Reactionary. Perhaps I was at one time. I'm not perfect, like everyone else. But I have always put my country's needs first."

"As do I," Meyerstein said.

"No doubt. Here's the thing. And this is a very important point. A point that has not been raised about this woman."

"This woman?" Meyerstein said. "Is that how you refer to her?"

O'Donoghue shifted uncomfortably in his seat.

Charles cleared his throat. "I have it on good authority, from a source with impeccable credentials, that Rosalind Dyer is an unhinged woman. She is very unstable."

Meyerstein shook her head. "Bullshit. I think you're lying. In fact, she's a highly intelligent woman, wouldn't you agree?"

"She's also delusional. And increasingly so."

"You're a lying son of a bitch."

"Listen, I've spoken to doctors about this. They have told me that she is on medication for schizophrenia. She has talked about hearing voices. And that's what this is all about. She's absolutely delusional, embarrassingly so."

"I don't believe it. This is a pretty low-down tactic. It's disgusting. And I don't buy it. Trying to pretend she's crazy? Oldest trick in the book."

Charles sighed. "It's hard to hear, I understand. I have a role to play in reaching a solution we can all live with. The optics don't look good, I get that. An old CIA guy trying to stop this woman from talking."

"Whatever happened to free speech?" Meyerstein said. "The First Amendment?"

"It's what this country is founded on," Charles said. "But Rosalind Dyer can cause incredible harm to this country if she takes the stand. Everyone at the DCIS knows she's out of her mind."

"Show me the proof."

"I'll get that to you."

"When?"

"I need to get the information cleared. Might take a day or two. Two government psychologists deemed her unstable after she bombarded the chairman of the Senate Armed Services Committee with emails morning, noon, and night. She's not well."

"Then why hasn't she been hospitalized before now?"

"She needs medical treatment. It's a sin that it's gotten this far."

"Do you mind explaining the killing of a young man down in a Miami warehouse, at the hands of masked men? Allegedly looking for copies of this memo outlining a plan to neutralize Rosalind Dyer? The memo written by your company."

Charles held up his hand. "Let's be clear one more time. The employee who wrote that had no authority to do so. He was a kid. It was irresponsible. And he was fired. I assume what he meant was that her threat to the country had to be neutralized. His language had zero finesse. But it's certainly not what you're making it out to be. And there is no connection between that innocuous private message and this act in Miami of which I know nothing."

"That strains credulity."

Charles shifted on the sofa, hands clasped, as if giving Meyerstein his full attention. "So what happened down in Miami?"

"A young hacker was shot by masked men in a warehouse loft in Overtown."

"I know that area well. That is an incredibly high-crime area. Home invasion, right?"

"That's not what we think."

"Really?"

"You were found to be communicating with the men after they came to DC. I have the voice audio. And we know who they are. I'll play it for you."

Charles's waxy complexion visibly sagged. It was as if the wind had been taken out of him. He regained his composure quickly, glancing at O'Donoghue before fixing his icy gaze on Meyerstein. "Is this some sort of joke? Some of these hackers, they're radicals. They want to overthrow our government by any means possible. Fabrication, fake news, phony stuff. It chips away at what's real and what's not. You know as well I do, Martha, that there's a thing called voice morphing. I'm assuming you've heard of it."

Meyerstein bristled at his patronizing tone. "Who the hell do you think you're talking to?"

"I'm sorry, I was just about to explain."

"Don't bother. I know all about voice morphing. Software that replicates speech patterns. Developed at Los Alamos. Are you seriously saying this recording isn't you?"

"What other explanation is there? It's bullshit. Sounds like someone is yanking your chain, Martha. I swear to God, this is the type of pervasive psychological operation that the Russians are so good at. I've got to give them their due. They had you fooled, pulling the wool over your eyes."

"No one is pulling the wool over my eyes. Believe me. Want to know something else? Jon Reznick discovered a weapon and ammo hidden under the floorboards of an apartment overlooking the Hart Senate Office Building. Was that part of a psychological operation carried out by foreign agents?"

"Who knows? Maybe."

Meyerstein shook her head. "You sound ridiculous."

"So where is this weapon?"

"Somewhere safe. I have photos."

"Are either the gun or ammo still in the apartment?"

"There was no trace of *anything* when we got to the apartment."

Charles shrugged. "No disrespect, Martha, but you need to check out that Jon Reznick and the people he hangs out with. I've seen this sort of thing before. A guy with an incredible track record like Reznick goes rogue. PTSD. Flashbacks. Are we sure he isn't behind all this and trying to cover his ass? I know people who worked with him and trained with him at Fort Bragg. Real tough guys. And they all say the same thing. Stay away from him. He's going to bring the FBI into disrepute. He's a fucking nutcase, Martha."

"That's enough!" Meyerstein snapped. "You are linked to this. And we are investigating. You need to lawyer up."

"Martha, listen to me. All you have is a paranoid little hacker, Trevelle Williams, and a crazy lady named Rosalind Dyer who's an embarrassment to the DCIS and a traitor to this country."

O'Donoghue cleared his throat. "Play the recording, Martha."

Meyerstein took out her cell phone. "Are you sure?"

O'Donoghue nodded.

Charles displayed empty hands, as if pleading for help. "Bill, come on, you can't be serious? I come in here to give the FBI a heads-up about the ramifications of this woman giving evidence, and now I'm hearing that I'm in the picture? Doesn't that strike you as strange?"

O'Donoghue said, "Play the recording, Martha. I want to hear what you've got."

Meyerstein scrolled to the audio clip that had been sent over, then pressed play. The conversation between Reznick and Charles was unmistakable. Pristine. The silence in the room afterward was deafening. "That's you, Max," she said. "Or should I say Thomas McAleese. Why didn't you like that name, Thomas?"

Charles stared at her with fury burning in his eyes. "No idea what you're talking about. But the faked voice is a very good match, I'll give you that."

"You want Dyer dead, you tried to bribe Jon Reznick—I'm sure the lawyers will have a field day with this, Max."

Charles stood. "I've tried to be nice and reasonable, and all I get back in return are lies. Fakery. I will be reporting back directly to the President's national security adviser. He's waiting, as we speak, on an update. And he'll be wondering why the FBI aren't looking for Rosalind Dyer. Now I hear that Reznick is hiding this traitor, working alongside this crazy hacker and his friends."

Meyerstein stared at Charles. She wondered how she was keeping herself in check.

"Are you dragging your feet on this because you're involved with him? Is that it, Martha? Do you have an inappropriate relationship with this Reznick? How would it look if that information came out?"

"Max, you're the one who's being completely inappropri—" O'Donoghue began, but Meyerstein interrupted.

"You listen to me, you piece of shit. My relationship with Jon Reznick is purely professional. Reznick is a true patriot."

"Are you sure? Not what I hear. People are talking about you two. About how you're very tight with Mr. Reznick." He looked from O'Donoghue to Meyerstein. "But . . . that's how it is? Then I need to speak to Mr. Firskin. Make no mistake: Rosalind Dyer needs to be tracked down and arrested without further delay." He turned to leave. "Nice talking to you, Bill. You'll be hearing from Firskin within the hour."

Thirty-One

The hours dragged on in the Georgetown townhouse, making Reznick restless. He sat in the kitchen by himself, thinking of the seven men Rosalind Dyer claimed had been killed for investigating the case.

The more he learned, the more he was concerned that Rosalind was going to be killed the following day.

He fixed two cups of coffee.

Reznick felt like he needed another face-to-face with Rosalind. She was in the living room by herself watching television, Fifi and Trevelle upstairs noodling on their computers.

Rosalind glanced up at him as entered the room. "I'm assuming you haven't sold me out yet."

"You assume correct."

Rosalind smiled. "What's on your mind?"

Reznick handed her a cup of coffee. "You look like you could do with some caffeine." He sat down on the sofa opposite. "I'm glad we've got another chance to talk, face-to-face, just me and you. And I'm glad I know the full story now. And this informs what I have to say."

"Jon, I've made up my mind."

"Hear me out. Seven men have paid with their lives already, trying to do what you're about to do."

"Which is exactly *why* I need to do it."

"The methods these people are deploying are terrifying. And I speak as someone who knows a thing or two about how this type of thing works. Max Charles, former CIA, is the guy who is orchestrating this, but on whose behalf? We haven't scratched the surface on that."

"I don't know what you mean."

"He is acting on behalf of an individual, corporation, or government. Maybe all three. And money is no problem for people like that. So is he working on behalf of the American government to suppress one of their employees, namely you?"

Dyer stared into her coffee.

Reznick forged ahead. "Charles is pulling strings. But who for? That's what worries me most."

"Jon, this isn't making me feel any better or stronger."

Reznick leaned forward, voice low. "You need to be sure, totally sure, that you know exactly the risks that you will face if you give evidence. Even if we can protect you from Charles's men, what's to stop whoever hired him from trying to get to you a different way?"

"That wouldn't surprise me. I think we've got to start with, who does my death benefit? The answer? The American government? Perhaps. The Joint Chiefs of Staff? The Pentagon? Most certainly. My revelations will be dynamite. Imagine what will happen when the committee is told about the links to the seven deaths."

"Not to mention your lawyer's."

"Precisely. And the Pentagon knows and has been trying to silence me internally for months. Sidelining me."

Reznick sighed. "They're not going to stop coming after you. I'm going to be up front with you. I found a couple of Guatemalan ex-military guys. Nasty bastards. But they won't be the only ones."

"You're making me nervous."

"I want you to understand the real threat you're under. The two men I took out will be just one of several teams tasked with making sure you don't testify. If one fails, the other will be activated. Plan A, plan B, plan C, and so on."

Dyer had her head in her hands.

"Your lawyer? Dead. That was a warning. Sometimes it's smart to heed warnings."

"Don't you see what I'm trying to do?" she said, raising her head. "I'm trying to tell the American people the truth about some of the most senior men in our military, who are supposed to be protecting the country and instead care more about enriching themselves than doing their duty as patriots. It's the military-industrial complex as the mafia."

Dyer shook her head. "I want to sit in front of the chair of the committee and tell him how the chairman of the Joint Chiefs of Staff, Franklin D. Ross, has somehow acquired assets totaling four hundred and fifty million dollars. On a salary of one hundred and ninety thousand dollars a year. I want everyone to sit up and take notice of the waste. But more than that, I want to bring justice to those seven men and their families."

Reznick sighed. "What about your family? Are you prepared to see your husband alone, without his wife?"

Dyer stared at him, shocked at his strident tone. "I'm sorry, what?"

"What if you die? What about the impact on your family? Your children. Your husband."

"This is about something bigger than my family."

"Nothing is bigger than your family. And trust me, I know what I'm talking about. I lost my wife on 9/11 and not a day passes that I don't grieve. Grieving for what we should have had. The years we should have spent together. I might've been a different person.

But instead I'm locked in this shadowy world. Do you really want your loved ones to lose you?"

"I can't believe you're saying this."

"Rosalind, goddamn, it's a wake-up call! I'm your alarm clock! Don't get me wrong, you are brave, fearless, and a true American. You know right from wrong. But sometimes it's better to just say fuck it, who cares about corruption? Accept that it's always going to be there."

"What about the seven men who died? I wouldn't be able to live with myself, Jon."

"That's not true. You would. We turn the other cheek, day in, day out. We have to."

"Haven't you put your life on the line?"

Reznick took a gulp of the hot coffee. "Yeah."

"And what about the impact on your daughter. You have a daughter, don't you?"

"Yes, I do."

"Your work has affected her, I'd imagine, in some ways?"

"In many ways, my world has encroached on hers. And I feel sick every time it happens. But you can make a different choice."

Dyer ran her hands through her hair. A faraway look came into her eyes. "My father, he always said I was headstrong. He wanted me to join the Feds."

"Oh yeah?"

"He was a special agent back in the 1980s and 1990s. Retired now."

"What was wrong with the FBI?"

Dyer shrugged. "I don't know. I think I was attracted to the stability of being based in DC. I'm not big on firing guns, honestly. I also didn't want to get assigned to a field office."

"Tell me about your husband. How does he feel about all this?"

"Travis? He works from home. He codes. He makes websites. And he looks after the kids. He drives them to soccer and the usual school stuff. But how does he feel? He thinks I'm doing the right thing. But he's starting to get worried. The FBI raiding our house with a warrant talking about stealing classified documents unnerved him. It's crazy, right?"

Reznick sensed she had already made up her mind and would not budge, no matter what happened. "You really are determined to see this through, aren't you?"

"I am . . . but what you're saying, it's true. What about the impact on my husband? What about my children? What if something does happen? I try not to think about it. I'm trying to block it out."

"Rosalind, the people after you are resourceful. I got lucky discovering their base near the Hart building. They had a direct line of sight that would make it a piece of cake for a sniper to take you out. That's the stone-cold reality. I hope I disrupted their original plan enough to make it tougher for them to pull it off tomorrow, but we'd both be naive if we thought eliminating their base of operations removed the threat."

Dyer nodded. "I guess I'm trusting in luck. And faith."

"Faith you can rely on. But luck? Luck runs out. And I fear for you."

She closed her eyes for a few moments, and Reznick saw a way to try a different path. One that would allow her to maintain her integrity. "I'm not going to desert you. I just want to find a different way."

Dyer looked at him long and hard. "OK. Currently, I either testify tomorrow or I cut and run. But you've got a different plan?"

"Maybe. Just hear me out. You said you want to sit in front of the chairman and tell him your story. Tell what you know. The corruption. The billions of missing dollars. And the seven dead accountants and auditors. Right?"

Dyer nodded.

"Then why don't we take the documents and hand them over in person."

Dyer looked bemused. "That's what I was going to do tomorrow."

"No, I mean, turn up to the chair of the committee's house, his private home."

"His home? You can't do that. Besides, we don't know where he lives."

Reznick grinned. "Yeah, but guess what? I bet our hacker friends next door do."

Thirty-Two

Three minutes later, Reznick—thanks to Trevelle and Fifi—had found the home address of the chair of the Senate Armed Services Committee. He lived in a gated mansion on the outskirts of McLean.

"That could be problematic," Reznick said. "I mean, getting to him. It can be done. But it's problematic getting access in such a tight time frame."

Fifi was tapping away at the keyboard. "Let me just check something for a minute. Hang on. Well, that's interesting."

"What is?" Trevelle said.

"He isn't there."

Reznick shrugged. "OK, so where is he?"

"Not surprisingly, the senator is here in DC. And he is . . . at the Hay-Adams. Very nice. Five-star deluxe."

Reznick said, "We need to be more precise. Is he having a drink at the hotel? Does he have a room at the Hay-Adams? Perhaps he has a place here in DC?"

Trevelle was nodding, chewing gum, tapping away at his keyboard. "So let's see if that's the case . . . What do you know, he does have a place here in DC. Apparently right here in Georgetown.

Thirty-Second Street Northwest. Two-bedroom townhouse. That would make sense during the week."

"Around the corner, virtually," Fifi said.

Reznick nodded. "OK, now that is good to know."

"So are we going to wait till he gets home before we speak to him?" Rosalind asked.

"I don't know," Reznick said. "Maybe we should sit tight for now. Not make any moves till nightfall. But we don't want to wait too long."

Fifi said, "I've got an idea."

"What kind of idea?" Reznick said.

"How about I check out his Georgetown place, just around the corner. Just so we're sure where it is."

Reznick didn't think that was such a great idea. "It would be better just to sit tight."

"Got another reason. I'm out of cigarettes."

"Can it wait?"

"I'll just pick up some cigarettes, get my bearings on where the house is . . . what's the number?"

"1651 Thirty-Second Street Northwest."

Reznick shook his head. "Sorry, but this is not a good idea. We can't have people wandering in and out. It's not a sorority house. We need to sit tight."

"You sound like my mom."

"Smart mom."

Fifi rolled her eyes just like Reznick's daughter did. "Hang on," she said, "there's a pizza delivery company. They do cigarettes. How about I order pizza, and I can get my cigarettes delivered?"

Reznick grinned. "They deliver cigarettes? And pizza?"

"You gotta love America."

Thirty-Three

Charles sat with his eyes closed in a rear pew. He was attending mass at St. Patrick's, a Gothic cathedral in downtown DC. He always attended when he was in town, business permitting. And today, of all days, as his men closed in on Dyer, he felt in need of divine intervention.

He was a devout Catholic, just like his mother. He loved the spirituality and God-fearing sermons. He loved the sanctity of the church. A place that had stood, carved in granite, unmoved by time and fashions.

The words of the priest washed over him and the rest of the congregation. About redemption. And the blood sacrifice of Christ.

Wherever he went in the world—El Salvador, Guatemala, Mexico, Spain, Italy, Germany, the UK—he attended mass. He had been a deeply religious man all his life. He remembered the catechisms. He remembered the quick slap on his head from his mother or a priest if his words were wrong. But eventually, he got it. They were engrained on his very soul. Into the fabric of his being.

He understood the power of prayer. It gave him his belief. His inner strength. His core.

Charles's thoughts turned back to Rosalind Dyer. She posed a real threat to Franklin Ross, a man he'd known for more than thirty years. A man who shared Charles's values. But perhaps more importantly, it wasn't just for personal reasons that he wanted to insulate Ross and those on the Joint Chiefs of Staff. Dyer was threatening to expose the way the machine of government, the machine of war, and the machine of commerce blended and merged as one. The nexus of power. The American people didn't need to know any of that. Dyer was threatening to expose a thread woven into the very fabric of American foreign and domestic policy. The sway of money. How people were bought and sold. Americans had an idea that Washington and their elected representatives had been compromised decades earlier by corporate interests. And it was true. But what they didn't know and shouldn't know was how their senior military officers, who were supposed to serve the country, had been groomed for years by corporate donors and foreign governments. Middle Eastern money. Saudis throwing hundreds of millions around left, right, and center. Lobbyists holding sway over the military-industrial complex. It was real. It was pervasive. And no one needed to know the true extent.

There was too much at stake.

Charles saw Dyer the same way he saw traitors like Edward Snowden, Daniel Ellsberg, and Chelsea Manning. Divulging national secrets. People like Snowden, now hiding in Moscow, protected by the Russian security services 24/7, were all criminals.

All had been trusted to work within the intelligence community. To have access to sensitive information. And they'd chosen to leak to the American public secrets they thought were important to expose, rather than consider the serious consequences of their actions.

They were all misguided idealists. Fuck it, he hated them all.

The mass finished, the smell of incense heavy in the air, the words of redemption echoing around the old stone walls.

Slowly Charles opened his eyes. He felt invigorated. Cleansed. He filed out of the church along with all the other worshippers. Shards of harsh sunlight pierced through the trees, and he put on his sunglasses, walked over to his car, and was ushered inside by his chauffeur.

The car pulled away, and Charles turned his cell phone back on. It rang almost immediately.

"Is it OK to talk?" It was Steve Lopez, his director of operations. "Been trying to contact you."

"What's on your mind?"

"We're working on a new plan. We've got the team now in place, in DC. And we can see how we're going to do this."

"Have you found the target?"

A beat. "We've narrowed it down."

"How long till you pinpoint where she is?"

"We've managed to find a Gmail account the target's husband uses. And from there we got into his phone. Also their daughter's. They've both sent messages, so it's just a matter of waiting for the target to reply, and then we can narrow down her location using cell tower triangulation, among other things."

"I'm heartened by that. Very heartened. So we're closing in."

"We will know where she is within the hour. Hang on . . ."

Charles waited impatiently as he was driven back to his suite at the Four Seasons.

"Interesting," Lopez said. "She's 100 percent in the Georgetown area of DC."

Charles felt his old heart begin to beat a bit faster. He was tempted to join the team when they went to neutralize the target. He loved the thrill of the hunt. The waiting. And the kill. "How long till we find the exact location?"

"Not long."

"Find her. Time's running out."

Thirty-Four

Reznick was looking at a street map of downtown Washington, DC, on Trevelle's MacBook. It showed the area around the Hay-Adams. He wanted to see the best way to approach the hotel.

His cell phone rang.

"Jon, it's Martha."

Reznick moved across to the other side of the kitchen and leaned against the counter. "Hey, how are you?"

"Worried."

"You're not the only one."

"Don't mention this to Rosalind. Perhaps I shouldn't even tell you. But under the circumstances, I feel I have to. Besides, I trust you."

"What is it?"

"Max Charles . . . the guy you were talking to? He was meeting with the Director a few hours ago, here in DC."

Reznick took a few moments to digest the information. It hardly seemed believable. "At the Hoover Building?"

"Yup. Apparently he's advising the President's national security adviser."

"Bullshit."

"Unfortunately not. I checked. I got confirmation from the deputy secretary of Homeland Security of that, and I quote: 'Max Charles is consulting on several matters of geopolitical importance and national security for the National Security Council.'"

"How is that possible?"

"He knows people of influence in the corridors of power. Has for years. And he's popped up in Washington all of a sudden."

"It's going to go down. He's in town to make sure this hit happens."

"I know."

"Martha, that is not good. Does this mean the office of the President has contracted Max Charles's firm to silence Rosalind Dyer? At the very least, the national security adviser must know the sort of work this man does."

Meyerstein said nothing.

Reznick began to pace the kitchen. "If Max Charles is that far on the inside, neither Trevelle nor Rosalind is safe. And there's no way the FBI can guarantee they will be."

"I give you my word they will be safe. But I can't protect them without knowing where they are. Without getting them to a safe house. Right now. Tonight."

"Rosalind is determined to testify tomorrow."

Meyerstein sighed. "Is that her final decision?"

"Yes, it is. Look, I've got to go. I'll talk to you soon." Reznick ended the call.

"Hey, Jon," Trevelle said, "you're wanted upstairs."

"What is it?"

Trevelle hesitated for a moment. "Fifi messaged me. She wants you upstairs to take a look for yourself."

Reznick found Fifi upstairs in a back room, the blinds drawn, an iMac showing multiscreen images from the townhouse's security cameras. "Check this out."

"What?"

"Have a look at what the security cameras are showing from the front."

Reznick pulled up a seat beside the monitor. Pin-sharp color footage captured the view from the front door. He scanned down the street and saw a Lincoln SUV with tinted windows. A guy wearing a leather jacket was talking into a cell phone. "How long has he been there?"

"I have no idea."

Reznick got up and retrieved his binoculars from his backpack. He cracked open the blinds and scanned the scene. "Florida plates."

"What does that mean?" Fifi asked.

"That's where Trevelle is from. That's where his friend was killed. This could be the Miami crew. And they're in town."

"We don't know that for sure."

"You don't want to hang around and find out, trust me. We need to move. Fast."

"So what do we do?"

Reznick took out his cell phone. "I want you to do me a favor," he said.

"What?"

"Write down the license plate number."

"Got it," she said.

"Call 911 with this cell phone. Give them the license plate. And report that you saw a guy with a gun. Give the street. Describe the car. Say it's very suspicious. That kind of thing."

Fifi just nodded. "OK, I'm in."

Reznick handed her the cell phone.

Fifi dialed 911. She gave the street and the license plate. "Black Lincoln. I saw guys with guns. One is still standing outside the Lincoln, waving his gun around. I'm scared. He's a very dangerous-looking guy. Please send the police." She ended the call and looked at Reznick. "How did I do?"

"Very convincing. Now it's time to move. We need to get the others. Get them out of here, Fifi."

Reznick got Dyer and Trevelle in the kitchen and gave them the lowdown on what was happening.

Trevelle shook his head. "Christ!"

Reznick looked at them both. "You guys need to move."

"What about you?" Fifi said.

"Head out the back on foot—there's no way to get the car out of here. You guys need to stick together. Find a cab. Get out of Georgetown. And meet up at the Hay-Adams hotel. You need to move, now!"

Fifi quickly picked up a wig belonging to her mother, makeup, and dark glasses and stuffed the items into a leather carryall. She led the way down a back hallway off the kitchen and through a sunroom to a garden shaded by live oaks. He watched as they scaled the wall at the rear of the garden and into a neighbor's backyard. Then they disappeared out onto the streets of Georgetown.

Reznick went back into the house. He heard the sound of police sirens getting louder. He went up to an attic room, cracked open the blinds, and raised the window. He quickly assembled the rifle he'd taken from the Guatemalans' apartment and trained the telescopic sights on the Lincoln's back window. He saw the lights of the police car a block away.

He took aim, looking through the rifle's crosshairs. Then he fired two shots into the SUV's rear window. Glass shattered, and the car alarm went off.

That would draw the cops to the car like bees to honey.

Reznick gathered up the shell casings and put them in his backpack. Then he quickly disassembled the rifle and put the parts away. He pulled on the backpack, bounded down the stairs, and headed out into the back garden. He hauled himself over the rear wall and disappeared down a quiet residential street.

It was late afternoon when Reznick walked into the lobby of the Hay-Adams. He spotted Rosalind Dyer, who was wearing a wig and dark glasses. *Pretty neat disguise,* he thought. He headed through to the bar.

Reznick sat down opposite her and ordered sandwiches for four, iced tea, and a bottle of wine. "Nice getup," he said.

Dyer took off the glasses and forced a smile. "I appreciate all you've done for me. It's above and beyond the call of duty."

"How you feeling?"

"I'm scared."

"I know. For what it's worth, we're here for you. I've got to be honest. The sooner you give your testimony and are in a safe house, the happier I'll be."

Dyer averted her gaze.

"What is it? Family?"

"Yeah, I miss them."

"I'm sure the Feds will have them in a safe place."

"I hope so," she said. She looked at Reznick, who was scanning the customers surreptitiously. "Do you ever relax?"

"Not often."

"You mind me asking you a question?"

"Shoot."

"Where're you from?"

"Why do you want to know that?"

"I always wondered about guys like you. We know what they do in far-off places. But you lead real lives, here, back home. Ordinary."

"I'm just a regular guy."

"From where?"

"A little place in Maine. Rockland."

Dyer smiled. "Rockland, Maine. What's it like?"

"Quiet."

"I've never been there. Is it near Camden? I visited there once."

"Not far. Rockland is mid-coast Maine, fantastic in the summer. The winter? Pretty brutal. But it's home. I can relax there. I know the place, the people. DC? I can never relax when I'm here."

"I know what you mean."

"Got a weird vibe. Don't know what it is."

"Maybe all the politicians. All the policymakers. The aphrodisiac of power seems to warp people's minds."

Reznick smiled.

"Your parents still live in Maine?"

Reznick shook his head. "Both passed."

"I'm sorry."

"My mother died when I was very young. My father died quite a few years ago. He was a character. A Vietnam vet."

Dyer nodded empathetically.

"He used to come down here to DC. I used to come with him when I was a boy."

"Did you visit the memorial?"

"That's exactly why he would come down here. To remember his friends who died out there. Just kids."

"Maybe the weird vibes are all those memories."

Reznick nodded. "Maybe. It all comes flooding back." He sighed. "A lot of memories. Some not so good."

They made small talk for the next twenty minutes. Eventually, Trevelle and Fifi walked in and joined them at their table in the bar.

Fifi smiled. "So we're all good."

Dyer nodded. "Fine. Thanks for helping out."

Fifi looked around at the political caricatures on the wall. "Haven't been here for a while. My parents hang out here occasionally. Pretty buttoned-up place."

Trevelle picked up a sandwich. He began to wolf it down. "Man, this is delicious. Who's paying for this?"

Reznick smiled and leaned closer, voice low. "I got this. Now listen to me, where exactly is our guy?"

"The chairman?" Trevelle asked.

"Keep it down."

Trevelle looked sheepish. "Sorry. He's got a junior suite on the top floor."

"What's the direct line to the phone in his hotel room? Not his cell phone. The phone in his suite."

Trevelle pulled out his cell phone. He took a few minutes to hack the hotel's systems. "I just sent it to you."

"Already?"

Trevelle shrugged, eating the rest of the sandwich.

Reznick checked his messages. He headed to the bathroom and made sure the stalls were empty before he called the number. It rang six times before it was picked up. "Senator Aldrich?"

"Speaking."

"Sir, apologies for disturbing you. My name is Jon Reznick. And I'm downstairs with a woman who is due to testify before your committee tomorrow."

"I beg your pardon?"

"We need to talk. Now."

"That's highly irregular."

"Sir, she is in fear for her life."

Dead silence echoed on the line. Reznick feared the senator would get spooked and call the cops.

"Sir, are you still there?"

"Who are you?"

"Sir, there is an ongoing situation. I consult for the FBI. I report to assistant director Martha Meyerstein. Please verify that with her."

"I know Martha."

"Good. Rosalind Dyer is here now, sir."

"Here at the hotel? How did you find me?"

"Long story. Sir, she would like to speak to you in person."

"In person? This is not the way things work here in Washington, Mr. Reznick."

"I know it's not. But the people she's going to testify against, they want to silence her for good. Do you understand what I'm saying?"

"I haven't been informed of that."

"Trust me, this is a real and present threat. The FBI is aware of it."

"Mr. Reznick, I know Martha Meyerstein. And I trust her judgment. You say you work for her?"

"Ad hoc basis, sir. Consulting. Please check with her."

"And how did you get involved in this, Mr. Reznick?"

"I can explain all that. But first Rosalind needs to speak to you."

"She's speaking to the committee tomorrow. She can say whatever she likes then. That would be the appropriate place. And it will be a closed session."

"Senator, we believe she will be killed before she testifies, sir. You have to believe me."

"Are you serious?"

"Deadly serious."

Fifteen minutes later, Senator Aldrich's aide, a young, fresh-faced college kid, escorted Reznick and Dyer upstairs to the chairman's suite. The aide knocked three times.

Aldrich opened the door to his suite, cell phone pressed to his ear. He ushered them inside.

Reznick sat down on a cream sofa as Rosalind sat down on a wine-red leather chair.

Aldrich continued his telephone conversation. He spoke for almost ten minutes about "protocol" and "standards." Eventually, he ended the call and put his phone in his pocket. "Sorry about that," he said. "Was just making sure that, legally speaking, my meeting with Mrs. Dyer wouldn't break any laws."

Reznick nodded. "We appreciate you seeing us."

Aldrich sat down on the sofa opposite Reznick, next to huge windows overlooking the White House. He looked at Reznick. "I was also checking your credentials with Martha."

Reznick nodded.

Aldrich leaned forward, hands clasped, and turned his gaze to Dyer. "The legal advice I was just given indicates that while I can meet with you, Mrs. Dyer, what you say within these four walls can't be accepted as evidence to the committee."

Rosalind said, "I understand."

"It's the best I can do."

"But I still want to talk to you. At least get you to listen to what I have to say."

Aldrich nodded and opened his palms. "No harm in listening, is there?"

Rosalind took a few moments to compose herself, taking a few deep breaths. She cleared her throat.

"Take your time. Trust me, I don't bite."

Rosalind smiled, tears in her eyes. "This is difficult." She cleared her throat again. "Sir, the last forty-eight hours have been very frightening."

"How so?"

"I've feared for my life. And my lawyer, who was supposed to be representing me tomorrow morning, has fallen to his death."

Aldrich stared at her. "I saw something on Fox. I'm so sorry. That was your lawyer?"

"Yes, it was. I've been receiving anonymous, silent calls for a while, and my lawyer had been approached by lawyers for the Pentagon who threatened to tell lies about me to the media and to get my pension revoked if I testify. Then he falls to his death shortly before I'm supposed to appear."

Aldrich looked thoughtful. "That doesn't mean those things are linked."

"True. But I believe they are."

"Is it possible he was under extreme stress and took his own life? It happens."

"I'm not buying it. Not one bit. Besides, there are seven others. Seven men who died. I want you to know that. The latest one, Andrew Boyd, died only three weeks ago. A partner at a DC accounting firm, Summersby and Grant."

Aldrich looked at Reznick. "Excuse me?"

"At the hearing tomorrow, I plan to talk about not only the financial malfeasance, but the deaths of seven men. Accountants. Auditors."

Aldrich went quiet for a few moments. "That's a lot to take in. First, let's start, if I may, with the chain of events that has led the two of you here. How did this all begin? And I don't mean Mrs. Dyer's investigation into financial irregularities within the Pentagon."

Reznick and Dyer filled Aldrich in on everything, starting with the hacked memo and the murder of Trevelle's friend Fernandez. They laid out the case for the links between each event. Aldrich listened silently through most of this, his brows occasionally skyrocketing toward his hairline, and when they'd circled back to the lawyer's death, he finally spoke, asking again, "How can you be so sure it wasn't just a tragedy? A terrible suicide."

"Trust me," Reznick said, "this was made to look like an accident. Just as Rosalind's death would have if that leaked memo hadn't screwed everything up. The head of Geostrategy Solutions is Max Charles. You might've heard of him."

"Max Charles? He used to work for the Agency, didn't he?"

"He did indeed. He now runs a private security company, and in addition to consulting for the Pentagon, he is currently working on behalf of Brad Firskin, the President's national security adviser."

"You've got to be kidding me. And you believe Charles is behind this?"

"I believe he's acting on behalf of elements in the American government who want to neutralize Rosalind Dyer."

"I find that a bit far-fetched, Jon."

"I don't."

Aldrich said nothing.

"Sir, Rosalind Dyer's life is at risk. You can believe it or not, but I've seen it firsthand. The Feds want her taken to a secure location. They're likely going to arrest her on the pretense that she's stolen classified documents. And she will allow them to do so. But only *after* she has told you what she knows."

Dyer continued, "Sir, I've taken the opportunity to upload the documents to a secure cloud server." She handed him the password details. "This will decrypt the contents. I've also saved a copy to a server in Switzerland as a backup if anything happens to me. The documents tell you everything. They also contain the names

208

of the seven men who have died. Boating accidents, suicide, car accidents, falls from great heights, et cetera. All of these men were investigating the irregularities in the Pentagon budget. And they all went to the inspector general. I'm the only one who took a different path."

Aldrich looked at the scrap of paper.

"There are two boxes of documents that I will have couriered to the committee tomorrow. That's been arranged."

Reznick said, "Sir, I understand all too well there are protocols. How you go about things. How you make sure it's legal. I get that. But Rosalind felt compelled to bring this to you. I hope you understand where we're coming from."

Aldrich sighed. "I appreciate this. And I fully understand your reticence about speaking in front of my committee tomorrow. It's a lot to take in."

Reznick said, "I have another favor to ask."

"What kind of favor?"

"Is it possible for Rosalind to give her testimony via videoconference?"

Aldrich shook his head. "That's not a possibility, I'm afraid. It's a closed-door session, and the security is excellent. There are some things we can't change."

"Can you guarantee her safety?"

Aldrich grimaced. "There are no guarantees in life. You probably know that better than anyone, Mr. Reznick." He looked at Rosalind. "You have submitted a written statement. But oral testimony is required. And there will be questions and answers and opportunity for the committee members to expand upon the statement, gathering their evidence as they see fit."

Dyer nodded. "I understand."

"I have discretion, of course. But in this case, I know the other members of the committee will insist that it be in person. Especially in light of what you've told me."

Reznick looked at Dyer, who was sitting quietly. "What do you think, Rosalind?"

"I will do whatever it takes to let the committee know what's going on."

Reznick's heart sank. He'd held out this last hope of changing her mind.

Aldrich stood. "Your testimony tomorrow is going to prove very powerful. Thank you for stepping forward and doing this brave thing. Now, I suggest we all rest up. The committee will see you at ten a.m. tomorrow?"

"I'll be there."

Thirty-Five

Meyerstein stared out her office window on the darkness of downtown Washington, DC. She felt drained by recent events, and she had a sense of foreboding like she hadn't felt for some time. Once Rosalind Dyer testified tomorrow, she, Trevelle Williams, and Reznick would all have to face a reckoning for their actions over the past few days.

Meyerstein felt mentally exhausted, running on empty. Week after week, month after month of intense work, investigations, and mounting pressure both within and outside the FBI.

What she wouldn't give for a long vacation.

It had been three, maybe four years since she had taken time off. She wondered if a couple of weeks down in the Keys would raise her spirits. The hot sun, the peace, and the water lapping onto the sand. The sound of the birds in the trees. Reading some books. Drifting off on the beach. The gentle breeze blowing in off the Gulf. She longed to be down there now.

She closed her eyes for a moment. Her mind flashed to her honeymoon in Europe with her husband. The Greek islands. The smell of wild chamomile and the hint of thyme in the breeze. All her senses were alive. It seemed so long ago.

Her desk phone rang, snapping her back to harsh reality.

"Ma'am, Abbie Silverman at Quantico."

"Hey, Abbie, how goes it?"

"We've been looking into the video recorded at the warehouse in Miami. The masked men who broke in and shot the kid."

"What've you got?"

"We couldn't figure out what language these guys were using. Really struggled with it. But we got it now. It's interesting."

"What'd you find out?"

"The guys in Miami. They were speaking a Mayan language, K'iche'. Spoken primarily in Guatemala, in the western highlands. About a million people in Guatemala speak this language, about 7 percent of the population. Second-most widely spoken language after Spanish."

"Mayan, interesting. Very interesting indeed."

"There are thousands, maybe tens of thousands who speak a Mayan language in the US alone."

"So these guys might originally, quite conceivably, have come from Guatemala, but because of the death squads and killings, they wound up in America?"

"There's a large concentration in California."

"Appreciate the heads-up."

Meyerstein ended the call and sat down at her computer. She pulled up the FBI's files on Max Charles. A lot of it was redacted. But she knew about the connections between the CIA and its "assets" in Central America. She knew there were many former death squad members from Central American armies who were on the CIA payroll. Past and present. She also knew that joint DEA and FBI investigations into Florida drug cartels sometimes uncovered former military officers from Central and South America who'd turned to importing cocaine from Colombia via Guatemala and into America.

She saw the link right away.

Meyerstein speed-read the file, then came back to what had caught her eye. An Associated Press photo of Max Charles with senior military officers in Guatemala City, 1981. He had been station chief of the CIA there in 1974. Charles knew the country well. He knew the Mayan people, the native people of Guatemala who had suffered at the hands of the military, spoke their own languages. But who were those Guatemalans that Reznick had taken down? Were they former army officers from a Mayan area of Guatemala?

She headed immediately to let the Director know. He was working late as usual.

O'Donoghue leaned back in his chair as he listened to what she had to say. "What do you want to do, Martha?"

"Ideally we need to speak to Max Charles. We need to get a warrant to search his company records, his calls. That's what we should do."

"Max Charles is seriously connected—you know that. You heard the same things I did when he was here. National Security Council consultant? Can you imagine how that would look?"

"I don't give a damn how it looks. We have enough to start with. And I believe he is bending the will of the National Security Council on this issue. For him it's not about the law or national security. It's about protecting senior military officers who are alleged to be accepting kickbacks."

O'Donoghue said nothing.

"Without fear or favor. We need to show resolve on this. No one is above the law. And Max Charles has operated with impunity, protected by God knows who, for years, probably decades. He's a law unto himself."

"I need to think about it."

"What's there to think about?"

"Martha, this is a time for caution."

"Sir, I believe undue caution could be construed by some as failure to take action."

O'Donoghue nodded. "That's fair."

"We have enough to question him. More than enough."

O'Donoghue was quiet for what seemed like an eternity before he finally spoke. "I agree. Let's find him. And bring him in."

"Thank you."

Meyerstein's cell phone buzzed. She thanked O'Donoghue and saw the caller ID was Frank Perino, who was leading the team to track down Reznick and Rosalind Dyer. "Frank, talk to me."

"We know where Reznick and Rosalind Dyer and their hacker pal are."

"Where?"

"Hay-Adams."

Meyerstein took a few moments to figure out what she should do. "First things first, let's make that hotel secure. Talk to the manager. And I want agents outside her room until she appears. But I also want serious security in and around the hotel."

"What about Reznick? You want to haul him in?"

"I'll deal with him later. Just keep Dyer safe. But also, Frank, I just talked to Bill. We have the go-ahead to get Max Charles."

"You got it. Anything else?"

"That's all for now."

Meyerstein ended the call. She gathered up her things, left the office, and drove back to her house in Bethesda. She was relieved to get home. She hugged her kids and spoke to her mom, getting an update on their day.

Almost immediately, her cell phone rang. *Are you kidding me?*

"Sorry," she said to her mother, "urgent business."

"Honey, you need to slow down. You're going to give yourself a heart attack."

"Tell me about it."

Meyerstein headed through to the kitchen, where she took the call.

"Ma'am." Abbie Silverman again. "Got something else."

"What?" Her tone was harsher than she intended.

"I just emailed it to you. It's a photo."

Meyerstein flicked open her laptop on the kitchen table. She logged on and scrolled through her FBI emails. She opened the one from Silverman and double-clicked on the attachment. A photo of Max Charles shaking the hand of a handsome military officer. "Got it," she said, cell phone pressed tight to her ear. "So what am I looking at?"

"You're going to love this. The military officer is Colonel Luis Molena, graduating from the School of the Americas in 1981."

Meyerstein's mind began to race. She knew that was where the US trained senior officers from militaries across Central and South America. "What's the relevance?"

"Molena now lives in Washington, DC, with his wife and five kids. He's originally from Guatemala. He speaks two Mayan languages. And he's Max Charles's son-in-law."

"You think he's the point man for this operation?"

"Guarantee it."

Thirty-Six

It was nearly midnight, and Reznick was nursing a bottle of beer by himself in the Hay-Adams bar. He was pleased that Dyer had managed to speak to the senator face-to-face. But he was wary that she was still insisting on testifying.

Reznick knew the threat was far from over. He had suggested to Dyer that she check in at another hotel nearer the Hart Senate Office Building. But she said she was stressed and tired. And besides, she said, the Hay-Adams had a nice room available and the FBI had secured the hotel. She had Meyerstein to thank for that, almost certainly. He guessed she'd given up on trying to arrest them. At least for now.

Reznick was also pleased to learn that the Feds had teams directly outside and in and around the lobby, vetting who went in and came out. He had already been allocated a room, while Trevelle and Fifi had gotten a double room between them.

The more he thought about it, the more he wondered, even though the Feds had beefed up security, if they shouldn't move, even at this late hour. He wondered how Dyer would react. But in the circumstances, with Feds protecting her room and the hotel until she reached the Hart Senate Office Building, it was maybe best to stay where they were.

Reznick had agreed to wake Dyer at seven, and they would get a cab at eight. His mind was still racing, and he wasn't tired. Probably the Dexedrine running through his system, since he popped three pills earlier in the bathroom. He didn't want to let his guard down now.

He wondered when he was going to cut the habit. He was doing amphetamines every day. He was wired every day. He knew it wasn't great for his health. But still he took them.

He thought about that.

Meyerstein had raised the issue with him before. She thought it was affecting him psychologically. Affecting his decision-making. Making him less cautious.

He realized better than anyone that amphetamines were a surefire way to self-destruct. Popping pills that kept you alert might be fine for a few days. Maybe. But each and every day, feeling wired, on edge, was taking its toll on him. He couldn't relax. Couldn't switch off. His mind was running fast. His heart rate was pounding. Palpitations. He had tried to ignore the rapid-fire beats in his chest. But it was always there.

A woman's voice behind him said, "Hey, Jon."

Reznick turned and saw Meyerstein. "I've been waiting for you."

"You have?"

Reznick shrugged. "Well, I thought you would have found us before now."

"A lot of cameras around the Hay-Adams. And the call from Senator Aldrich pretty much confirmed where you and Rosalind were."

"Appreciate the protection you've put in place. I know you could've hauled us all out of here. So thank you for that."

Meyerstein sat down, and Reznick ordered a couple of glasses of red wine from a passing server. "A few things. First, Dyer would have been better off with us when this all started."

"I'm not disagreeing with that. You guys would have gotten her to a genuinely secure location. I get that."

"Second, just so you know, when she has finished her testimony tomorrow, we're taking her in. There's an arrest warrant that needs to be executed. And I don't care what you say. Are we clear?"

"I think she's fine with that."

"Are we clear?"

"Crystal."

Meyerstein nodded and looked at him. "Are you OK? You look awful."

"Haven't had much sleep in the last forty-eight hours. But I'll live."

Meyerstein pulled her chair close and leaned in. "Your eyes are like pinpricks. You need to ditch the Dexedrine. It'll kill you."

He grinned. "Does it help if I tell you I've been hearing your voice in my head telling me that?"

She smiled. "I'm glad to know at least some of my advice sticks with you. Anyway, after your meeting, Senator Aldrich mentioned you'd made allegations about the deaths of seven accountants and auditors who have investigated the Pentagon's books. He was curious if any of their deaths had made the FBI's radar. They hadn't, but we've started our own investigation into them."

"Excellent."

"Can I ask, Jon—it's just that I'm curious—why did Dyer want to speak to Aldrich before the hearing tomorrow? What was that all about?"

"That was my idea." Reznick shook his head, then gestured around the hotel. "No matter how much security you throw at her, no matter how many precautions we take, I think something is going to happen to her. There's too much at stake. So I suggested she tell the chairman what she knows, face-to-face. And also give him details of where she sent all the files."

"So she wouldn't have to give evidence tomorrow?"

Reznick nodded. "I had hoped that would be the outcome. Unfortunately, the chairman said she needed to be there so the other senators could question her, cross-examine her evidence."

"I wish they didn't need to do that. The sooner she's out of sight, the better."

The server returned with two glasses of red.

Meyerstein waited until the server was out of earshot. "I thought you'd like to know. We've got a connection. A firm connection. To Max Charles."

"You do?"

"Quantico has been looking at the forensics side of things. The clip in Miami from the warehouse?"

Reznick nodded.

"The language the guys used? It's a Mayan language."

"Guatemalan?"

"Got it. And Charles was based there. But one final thing. His son-in-law was a colonel in the Guatemalan army back in the early 1980s. Luis Molena. He was involved in a massacre at a village called Dos Erres. Two hundred men, women, and children butchered. Now he's a naturalized American. Living here in DC."

Reznick ran some scenarios through his head. "Interesting. But it doesn't prove anything."

"True. But it's building a compelling picture. We think he's the guy pulling strings, hiring his old buddies from the Guatemalan death squads who are hiding out in America. The FBI has secured a warrant, and we're looking through his house, his business interests. We're speaking with immigration too. And we're in the process of finding Charles so we can serve a warrant."

"You got him in custody?"

"Not yet. But we will."

"What are your analysts saying about this Guatemalan colonel?"

"We believe that he was, from what I've read, involved in an elite unit known as the Kaibiles. Human rights groups have documented abuses that the colonel's men committed."

"So why was he never sent back to Guatemala to face charges?"

"Redacted letters sent by Max Charles and two members of the Joint Chiefs of Staff, saying this wouldn't be in American national interests."

Reznick rubbed a hand over his face, then sipped some wine. "We have no idea how many of these guys are out there gunning for Rosalind."

"We have plainclothes FBI throughout the hotel. We have two agents from the field office outside her door. It's as close to lockdown as we can get."

"At least it's something."

"And by the end of tomorrow, she can join her family. She will also need to answer for the hundreds of classified documents she has allegedly stolen."

"She's not disputing that. But you have to look at it from her point of view. She couldn't have evidence of corruption without official documentation."

"I'm interested in the law. She's broken the law. And she needs to answer for that."

Reznick took a few moments to study Meyerstein's features up close. Even at that late hour, her eyes were sparkling, her posture in the leather seat upright, and the navy suit she wore impeccable. Her nails were freshly painted. A woman who always looked her best, no matter the time or occasion. He saw the faintest lines around her eyes, which she had tried to conceal with makeup. He felt calm in her presence. He always did.

He wondered why he had never broached the subject of a serious date, just them. He knew her divorce had come through. It seemed crazy but, in all these years, despite their lives being interwoven through their work, they had both always kept their distance. It was as if he feared she would politely decline. Was that it? But he sensed that she cared about him too. A lot. Initially, he felt uncomfortable with that. But he had begun to realize, helped by his daughter's finely tuned intuition, that it was OK to let another woman into his life. That was the problem. He hadn't let anyone, let alone another woman, into his life since his wife died all those years ago.

"Are you OK, Jon?" she asked.

"Me? I'm fine, thanks. Why do you ask?"

"You seem miles away."

Reznick smiled. "A lot on my mind."

"I can imagine."

Reznick leaned closer. "Listen, I'm not very good at this sort of thing. But I just wanted to say, I've got a lot to thank you for, Martha. I really do."

Meyerstein blushed. "Gimme a break, what are you talking about?"

"I mean, you instinctively know how to walk that thin line. You put your neck on the line for me. I love that about you. I don't trust many people. But I trust you. With my life. I guess what I'm trying to say is that, despite the circumstances, I'm glad you're here tonight. You didn't have to be."

Meyerstein tucked her hair behind her right ear. She gazed at him long and hard. "No, I didn't have to be. But I wanted to be." She shifted in her seat and cleared her throat. "And here I am."

Reznick took a gulp of the red wine, savoring the taste.

"This hotel your idea?"

Reznick nodded.

"Very expensive tastes you have, Jon."

"What can I say? I don't get out too often."

Meyerstein laughed. "Yeah, right. So, are you picking up the tab for this tonight?"

Reznick nodded.

"Including Rosalind, Trevelle, and the girl?"

"I'm a bit of a soft touch, if you must know."

Meyerstein rolled her eyes. "Next time, my treat, what do you say?"

"You asking me on a date?"

"Maybe."

Reznick clinked his glass to hers. "Then you've got a deal."

Thirty-Seven

Rosalind Dyer was floating on a dark sea, staring at the inky-black sky. She looked at the billions of stars twinkling like pinpricks of light. She began to drift downstream, taken by the water. Ripples washing over her.

A voice was talking softly.

She opened her eyes. The luminous red dial on the radio alarm clock showed it was 4:30 a.m. The radio was tuned to a talk program discussing gang violence in DC.

Dyer pushed back the covers and walked to the bathroom. She looked at her face in the mirror. Ashen. No makeup. Eyes bloodshot. She looked awful. But she was ready. She had gotten four hours of sleep. That was enough. "You can do this, Rosalind," she said to her reflection in the mirror. "You will do this. Be strong."

She turned on the shower and stepped into the glass cubicle. The hot water was reviving her. The hotel shower gel refreshing her. Cleansing her. She felt sharper.

Dyer tilted her head back, enjoying the sensation of the water splashing onto her face. She leaned forward, hands pressed against the tiles, luxuriating in the powerful jets of water on her body. She thought of her father. The commitment he had made to the country over the years. She thought of her brother. A man who served his country with distinction. And she thought of her husband. The thread that ran through them and her was love of country. She had felt torn and more than slightly scared. But her mind was settled. She was doing the right thing.

The talk the previous afternoon with the chairman, face-to-face, had helped her realize her fears. But also unburden herself before today's events. She wanted to tell the committee about the seven men. She had to.

Dyer stepped out of the shower, dried herself, and put on a new set of clothes the Feds had brought over from her house. She dried her hair and applied her makeup. She was ready.

She called room service and ordered breakfast.

"It'll be about twenty minutes, ma'am," a female voice said on the other end of the line.

"Thanks."

Dyer opened the blinds. In the distance, the White House was illuminated in all its alabaster glory. She thought of what lay ahead for her today. She was going to hold some of the most senior military men and, indeed, the United States government to account. It was her duty. As an American. As a patriot. She wouldn't let herself down.

She sat down in an easy chair and turned on Fox News, sound low. Her picture was up on the screen as a reporter spoke about her upcoming secret testimony.

Dyer's heart skipped a bit. It was surreal. She began to feel butterflies in her stomach. The full magnitude of what she was about to do hadn't yet hit her. The reporter stood among a crowd of other journalists outside the Hart Senate Office Building.

She thought again of what Reznick had told her about the apartment and the two men with a sniper rifle within range of the building. It had unnerved her, although she'd tried not to show it in front of Reznick.

All of a sudden, she felt panicked. Her heart was racing. Her mind was going in a million different directions. How would she perform in front of the committee? Would she screw up? Would she inadvertently incriminate herself?

Dyer closed her eyes and began some meditation exercises. Deep breathing. Imagining a positive experience. She visualized a beautiful meadow. And a lake, ice-cold water. A few minutes later, she felt a sense of calm return. She had this.

She knew her subject. Inside out. The faces of the men flashed through her mind. Honest men. Americans who had all died unexpectedly in different circumstances. But all linked to the same huge investigation into the corruption, the complicit generals, and the trail of money and foreign bank accounts. It was sickening.

She'd gone over the files and report with a fine-tooth comb. Frank had grilled her in practice sessions. She would feel his loss this morning, without him at her side. His associate would be sitting in, but the fresh-faced young lawyer would not have the same intimate knowledge of her report. She hadn't even gotten around to trying to contact Frank's widow—she vowed that it would be the first call she made after her testimony.

Dyer stared blankly at the TV as her thoughts turned to her own family. She picked up the remote control and turned down the volume. Her husband had wanted to sit by her side that day. But she didn't want him embroiled in her fight. She wanted him to look after their family, to remind her of what she had to go home to.

She checked her watch. A few minutes until her breakfast would arrive. She wondered what her husband was doing. She knew he was an early riser. She missed his voice. His slow Carolina drawl. It always reassured her. Calmed her.

Dyer reached over to her bed and picked up her cell phone. She wanted to hear his voice again.

"Honey, thank God, I've been worried sick."

Dyer felt her throat tighten. "I hope I didn't wake you."

"I've been awake all night. Did you sleep?"

"Yeah . . . I managed four hours, so I'm good."

"That's a relief. Excellent. Rosalind, I was going to call you, but you beat me to it. I just wanted you to know that you're incredibly brave. And I'm going to be thinking of you every step of the way."

"I'm sorry about everything that's happened. The Feds coming into our house and taking away all my stuff. It must've been very unsettling for you and the kids."

"Rosalind, relax. The Feds couldn't have been nicer. Very apologetic. But they're doing what they have to do, I guess. And they've moved us. But we're somewhere safe."

Dyer closed her eyes, tears welling. "I miss you, honey. And the kids. Tell them I miss them and I'll see them later today. Once it's all over. Then we can all catch up."

"Everything's gonna be fine. You'll see. You all set with your testimony?"

"I got this, honey. Trust me."

"You're going to be great. You're going to knock 'em dead. You know all that stuff."

"I hope so."

"I know so. I'm the one who's had to listen to it for the better part of a year."

Rosalind smiled. Her husband was a good man. He was a great husband. And a fantastic father. She was lucky.

"When this is all over, we're going to take a long, long vacation."

"Where do you have in mind?"

"Italy. You always wanted to go to Italy, right? So how about the Eternal City? Rome. Lake Como?"

"I'd love that."

"Just me and you. And my mother can look after the kids."

"I want to go to Capri."

"Two weeks in Rome, followed by two weeks in Capri."

"You got a deal."

Her husband was quiet for a few moments. "Anyway, I just want you to know that the kids and I wish you the very best for today. I'm thinking of you."

"I love you. Take care."

Dyer ended the call as tears threatened to fall. She turned up the volume on the TV. The news was now discussing the death of her lawyer again. She felt the wounds begin to open. The bad memories flashing through her head.

She wondered if Frank's widow blamed her.

The more she thought about it, the more she realized how obsessed she had been with her investigation. She had pushed aside concerns for her own family and for her lawyer as her investigation had proceeded. And despite the silent calls and the low-level intimidation, she'd pressed on.

What was the end result?

Her lawyer was dead, and her husband and kids were in an FBI safe house, unable to return to normal life for months, perhaps even years.

Had it really been worth it?

Dyer got up and walked to the bathroom, switched on the light illuminating the mirror. Despite the makeup, she could still see the dark shadows under her eyes. Her skin was bone white. She looked drained. Exhausted. She had been killing herself with fourteen-hour days, seven days a week. But she needed to get it together today.

She needed to be sharp. *Be sharp*.

Dyer reapplied her makeup, and she looked a bit better.

Three sharp knocks sounded on the door.

Dyer walked over to the door and pressed her eye against the peephole. The Fed guarding her door was standing next to a smiling Latina room service lady and a trolley of food.

Thirty-Eight

It wasn't even dawn, and Reznick was standing in the lobby, wearing a black polo shirt, jeans, and black sneakers. He wore an FBI earpiece and was shooting the breeze with a couple of young Feds in navy suits. "So when's the shift change for you guys?"

The taller of the two stifled a yawn. "I was on a split-shift yesterday. Three hours of sleep yesterday afternoon. And I'm hoping I'm out of here by seven."

Reznick checked his watch. "Two hours."

"You gotta love this job."

Reznick's earpiece buzzed, and he stepped away from the Feds to get a bit more privacy. "Hi, Jon, it's Martha. You're up early."

"Where are you?"

"Still in my office."

"All night? Do you ever sleep?"

"Not as much as I want."

"Why the early start?"

"Lot of stuff happening overnight. We're interviewing the son-in-law of Max Charles. Very slippery character."

"You guys using the immigration card as leverage?"

"Got it. We told him we want to know everything. And in return, we could come to an arrangement. Time in white-collar prison in the US in exchange for telling us the full story."

"How did he react?"

"Not well. But his lawyer is confident we can turn him around. Just a matter of time."

Reznick was impressed. "It seems to be coming together now."

"It's about time."

"What about Max Charles?"

"A bit more elusive. We believe he's still in DC. We're already in his office in Manhattan, couple of his team arrested. The net is closing in on him."

"It's not over, Martha. The operation would be heavily compartmentalized. Need-to-know basis. Different cells with different jobs. One handler. Who knows, maybe two just in case?"

Martha sighed. "We're bringing Dyer in the moment this is over. I've got twenty people inside the Hart Senate Office Building."

"What about outside?"

"Blocking off access roads. She'll be protected from the moment she steps out of her room."

Reznick said, "Speaking of which, I'm going to head upstairs to make sure she's up and ready."

"You got the route we want you to take through the hotel?"

"I've also got two alternate routes just in case."

"Jon, I'm glad you're going to be with her. Keep in touch. And we'll be watching."

Thirty-Nine

Once the Fed outside Dyer's door had electronically scanned the ID badge on the lanyard around the room service attendant's neck and confirmed her identity matched the hotel's employee database, a female Fed frisked the woman for weapons.

The Fed knocked again. "No problem, Rosalind."

Dyer opened the door, and the woman wheeled in the trolley. On it was a tray with a mug of black coffee, different packets of sugar, toast, and marmalade.

"Morning, ma'am. You ordered breakfast?"

"Yes, thank you. I'm starving."

The Fed shut the door.

Dyer handed the woman a ten-dollar tip. "Muchas gracias, señorita."

The woman gave a slightly subservient nod. "Thank you, señora."

Dyer sprinkled the sugar into the mug of coffee. She stirred it and picked up the cup. She took a sip as the woman placed the tray on the writing desk.

"This OK, señora?"

"Perfect."

"Do you want me to tidy or clean your room just now, señora?"

Dyer smiled. "No, thank you." She sat down at the writing desk and spread some marmalade on her toast. She took a bite. It tasted delicious. Then another bite. She didn't realize how ravenous she was. The taste of tangerine was sweet on her tongue.

She picked up the remote and turned up the sound of Fox News. It was reporting on the Dow Jones.

"Anything else I can get you, señora?"

Dyer tried to turn around to answer, but realized she couldn't. She felt a wave of exhaustion sweep over her. Her eyes felt heavy. She felt paralyzed.

"Excuse me, señora, what was that?"

Dyer tried again to turn her head but couldn't. The room seemed to tilt on its side. She looked at the reflection on the TV. She felt incapacitated but strangely awake. Out of the corner of her eye, she saw the room service attendant. Dyer tried to speak.

The woman was smiling, standing over her, putting on forensic gloves, syringe in hand.

Forty

Reznick was waiting to take the elevator to the seventh floor. He pressed the button repeatedly on the ground floor, still waiting two minutes later. Eventually, the door opened and he got in. He rode the elevator up. A short while later the doors opened, and he headed down the carpeted corridor to the suite at the end.

Two Feds, a man and woman, were sitting on wooden chairs on either side of a small table with two Styrofoam cups of coffee. "Morning, Agents. Nice and quiet overnight, I'm assuming."

"All good. Breakfast was just delivered a few minutes ago."

Reznick felt as if his guts had been ripped out. "What? Room service?"

"Yeah, she ordered breakfast."

Reznick thought he was going to throw up. "Guys, are you kidding me? The door doesn't open to anyone. That's the rules."

They looked at each other, and the male agent shrugged. "No one told us."

"What are you talking about? That's bullshit."

"We came on at two. We were told she doesn't leave the room. Only photo ID staff on this floor. And the client opened the door this morning. Nothing out of place."

"And the room service attendant?"

"She's just left the room. We checked her credentials. They were fine. And we searched her."

Reznick had a bad feeling. He knocked sharply on the door. "Rosalind, it's Jon! Open up!"

No answer.

Reznick knocked hard three more times, feeling anxiety rising within him. "Rosalind! It's Jon Reznick. Open up!" He tried the door, but it was locked. He turned to the Feds. "You got a card to get into the room?"

"No."

"Out of the goddamn way."

The Feds got up and took a couple of steps back. "What the hell are you going to do? I think you're overreacting."

Reznick had seen enough. He took two steps back before kicking the door hard. It burst open and Jon ran in.

The TV was on. Rosalind was sitting slumped at the writing desk, head hung low, fully dressed. A tray of food and a cup of coffee were on the writing desk. He grabbed her wrist and checked her pulse. "No! Come on! Come on!" Nothing. But her skin was warm. He turned around. "Call 911! Get paramedics! She's not breathing. And seal off the hotel! Now! Get the manager! And get that fucking room service woman!"

The Feds got on their cell phones, frantic, calling for emergency help. "Target down!" one shouted. "Not breathing. Seventh floor."

Reznick lifted Dyer up and placed her on the floor. He frantically began to do chest compressions. But he knew it was too late. "Wake up, Rosalind!" he said, pressing harder and harder down onto her chest. "Come on, Rosalind!"

It seemed like an eternity before the duty manager, three Feds, Trevelle, and security burst into the room. A female security guard kneeled down and signaled for Reznick to stand aside as she continued CPR. Trevelle was holding Rosalind's hand, tears streaming down his face.

"She's not responding," Reznick said. "I've tried that."

The female security guard kept at the CPR. "Come on, honey," she said. "You can do it."

Trevelle turned and looked at Reznick. "What the hell happened, Jon?"

"Someone got to her. Room service woman."

Trevelle sobbed, still holding Rosalind's hand. "She can't die," he said. "Not now. Not today."

The Feds were on their radios, cheeks flushed.

Reznick pulled the manager aside. "I work for Martha Meyerstein, FBI assistant director. Where is the room service attendant?"

The manager got on his cell phone and spoke with an assistant duty manager. "Find her! Now!" He ended the call. "Apparently she went outside for a cigarette. But she's gone."

Reznick stepped out of the room and tore down the corridor. He was headed down in the elevator when his earpiece buzzed.

"Jon, what the hell is going on there?" Meyerstein said.

"Rosalind is dead. Repeat, she is dead. Room service woman delivered breakfast. Find her!"

Reznick ran into the hotel lobby and signaled for one of the Feds to join him. He pointed at the guy by the door. "A woman in a hotel room service uniform. We need to find her!"

The earpiece buzzed again. "Jon," Meyerstein said, "three minutes ago, the room service attendant was picked up in a silver Mercedes SUV down at the rear of the hotel. They're already on the move. They're headed west on the E Street Expressway." She gave him the license plate number.

Reznick ran out of the hotel with one of the Feds in tow. An FBI Lincoln screeched to a halt outside. He slid into the front passenger seat, the young special agent in the back. "E Street Expressway going west! Now! What the fuck are you waiting for?"

The driver nodded and they sped off.

Reznick pulled out his Beretta and ran his thumb along the grip. "Motherfucker!"

The driver glanced anxiously at him and accelerated hard, racing through predawn traffic, jumping red lights.

The earpiece buzzed. "Jon, we've tagged her, so we'll have a continuous fix on her and the vehicle."

"That's a start. Where exactly is the vehicle?"

"They're on I-66 westbound and approaching the Teddy Roosevelt Bridge."

The driver glanced in her rearview mirror. "Shit."

Reznick said, "What is it?"

"Right behind us. We got a tail. I don't like it."

Reznick turned and looked through the back window. A Humvee was closing in. He could make out a couple of silhouetted figures inside. "How long have they been there?"

"I'm not sure."

"Guess."

"Shortly after we left the Hay-Adams. I'm sure I saw them a few moments after picking you guys up."

Reznick snapped. "So what are you waiting for? Hit the gas!"

Forty-One

Forty miles from DC, the Gulfstream was waiting outside the terminal at Manassas Regional Airport in Virginia.

Max Charles was wearing shades as he walked through the terminal with Malcolm Black. He wore a single-breasted gray Zegna suit, a white shirt, a black tie, and shiny black shoes; his longtime confidant preferred jeans, sneakers, and a black hooded sweater.

They stepped out of the terminal and took the short walk to the steps of the plane, whose engines were already running.

Charles went first, Black close behind. He took his usual seat at the table in the middle left of the plane. A satellite phone and laptop were on the table waiting for him. He took a few deep breaths and sighed. He felt elated. Relieved. Euphoric, even. The job had been done. The job his company had been paid $23 million to carry out, on delivery. And with a $10 million personal bonus for Charles.

Black served up a club soda with ice as they waited for the final passengers to join them. His confidant sat down diagonally across the table from Charles and smiled. "I think we're good."

The engines were revving as the pilot went through the preflight checks.

Charles sipped his drink. He didn't like tempting fate. He looked across at Black, who was sending messages from his cell phone. "I hope so. Are we 100 percent sure Rosalind Dyer is dead?"

Black nodded. "Jamie has been scanning police radio and all 911 traffic in DC, and we have three confirmations from cops and 911 controllers. Dyer was dead on arrival. Heart attack. Stress. That's what they'll say."

Charles grinned. "Triple bonus for you, as promised. Buy that new wife of yours whatever she desires."

Black rolled his eyes. "I'd be broke if I did that."

"Tell me about the girl who carried out the wet work."

"As cold as they come. Very plausible. Appears warm and friendly. Second cousin of one of the Miami crew. Also the pilot's sister. But she'll kill you as soon as she looks at you."

"Sure it wasn't your ex-wife?" Charles joked.

The aide laughed. "Actually, now that you mention it . . ." He looked at his watch. "We really need to get moving."

"I know."

"We're cutting it tight."

Charles's satellite phone rang, interrupting the conversation. "Yes?"

"Sir, we have a problem."

Charles shook his head. "I don't want to hear about problems. I want to hear that the target is dead."

"Affirmative, target is dead. DOA. Repeat, target is neutralized."

"Wonderful. So what's the fucking problem?"

"We've got a tail."

"What? How is that possible?"

"Fuck knows. But they're after us. I think they've locked on to us. You wanna know who?"

"Of course!"

"Reznick."

"Christ, gimme a break. OK, you need to go to plan B."

"Copy that, sir. Plan B. Understood."

"Stay safe. And get the hell out of there."

Charles ended the call, feeling a burning sensation in his stomach. He popped a couple of Zantac to calm his ulcer. "Never a fucking break."

"What's going on?"

"They've got a tail. It was supposed to be a simple drive to the airport. Nice and smooth."

The aide nodded. "Let's not get ahead of ourselves. Relax, we got that covered."

"We better have. Jon fucking Reznick is on this."

"He couldn't stop us neutralizing Dyer."

"Very true. So what is plan B?"

"Plan B? They dump the car and move to the new vehicle. It's all in place. Just in case. Like always."

Charles pointed at his aide. "What do I always say?"

"Check. Double-check. And then check again."

Charles picked up his cell phone and called the driver of the waiting backup vehicle. "You expecting a pickup soon?"

"Already en route. I got this."

"Get a move on. I want her out of sight and out of the country. And on this plane in fifteen minutes. You're on the clock. One minute late, and we're out of here."

Forty-Two

Reznick turned around as the Humvee accelerated hard and nudged their rear bumper. He checked the sideview mirror. The bastard was closing in. And fast. He turned to the Fed in the back. "Get your head down, pal."

The Fed slid lower down in his seat, head out of sight.

The driver said, "Are these guys part of the same crew we're after?"

"Guaranteed," Reznick said. "They're trying to stop us getting to the car with the girl in it. They're making sure the target vehicle is unhindered."

The driver peered ahead. "I think I lost them. Goddamn it!"

Reznick knew he had to get their tail off them. And quick. He wound down his window, and a bullet whizzed past. He thumbed off the safety. "Meyerstein!" he shouted into his lapel microphone, "we've got someone on our tail! And it seems like we've lost the vehicle with the girl in it! Where the hell are they?"

"Copy that, Jon. The car you're following is about a mile up ahead. GPS will have the precise details."

"Fuck. We've got some serious heat on our tail."

"Trying to take you out?"

"No doubt about it. I want them off our tail. I want authorization."

"Do what you have to do. Priority is to catch the woman. We've got everyone and their dog working on this."

A shot was fired, shattering the rear glass.

"What was that?" Meyerstein said.

"Rear window shot out, what the hell do you think?"

The Fed in the back seat was gritting his teeth. "Goddamn!" he said, shaking glass out of his hair.

"Take them out, Jon!" Meyerstein ordered.

Reznick unbuckled his seat belt and turned around. He aimed through the shattered rearview window, through shards of glass, to the driver following them. He could make out a figure behind the wheel. He fired two shots. The Humvee's windshield exploded. The driver slumped forward, bullet in the head. Then the truck careered off the highway and into a concrete divider in the middle of the road, bursting into flames. "Bingo!"

The driver glanced in the rearview mirror. "God almighty!"

Reznick flicked on the safety.

His earpiece buzzed. "What the hell, Jon?"

"The tail is gone."

"So I see. You're about half a mile behind the target car. A parking garage up ahead."

"Copy that."

The driver beside him nodded. "Yeah, on it."

"Stay safe, Jon."

Reznick turned and looked again at the Fed in the back seat. The special agent was brushing fragments of glass off the shoulders of his jacket. "You OK?"

The Fed just nodded.

Meyerstein's voice was in his earpiece again. "Find that car, Jon. And find that woman."

Forty-Three

The drone footage on the big screens on the fifth floor of the Hoover Building showed the blazing Humvee being hosed down by firefighters. Meyerstein turned and looked at the analysts and agent who were watching the footage with her. "Where is that woman? Number one priority! She was in the silver Mercedes. Where in God's name is the Merc?"

A young female analyst looked up from her computer. "Ma'am! I think we got it. Footage from the North Highland Parking Garage, level four. Up on the screen. Four miles after they crossed the Potomac. They headed off the freeway. I've slowed it down. It's them."

Meyerstein turned and stared. The silver Mercedes pulled up. The young Hispanic woman, who, only minutes earlier, had snuck out of the hotel after poisoning Rosalind Dyer, got out of the car. The image was freeze-framed. She wore dark glasses and a red Washington Nationals ball cap pulled low. "This her?"

"One hundred percent. Matches the woman from the hotel."

"Who is she?"

"We're working on it, ma'am. A fake ID and passport were given to the employment agency who supplied her to the hotel."

Meyerstein watched as the footage rolled on. The young woman climbed into the back seat of a black Subaru SUV. Meyerstein called out the license plate. "Everyone, I want this license plate out to all our people! We need this car. Pull it up. She is now in a black Subaru SUV. Maryland plates. She's out there."

A middle-aged special agent shouted, "We got a fix. A good fix. We're on it."

Meyerstein looked over toward her computer specialist. "Where?"

"I-66 westbound. I repeat, I-66 westbound. One mile west of Arlington."

Meyerstein passed the news on to Reznick. "You hear that, Jon? Black Subaru SUV."

"How far away are we?"

"It was a superquick change into the new vehicle . . . they're moving. A mile ahead of you."

"What's their next move?" Reznick pondered.

"They've left the city."

"I'd guess the escape route is already in place."

"We need to apprehend and take them down, ideally without loss of life."

"These guys are not going to just meekly surrender, trust me."

"Do what you have to do, Jon."

Meyerstein stared ahead at drone footage of the two cars, a mile apart, weaving in and out of traffic, emergency vehicle lights blazing. She kept imagining Rosalind Dyer's prostrate, lifeless body in the hotel room. And she knew Reznick must be feeling even worse than she was.

A sense of foreboding washed over her as the FBI vehicle accelerated faster.

Forty-Four

Fifteen minutes later, Reznick's earpiece buzzed.

"Jon, they've gotten off the highway at Centreville, on Route 28 headed south."

Reznick checked the GPS as they headed onto Route 28. "Got it. We're about, what, a minute from them?"

"If that. You're closing in."

They whizzed through Centreville and sped out of the town. "Where are they headed, Martha? Gimme something."

"Comptons Corner."

"Then what?"

A beat. "Hang on, Jon, I've got two analysts trying to get through." A few moments later: "After Comptons Corner, we have Manassas."

Reznick's mind began to race. "The name rings a bell. Why is that?"

"It's rural Virginia."

"I got it now," he said. "Airport. There's a tiny little airport."

"What?"

The realization crashed through Reznick's head like a rock. "Martha, listen to me. I remember the place."

"What? This is a bad line. Say again?"

"I remember the place. The airport is occasionally used for clandestine operations by the Agency. I know; I've flown out of there several times."

"Copy that, Jon. Bear with me, we're working on this angle. Hold on . . ."

"Executive jets and all that based there. But the Agency has been known to use that particular airfield. And Max Charles is former CIA, isn't he?"

"Copy that, Jon. Stand by. Did you hear what Jon said, people?"

Reznick checked the GPS, which showed them closing in on the target vehicle. Suddenly, up ahead, they saw the black Subaru. They sped on past the fields. "Got a visual, Martha! I repeat, we've got a visual! I repeat, we have eyes on the black Subaru!"

The car hit a hundred ten as they sped south of Manassas and swerved to avoid a slow-moving truck.

"Copy that, Jon."

Up ahead, Reznick saw a sign for the airport and checked the GPS. "We seem to have lost them. No visual."

"Damn!" Martha shouted.

"What is it?"

"They just smashed into a SWAT truck, and it took out two of our guys."

Reznick felt his nerve ends twitching. He stared ahead. A few moments later, they drove past the burning SWAT truck. "Goddamn!" Suddenly, they turned a corner. The black Subaru was in the distance. It had stopped. Three guys running from the Subaru after the accident. "Got a visual on those fuckers!"

The driver shouted, "Two o'clock, Jon, we have three runners! I repeat, we have three runners. All males. Two agents down. Repeat, two agents down. Confirm."

Reznick sat in the front seat, ready to explode. He could only watch as they closed in on the three runners. Then, in the distance, he saw them scaling the fence adjacent to the Global Jet compound.

The driver said, "Southeast of the terminal. We are now southeast."

Reznick could see it wasn't three males. "Got it!" It was two males and a female. He pointed to the chain-link fence. "Smash through the fence. I see the girl!"

The vehicle went onto the grass, plowed through the fence, and accelerated toward the trio of runners.

Reznick felt the adrenaline coursing through his veins. He felt his mind switching. Focusing on the targets. He wound down his window. The car was headed straight for the runners.

Suddenly the two guys turned around with handguns aimed at their swerving vehicle.

Reznick fired two ear-splitting gunshots through the passenger side window. He hit the chest of the bulkier of the two. The guy collapsed, blood spilling onto the blacktop. But the second dropped to the ground and got a shot off.

The driver's-side window shattered, and the FBI agent slumped forward onto the steering wheel. The vehicle went into a skid.

"Christ!" Reznick shouted. "Driver hit! Repeat, our driver is hit."

The Fed in the back seat leaned forward and pulled on the hand brake, screeching the vehicle to a halt.

Reznick jumped out of the car and aimed at the second guy running away. He fired two head shots. The guy fell to the ground, brains spilling out onto the asphalt. Reznick fixed his gaze on the girl in the distance. He ran hard after her. He could hear the Fed from the back seat panting close behind.

The girl was sprinting past a huge gas tank, toward an executive jet idling near the far terminal, occasionally glancing backward.

Reznick sprinted after her. "Freeze!"

The girl didn't stop. She was frantic as she ran, glancing behind her once more.

Reznick stopped, took aim, and fired off two shots. Both hit her back. The girl collapsed on the ground, a gun falling from her hand. Reznick ran toward her.

The girl was writhing in pain and reaching for the gun.

Reznick didn't hesitate. He simply drilled a single shot to the side of her head. He stared down at her, feeling nothing. The girl who had poisoned and killed Dyer was dead.

His earpiece crackled into life as the executive jet's engines revved into life. "Jon, it's over," Meyerstein said. "Stand down. Do you hear?"

Reznick's eyes were focused on the plane. "Who's on board? We need to know."

Silence.

"Registration says . . . the aircraft belongs to Max Charles's company. Passenger manifest says he's on the plane." Reznick was about to take off running when Meyerstein added, "But the decision has been made. You must abort. I repeat, abort. Mission is finished."

Reznick couldn't believe what he was hearing. "No."

"Jon, that's an order! We can pick up Charles wherever he lands."

"And what if he lands outside US jurisdiction? Then what?"

"Jon, you need to stand down."

Reznick said nothing.

The roar of the engines in the distance was the only thing he could hear.

Forty-Five

Charles picked up the binoculars and stared out the Gulfstream's window. "Are you fucking kidding me? Christ, they're lying on the ground near the perimeter. All three of them are dead."

Black stared through the glass and flushed a deep red. "We need to get out of here."

Charles unbuckled himself.

"Where are you going?" Black asked.

"We need to get this show on the road." He slid out of his seat and walked up to the locked flight deck door. He pressed his thumb against the biometric scanner.

The Guatemalan pilot, a naturalized American, turned around as the door opened.

"We need to move," Charles said. "The mission has been compromised."

"Where's my sister? We're not leaving without her."

"She didn't make it," Charles said. "I'm sorry."

The pilot stared at him. "What are you talking about?"

"They were running for the plane when the FBI breached the perimeter fence. All three of them are dead."

"I'm not leaving without her. No way."

"She's dead!" Charles handed him the binoculars. "Take a look for yourself."

The pilot was shaking as he scanned the perimeter fence. He lowered the binoculars, tears filling his eyes. "My sister! I have to go get her." He started to unbuckle his safety belt.

"Listen to me. There's no time. You need to get us out of here! Right now."

"I cannot leave without the body of my sister. I couldn't live with myself."

"She's gone. Get us the fuck out of here!"

"I can't. They haven't given us clearance yet."

Charles pulled out his gun, aimed it at the pilot. "Fuck them. We take off. Now!"

The pilot shook his head, tears streaming down his face. "I cannot. I will not."

"Wrong choice, son." Charles pulled the trigger. Blood and brain matter exploded onto his fresh clothes. The sound nearly deafened him in the enclosed space. The acrid smell of gun smoke filled the cabin.

He hauled the dead pilot from his seat. "You stupid motherfucker!" He dragged him through the cockpit to the back of the plane, a trail of blood on the carpet.

Black stared at Charles. "You killed him?"

"He wasn't going to move without his sister. Strap this fucker into a rear seat, then get yourself strapped in."

"What?"

"That's an order!" Charles shouted.

"Yes, sir."

"I'm going to fly us out of the country."

"Do you have clearance?"

"Let me worry about that."

Charles went back into the cockpit, locked the door, and slumped down in the pilot's seat. He wiped down the mess with some paper towels, then put on the headset. He'd been flight certified by the CIA and the Federal Aviation Administration.

He punched in the dials he knew so well. Then he edged the Gulfstream into position for takeoff at the far end of the runway.

Forty-Six

Reznick had officially gone rogue. Batshit rogue. And he didn't give a damn.

He raced along a perimeter path that ran parallel to the fence surrounding the airport. He had a good line of sight on the Gulfstream on the runway in the distance. He got into position. Then he unzipped his backpack.

He quickly assembled the sniper rifle with its laser sights. Locked and loaded. He thumbed off the safety.

Reznick lay down in the low grass and peered through the crosshairs. He focused. He had the flight deck in his sights. "Martha, the plane seems ready to take off. It's getting into position. I've got a shot. Clean shot."

"Copy that, Jon. The plane does not have takeoff clearance."

"I copy that. But that doesn't seem to have fazed them. I'm telling you, they're ignoring that. They're in position on the runway. I'd guess they're doing final checks. Then they're ready to disappear."

The Gulfstream moved slowly forward.

"It is moving forward down the north runway." Reznick stared through the crosshairs. He saw the face of Max Charles in the pilot's seat. He relayed the information.

"That's impossible."

"Negative. It's happening. He is at the controls. He's running the show."

"Jon, there is no clearance."

"I want to take a shot. It's moving. Do you hear me?"

"Jon, I hear you. Yes, I can see it."

"I want the shot." Reznick trained the crosshairs on the plane. Silence.

The Gulfstream was gathering speed on the runway. "Martha . . . I have a clean shot. Repeat, clean shot. Innocent people's lives have been lost. This fucker could crash the plane into a building. He might land at another airport and kill whoever is in his path. We need to stop him!"

"Do what you have to do. Do you copy?"

"Copy that." Reznick took careful aim as the Gulfstream picked up speed down the runway. He focused on the flight deck windshield. "OK, you bastard!" He held his breath. Squeezed the trigger. He fired five shots in quick succession, exploding the Gulfstream's windshield.

The plane was still accelerating, gathering speed.

Reznick aimed for the right engine. He fired multiple shots, each ripping through the metal. He then fired at the plane's passenger windows. He needed to decompress the plane. And quick.

The Gulfstream continued accelerating fast. Getting farther and farther away.

Reznick locked on to the plane's right wing through the crosshairs. He guessed he had only one more chance before the plane would be out of range. He fired. Three hard shots.

A ball of flames erupted out of the Gulfstream's fuel tanks. The plane veered off the runway, engulfed in a fireball. The blazing jet, still gathering speed, plowed through a perimeter fence, exploding again with a thunderous bang. The ground shook.

Flames licked the sky as an inferno spread through the adjacent woods.

Forty-Seven

The sky turned burnt orange as the acrid smell of jet fuel and choking black smoke filled the rural Virginia air. Two fire engines, sirens blaring and lights blazing, rushed to the scene.

Reznick quickly took the rifle apart. He placed the components carefully in his backpack and slung it over his shoulder. He got up, turned, and walked back down the perimeter path. He spotted a group of cops swarming through the fence, guns trained on him.

A burly Fed stepped out of an SUV, badge raised, to intercept them. He pointed to Reznick. "He's with us! He's one of us! Stand down!"

Slowly, the cops lowered their weapons as Reznick approached. The Fed put an arm around Reznick. "You OK, Jon?"

Reznick nodded as he brushed past the cops. He walked past the bodies of the woman and the two men he had gunned down.

"What the hell happened?" the Fed asked.

"Long, long story, my friend."

"Glad you're OK, man."

Reznick looked around. Black smoke was still rising.

Forty-Eight

Just over an hour later, Reznick was being debriefed by an ashen-faced Meyerstein in her office on the seventh floor of the Hoover Building.

"What in God's name, Jon?"

Reznick was slumped in a seat, head bowed. He didn't want to talk. His thoughts were only for Rosalind Dyer. Also for her grieving family in protective FBI custody.

"I asked what happened."

"The threat was neutralized. Contained within the airport."

Meyerstein was quiet as she got up from her seat and stared out the window. "Do you understand what you did? I gave permission for you to take him out, not blow everything to hell."

"It had to be done."

"This will be difficult to contain—the story, I mean."

Reznick said nothing. He understood why Meyerstein saw the airport incident and deaths only as a disaster. He didn't blame her. It was a mess. But he couldn't help wondering if it was a mess that could have been avoided.

He should have just told the Feds where Dyer was and gotten her to safety. But it was pointless to beat himself up over what might have been. He knew that. The reality was Dyer was dead and the fallout at the airport would rumble on. There was nothing he could do to change that now.

It was a damn mess.

"The press are going to have a field day over this."

"Don't they always."

"They will have questions. But so do I. A lot of questions, about how we took down Max Charles and at what price."

Reznick stayed silent.

"What have you got to say for yourself, Jon?"

"I think there are a lot of questions, sure. About how Max Charles could be allowed to act on behalf of the Pentagon. The only reason this went on for so long was because he was working on the inside but accountable to no one. He was doing their dirty work. And what about the deaths of the seven men? What about that?"

Meyerstein shook her head.

"You know who we're forgetting in all this? Rosalind Dyer. Her bravery. Who's talking about how this operation to silence her was carried out? And how she was killed while under FBI protection?"

Meyerstein shook her head. "Jon, that's enough!"

"Martha, this was a fuckup. An FBI fuckup. No one should have been allowed in her room. No one. That's the reality."

"Now is not the time or place."

"Isn't it?"

"Jon, please."

"They were determined to take her out. We had ample warning. And still this happened."

Meyerstein turned and stared at him. "I have to take responsibility for this. I told you to do whatever it took. I will shoulder the responsibility. I just imagined you had a clean shot."

Reznick sighed. "It didn't work out like that. But what choice did I have? To let Max Charles and his goons fly off to Guatemala?

Never be seen again? Maybe land at another American airport? Then what? He would've killed anyone who got in their way."

"You did your best, as always, Jon. We fell short."

"The teams that Charles assembled. Is the threat over?"

"We believe the threat is over for now. But in light of what happened, Trevelle will need to find a new base."

Reznick knew that made sense. "I want to call in one last favor."

Meyerstein stared at him, unblinking.

"I don't want any charges brought against Trevelle or Fifi."

"That's not my call to make, Jon."

"Make it your call, Martha. They risked their lives for Rosalind so she could tell her story."

"I can't do that, Jon, you know that."

"I'm asking you to make sure that those two individuals do not face charges or any trial. That would be a travesty."

Meyerstein sighed and nodded. "It's not going to be easy."

"Nothing ever is. For me, that's all I'm asking. The very last favor I'm calling in, I promise."

"I'll see what I can do."

A knock at Meyerstein's door snapped them out of the tense discussion.

Meyerstein's assistant popped her head around the door. "Ma'am, check out C-SPAN. The chairman of the SASC is about to make a special announcement. It's live."

Meyerstein nodded. "Thanks, Sharon."

Sharon closed the door behind her.

Meyerstein picked up the remote control from her desk and switched on the large-screen TV on the wall. She channel-surfed until she got to C-SPAN's live broadcast.

Tom Aldrich, chairman of the Senate Armed Services Committee, was adjusting the microphone in front of him, photographers crowded around. "Ladies and gentlemen, we learned earlier this morning that Rosalind Dyer, who was supposed to give evidence during a closed session before the committee, tragically died before she could appear before us. The police and the FBI have begun an investigation into her death. I have had several requests from other members of the committee to postpone this hearing out of respect for the memory of Rosalind Dyer. But after much deliberation and soul-searching this morning, I have decided that we will not postpone. We will adjourn, but only for two hours. We have before us today evidence compiled by Rosalind Dyer. She not only managed to secure a vast amount of documentation about these grave allegations of corruption and kickbacks within the American military, but she has also passed on information, which I feel is credible, that outlines the highly suspicious deaths of seven accountants and auditors who have all been linked in some way to this investigation over the years. Seven deaths."

Audible gasps from others on the committee.

"Trust me, we will get to the bottom of this. My committee will not be intimidated. We will be calling witnesses. The government is on trial. We owe it to the bravery of Rosalind Dyer." His voice cracked for a moment. "I, for one, want to go on record and express my admiration for her integrity, courage, and patriotism, not to mention her exemplary service to this great country of ours."

Meyerstein stared at the TV as the camera panned across the faces of the other members of the committee. She switched off the TV, tears in her eyes. "Damn."

Reznick shook his head. "God bless her."

"I feel so bad, Jon. For her, for her family. I should've hauled her in."

"She didn't want that. She wanted to tell what she knew. She knew she was at risk. We all warned her."

"She's dead."

Reznick nodded. "Yes, she is. God rest her soul."

Meyerstein closed her eyes, tears spilling down her cheeks. When she opened them, she said, "I think your instincts were right on this, Jon. I was wrong. Or rather we, the FBI, were wrong. We came up short. I'm starting to wonder if our response was bureaucratic. We didn't seem to connect the dots. I'm starting to doubt what the hell we were doing. Missing the big picture. Going after the wrong people. The point is, you didn't."

Reznick sat quietly.

"You know the small consolation I take from this whole terrible episode?"

"What's that?"

"Rosalind Dyer couldn't be silenced. She paid for it with her life. But they could not silence her. Her story is going to be told. What she knew. And that's what she would have wanted."

The late-morning sun was streaming through the blinds.

Reznick squinted against the glare of the sun. "She made the ultimate sacrifice."

"Amen to that."

Epilogue

Three months later, Reznick was sitting on his deck, drinking a beer, watching the burnt autumn sun set over Penobscot Bay, when his cell phone rang. He checked the caller ID but didn't recognize the number.

"Yeah?"

"I'm looking to speak to Mr. Reznick." The man's voice was calm. "Mr. Jon Reznick."

"Who's this?"

There was a long silence before the man spoke again. "You don't know me. My name is Travis Dyer. My wife was Rosalind Dyer."

Reznick sat up and put down his beer. "Travis, hi."

"I hope you don't mind my calling."

"Not at all. I was actually thinking about you and your family just yesterday when I was out doing some fishing."

Travis sighed. "Jon—I hope you don't mind me calling you that."

Reznick smiled. "Not at all."

"I've been thinking about calling you for quite some time. But I've just never found the right moment or . . . I don't know. I think I was a little scared. Just that it brings back a lot of memories."

"It must, man. You mind me asking how you got my number, Travis?"

"I was given your number by Assistant Director Meyerstein. I hope it's OK that I called you."

"Really nice to hear from you. I don't mind at all."

"I'm still trying to come to terms with losing Rosalind. My kids with losing their mom. I guess it'll take more time."

"It's a terrible loss, I know."

"Jon—" Travis's voice broke with emotion. "It's only now that I can even talk about this, not only about what happened to her, but to try to understand the events that led up to it. I'm still trying to make sense of it."

Reznick sighed. "What do you know?"

"I know she had compiled a compelling case against at least one member of the Joint Chiefs of Staff. Double accounting, Swiss bank accounts. A whole host of stuff. And because of that, an operation was put in place to neutralize her. But she was also investigating the deaths of seven other people."

"That's correct. I haven't heard much about the committee and their findings. It's all been quiet on that front." Reznick knew why, or at least what had been stated publicly. "The chairman has been ill, apparently."

"The hearings are finished. They've been postponed indefinitely. Which means it's over. That's what I've been told."

"I'm sorry."

"Yeah . . . anyway, Jon, the reason I wanted to speak to you is that no one has really spoken to me about the last couple of days. Her last days. I guess I just want to hear it firsthand. Just for a bit of closure."

"I understand. What do you want to know?"

"How did you get involved?"

259

Reznick sighed long and hard. "Well, I was approached by a hacker I know . . ."

Reznick sketched out the events that had taken him and Trevelle to New York, then down to DC to warn Rosalind. How committed she'd been. How grateful that her family had supported her decision to testify.

A silence stretched between them for what seemed like an eternity, as if Travis was absorbing the picture of his wife's last few days. "I want to thank you for doing your best to protect her."

"I wish I could've done more."

"There's something else. I've been told by various people that you were the one who killed Max Charles."

Reznick sighed. "I'd rather not go into that."

"That's all I need to know. Jon, I know what you did. And my children know. Not only protecting Rosalind, putting your own life on the line, but also ensuring her investigation had a chance to see the light of day."

"I hope another committee renews the hearings."

"I do too."

"We owe it to Rosalind's memory."

"My family owes you a lot."

Reznick felt his throat tighten.

Travis broke down and began to cry. "I'm glad you killed him, the son of a bitch. Maybe I shouldn't say that. It doesn't sound like the Christian thing to say. Rosalind was a great believer. And I hope it's true that she's at peace in heaven."

"I hope so too."

Travis sniffed. "Sometimes I don't want to go on without her. It's like I'm in a tunnel and there's no light."

"I know that feeling. But we do go on. It's the human spirit within us. I think that was something Rosalind understood better than most."

"You're right about that. Thank you, Jon. And I hope we can meet up sometime."

"I'd like that."

After he hung up the phone, Reznick picked up his beer and took a large gulp. Out on the bay, the cold, dark waters off the coast of Maine were turning bloodred as the sun dipped lower in the sky.

Acknowledgments

I would like to thank my editor, Jack Butler, and everyone at Amazon Publishing for their enthusiasm, hard work, and belief in the Jon Reznick thriller series. I would also like to thank my loyal readers. Thanks also to Faith Black Ross for her terrific work on this book, and Caitlin Alexander in New York, who looked over an early draft.

Last but by no means least, thank you to my wife, family, and friends for their encouragement and support.

About the Author

Photo © 2013 John Need

J. B. Turner is a former journalist and the author of the Jon Reznick series of action thrillers (*Hard Road, Hard Kill, Hard Wired, Hard Way, Hard Fall, Hard Hit,* and *Hard Shot*), the American Ghost series of black-ops thrillers (*Rogue, Reckoning,* and *Requiem*), and the Deborah Jones political thrillers (*Miami Requiem* and *Dark Waters*). He has a keen interest in geopolitics. He lives in Scotland with his wife and two children.